JOHN CARPENTER PRESENTS

STORM KIDS

Series created by
JOHN CARPENTER and SANDY KING

STORM
KING

JOHN CARPENTER PRESENTS

STORM KIDS

FETCH
BOOK ONE: THE JOURNEY

Written by MIKE SIZEMORE
Art by DAVE KENNEDY
Colors by PETE KENNEDY
Lettering by JANICE CHIANG
Edited by SANDY KING
Cover art by DAVE KENNEDY

Book Design by SEAN SOBCZAK
Title Treatment by JOHN GALATI

Publishers: John Carpenter & Sandy King
Managing Editor: Sean Sobczak
Storm King Office Coordinator: Antwan Johnson
Publicity by Sphinx PR - Elysabeth Fulda

John Carpenter Presents Storm Kids: FETCH: BOOK ONE: THE JOURNEY, February 2023.
Published by Storm King Comics, a division of Storm King Productions, Inc.

AGES 8 AND UP
STORMKINGCOMICS.COM

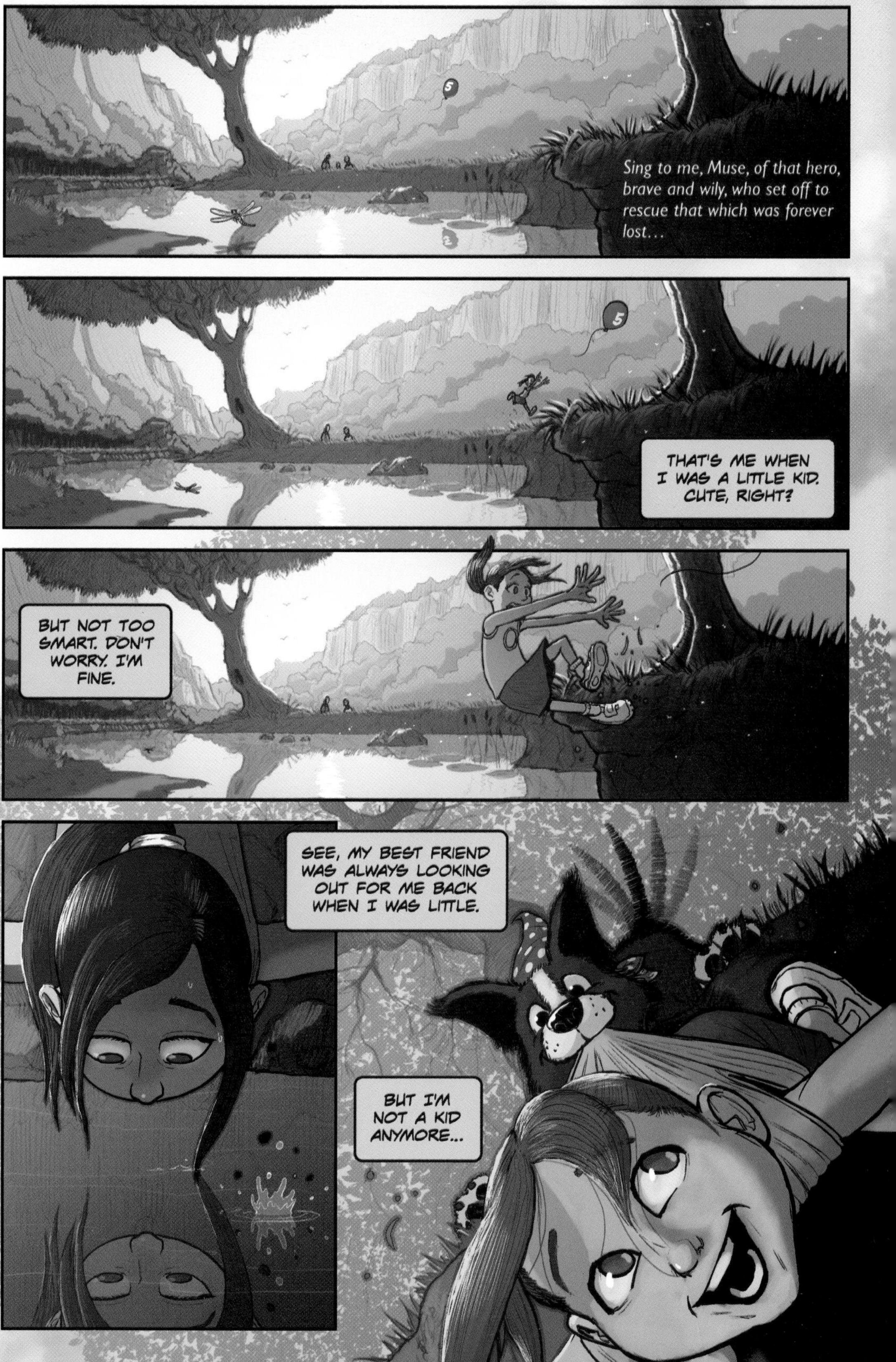

Sing to me, Muse, of that hero, brave and wily, who set off to rescue that which was forever lost…
THAT'S ME WHEN I WAS A LITTLE KID. CUTE, RIGHT?
BUT NOT TOO SMART. DON'T WORRY. I'M FINE.
SEE, MY BEST FRIEND WAS ALWAYS LOOKING OUT FOR ME BACK WHEN I WAS LITTLE.
BUT I'M NOT A KID ANYMORE...

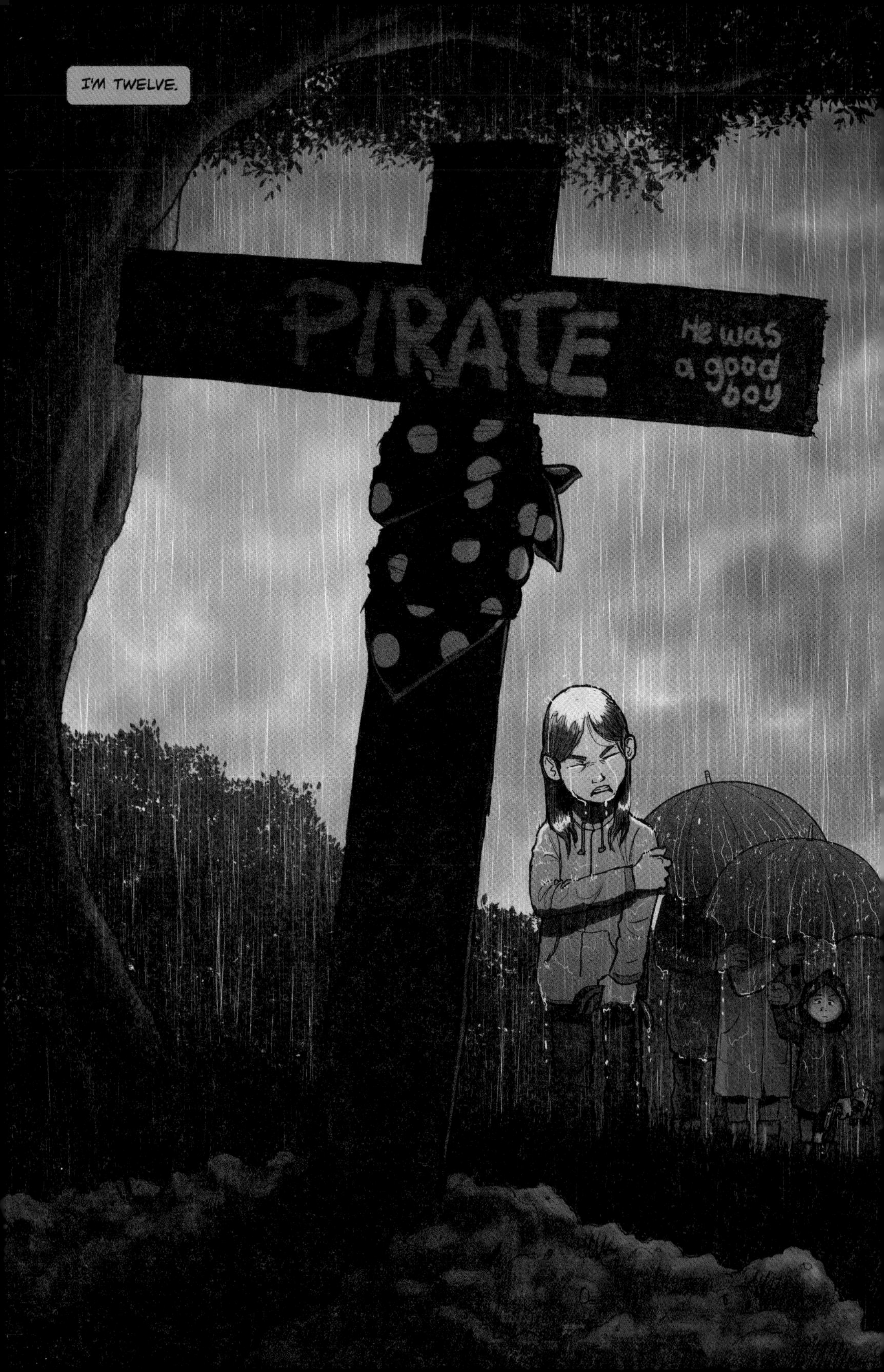
I'M TWELVE.
PIRATE
He was a good boy

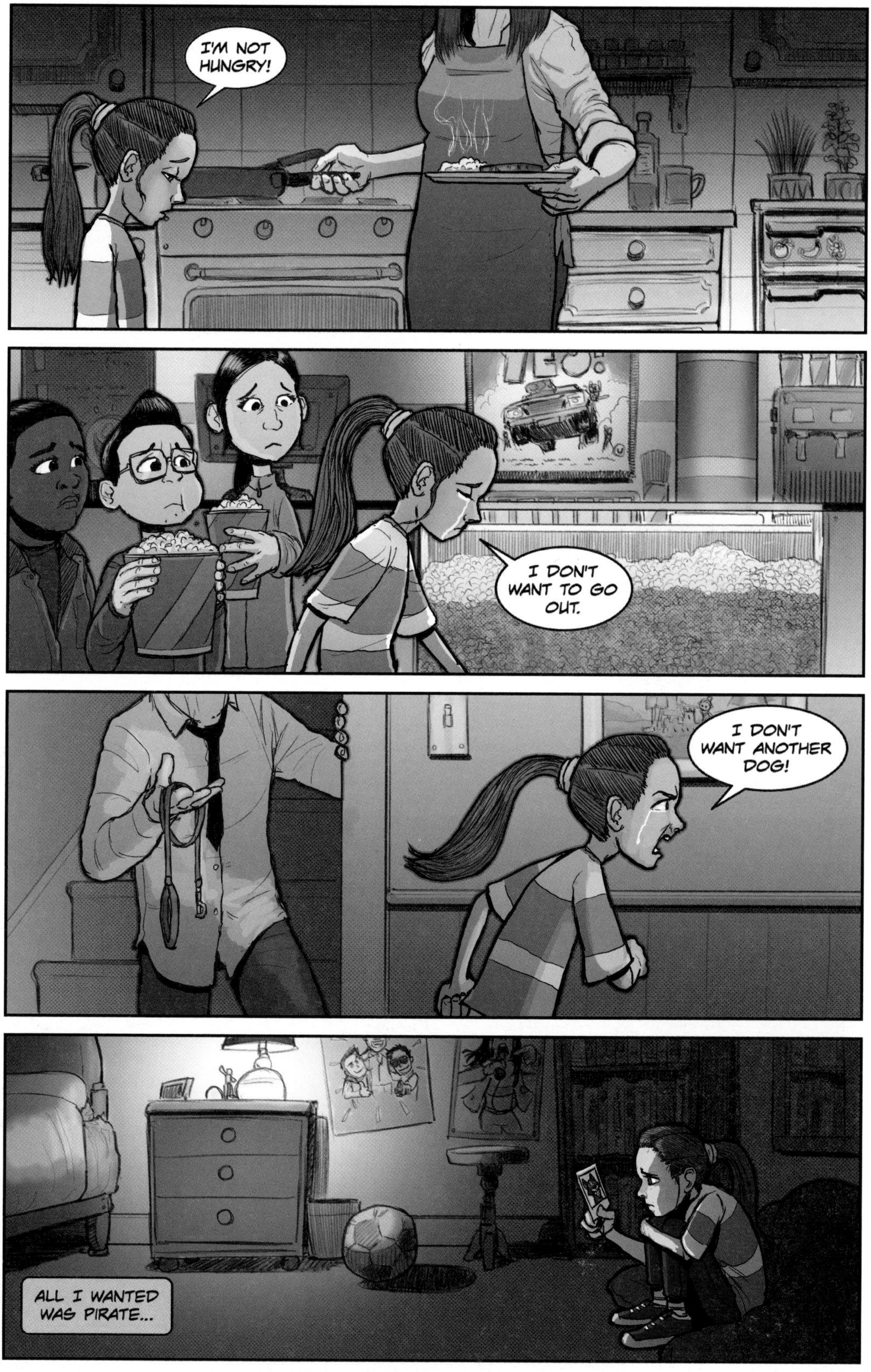
I'M NOT HUNGRY!
I DON'T WANT TO GO OUT.
I DON'T WANT ANOTHER DOG!
ALL I WANTED WAS PIRATE...

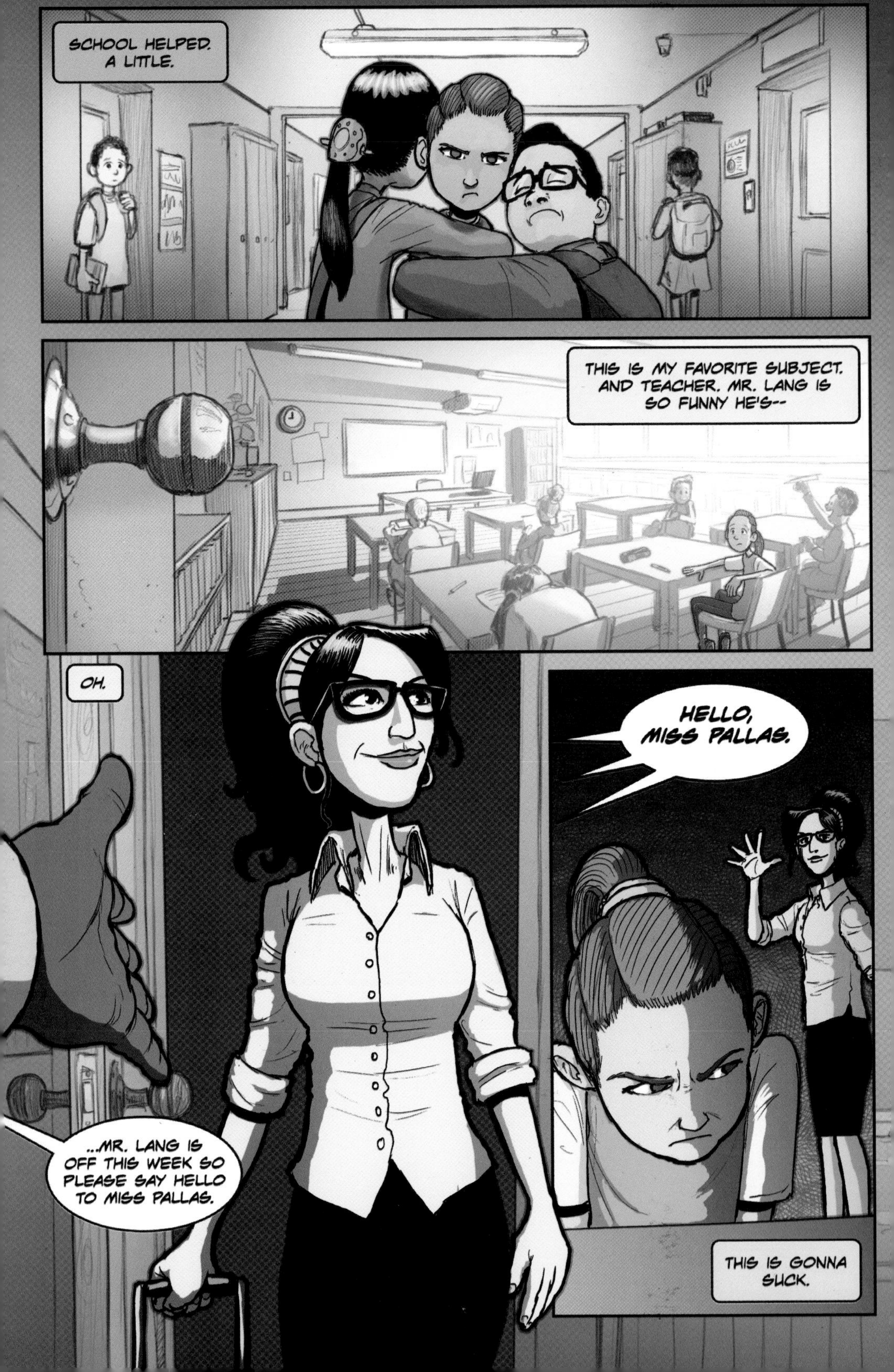

SCHOOL HELPED. A LITTLE.
THIS IS MY FAVORITE SUBJECT. AND TEACHER. MR. LANG IS SO FUNNY HE'S--
OH.
...MR. LANG IS OFF THIS WEEK SO PLEASE SAY HELLO TO MISS PALLAS.
HELLO, MISS PALLAS.
THIS IS GONNA SUCK.

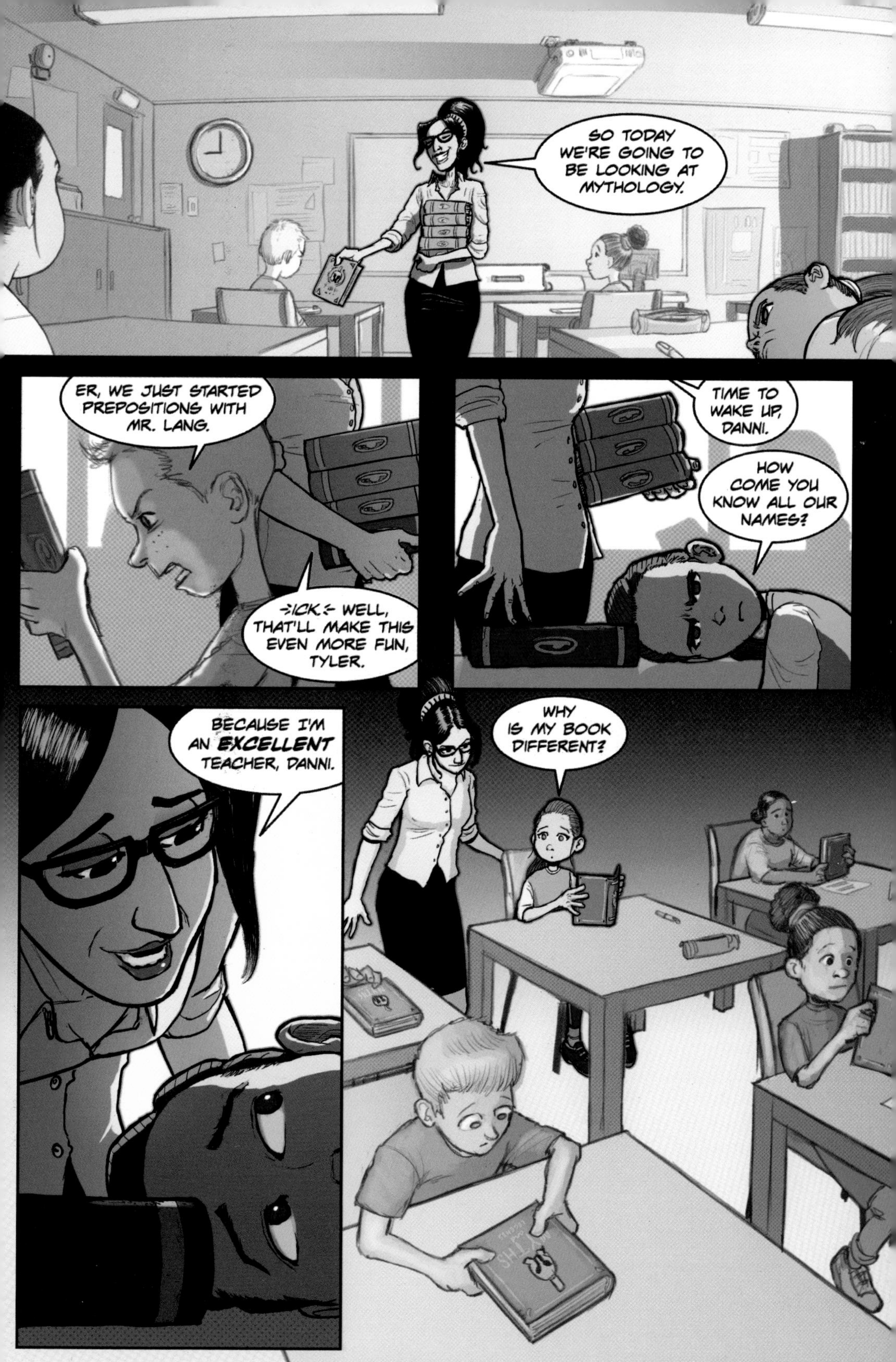
SO TODAY WE'RE GOING TO BE LOOKING AT MYTHOLOGY.
ER, WE JUST STARTED PREPOSITIONS WITH MR. LANG.
≈ICK.≈ WELL, THAT'LL MAKE THIS EVEN MORE FUN, TYLER.
TIME TO WAKE UP, DANNI.
HOW COME YOU KNOW ALL OUR NAMES?
BECAUSE I'M AN EXCELLENT TEACHER, DANNI.
WHY IS MY BOOK DIFFERENT?

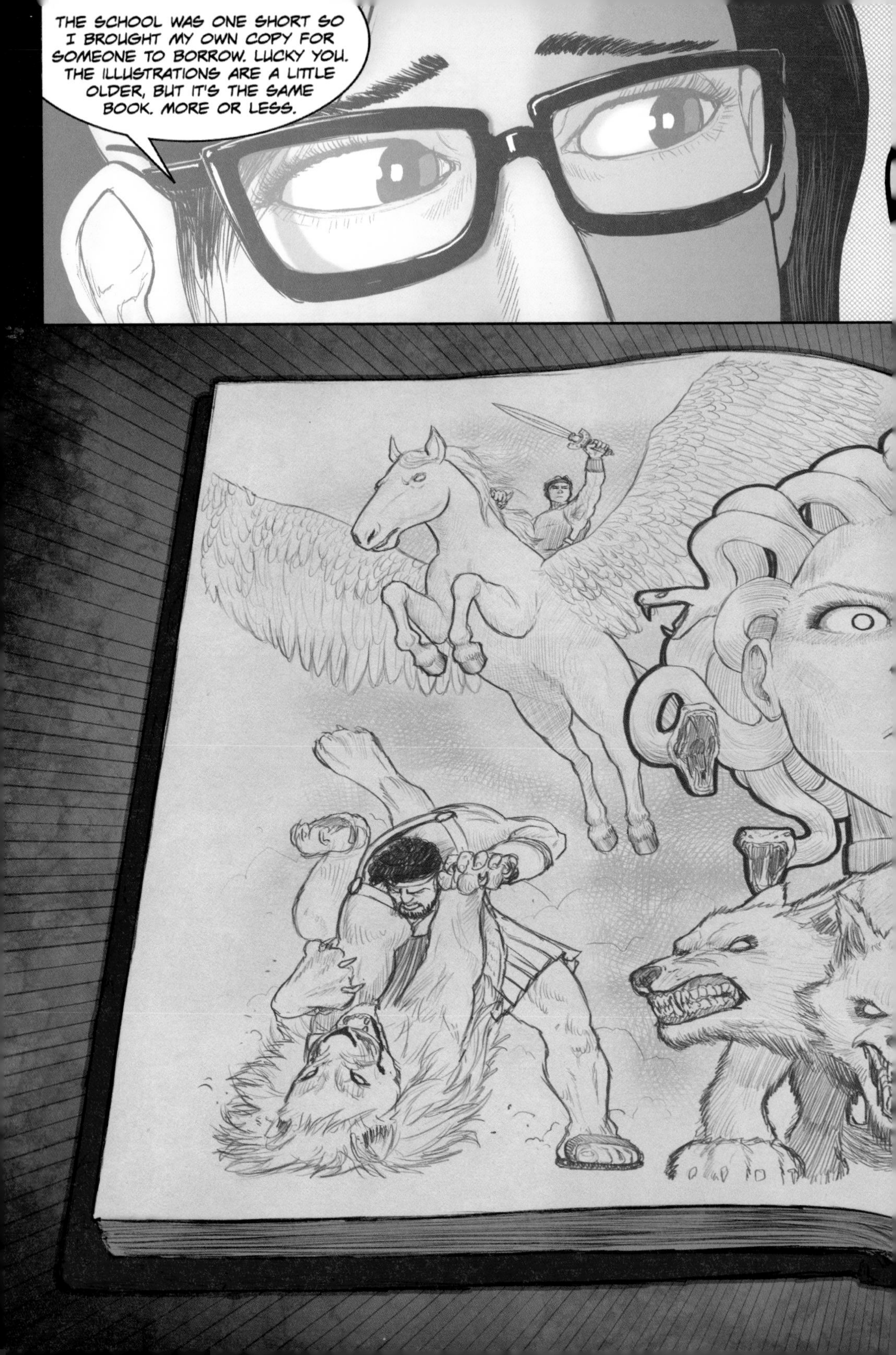
THE SCHOOL WAS ONE SHORT SO I BROUGHT MY OWN COPY FOR SOMEONE TO BORROW. LUCKY YOU. THE ILLUSTRATIONS ARE A LITTLE OLDER, BUT IT'S THE SAME BOOK. MORE OR LESS.

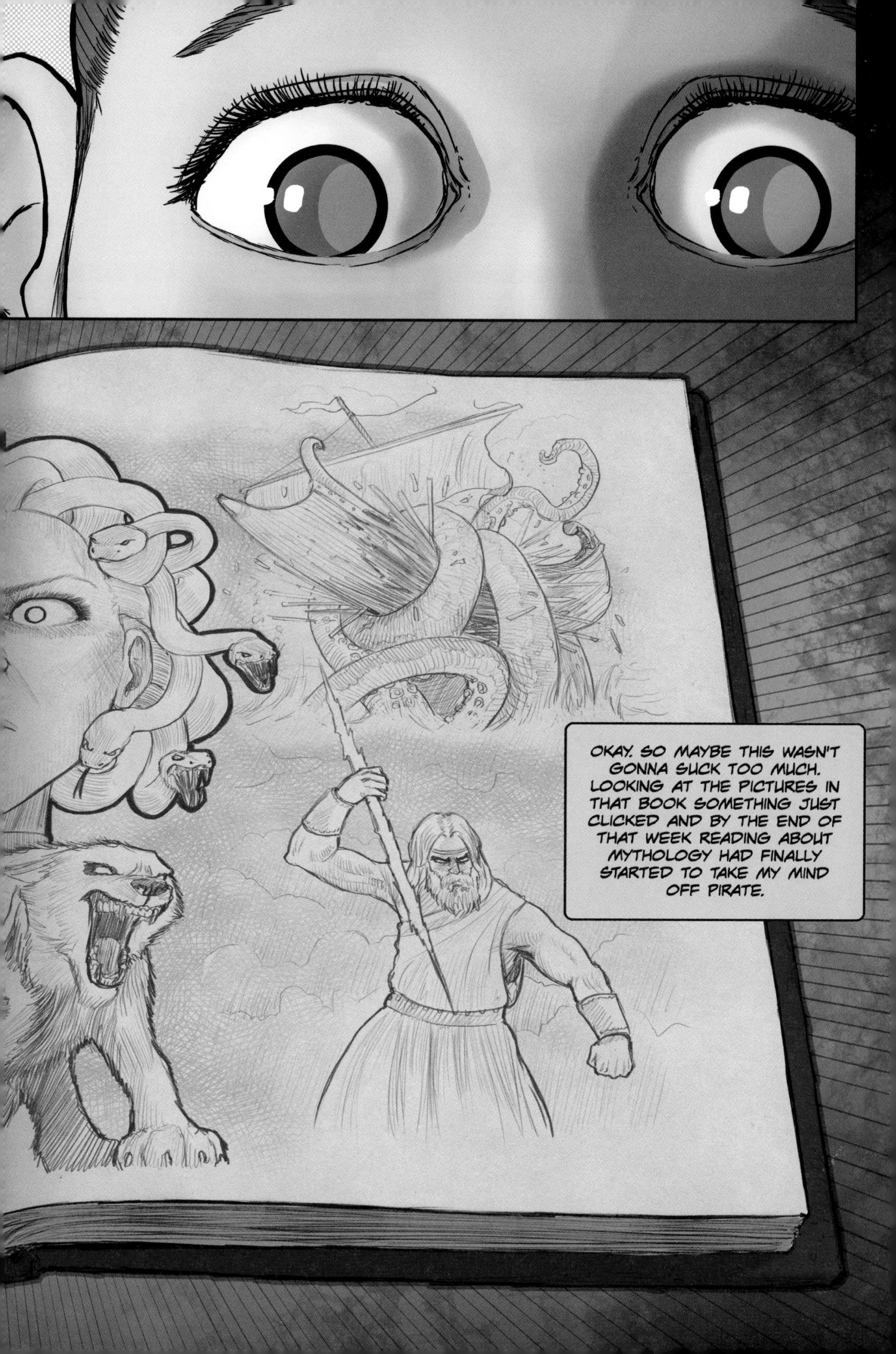
OKAY. SO MAYBE THIS WASN'T GONNA SUCK TOO MUCH. LOOKING AT THE PICTURES IN THAT BOOK SOMETHING JUST CLICKED AND BY THE END OF THAT WEEK READING ABOUT MYTHOLOGY HAD FINALLY STARTED TO TAKE MY MIND OFF PIRATE.

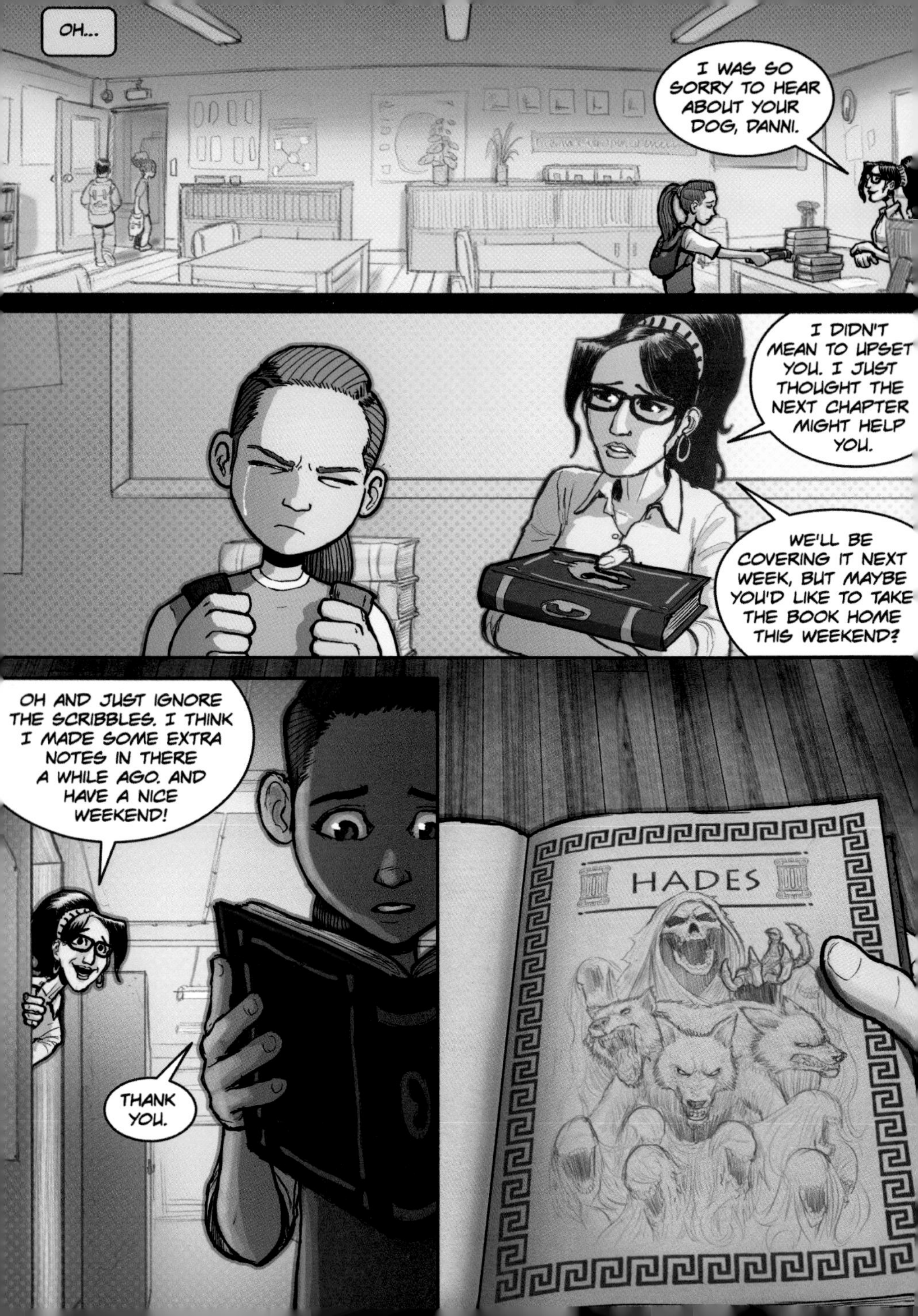
OH...
I WAS SO SORRY TO HEAR ABOUT YOUR DOG, DANNI.
I DIDN'T MEAN TO UPSET YOU. I JUST THOUGHT THE NEXT CHAPTER MIGHT HELP YOU.
WE'LL BE COVERING IT NEXT WEEK, BUT MAYBE YOU'D LIKE TO TAKE THE BOOK HOME THIS WEEKEND?
OH AND JUST IGNORE THE SCRIBBLES. I THINK I MADE SOME EXTRA NOTES IN THERE A WHILE AGO. AND HAVE A NICE WEEKEND!
THANK YOU.
HADES

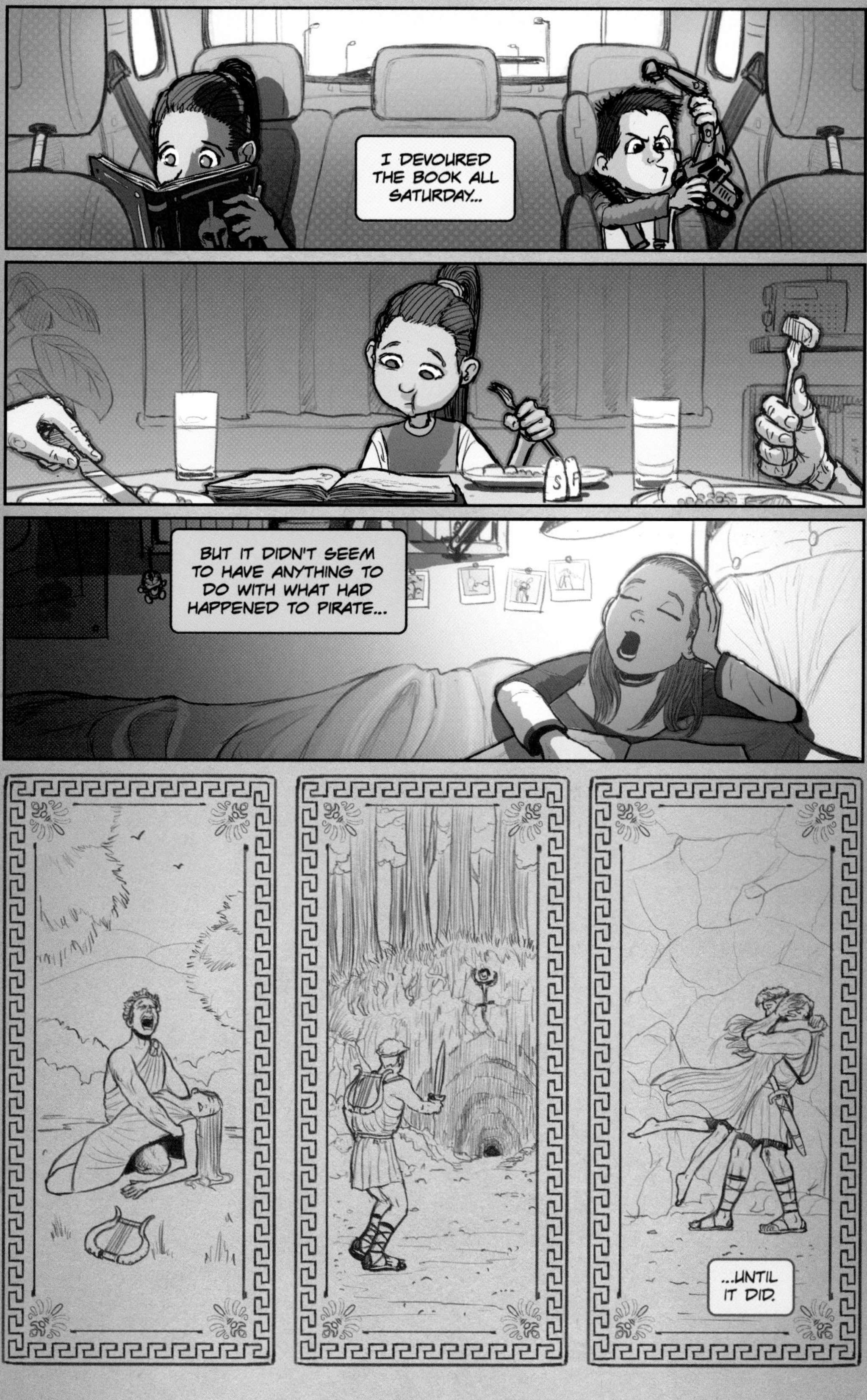
I DEVOURED THE BOOK ALL SATURDAY...
S
P
BUT IT DIDN'T SEEM TO HAVE ANYTHING TO DO WITH WHAT HAD HAPPENED TO PIRATE...
...UNTIL IT DID.

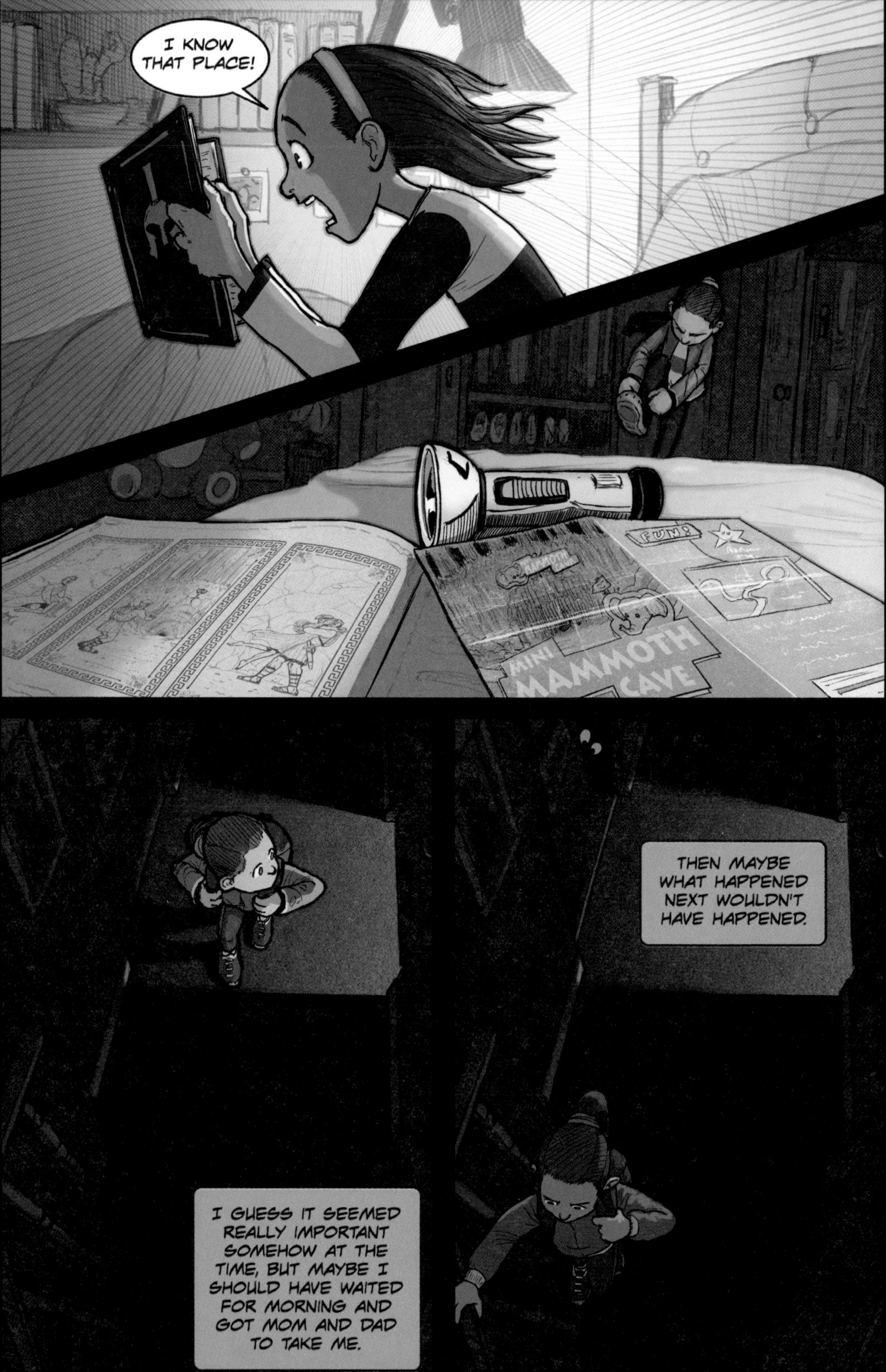
I KNOW THAT PLACE!
FUN!
MINI MAMMOTH CAVE
I GUESS IT SEEMED REALLY IMPORTANT SOMEHOW AT THE TIME, BUT MAYBE I SHOULD HAVE WAITED FOR MORNING AND GOT MOM AND DAD TO TAKE ME.
THEN MAYBE WHAT HAPPENED NEXT WOULDN'T HAVE HAPPENED.

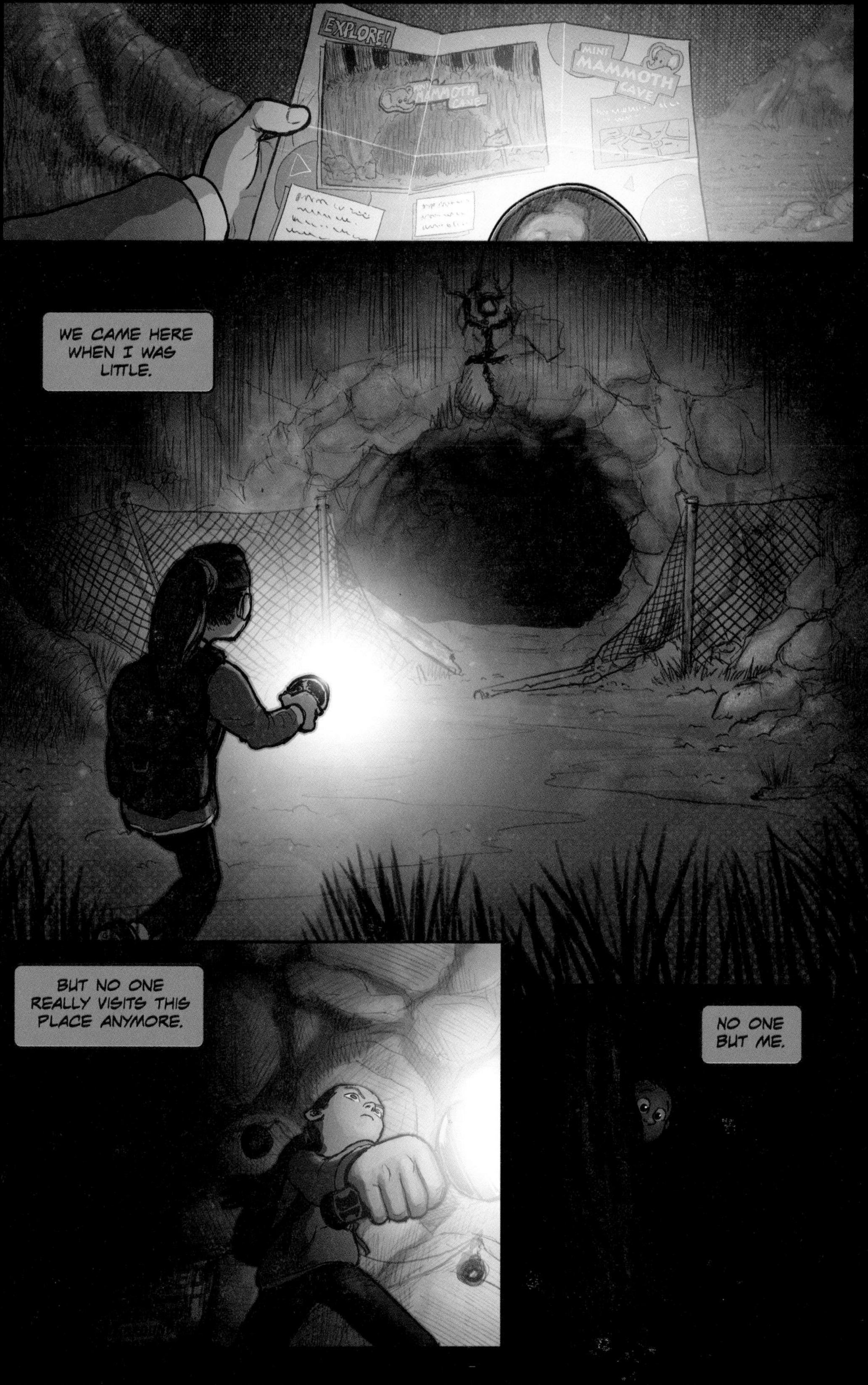
EXPLORE!
MINI MAMMOTH CAVE
WE CAME HERE WHEN I WAS LITTLE.
BUT NO ONE REALLY VISITS THIS PLACE ANYMORE.
NO ONE BUT ME.

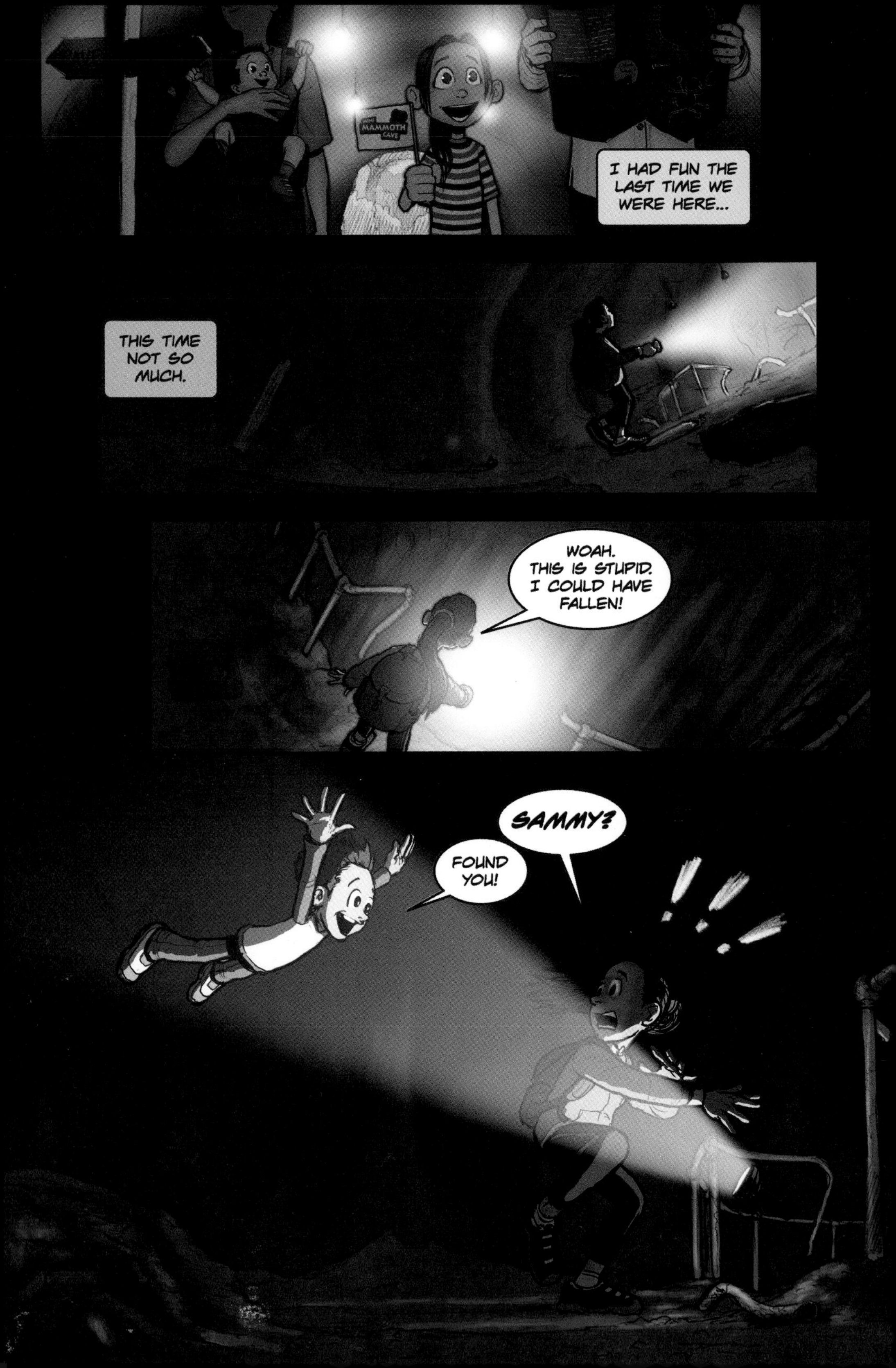
MAMMOTH CAVE
I HAD FUN THE LAST TIME WE WERE HERE...
THIS TIME NOT SO MUCH.
WOAH. THIS IS STUPID. I COULD HAVE FALLEN!
SAMMY?
FOUND YOU!

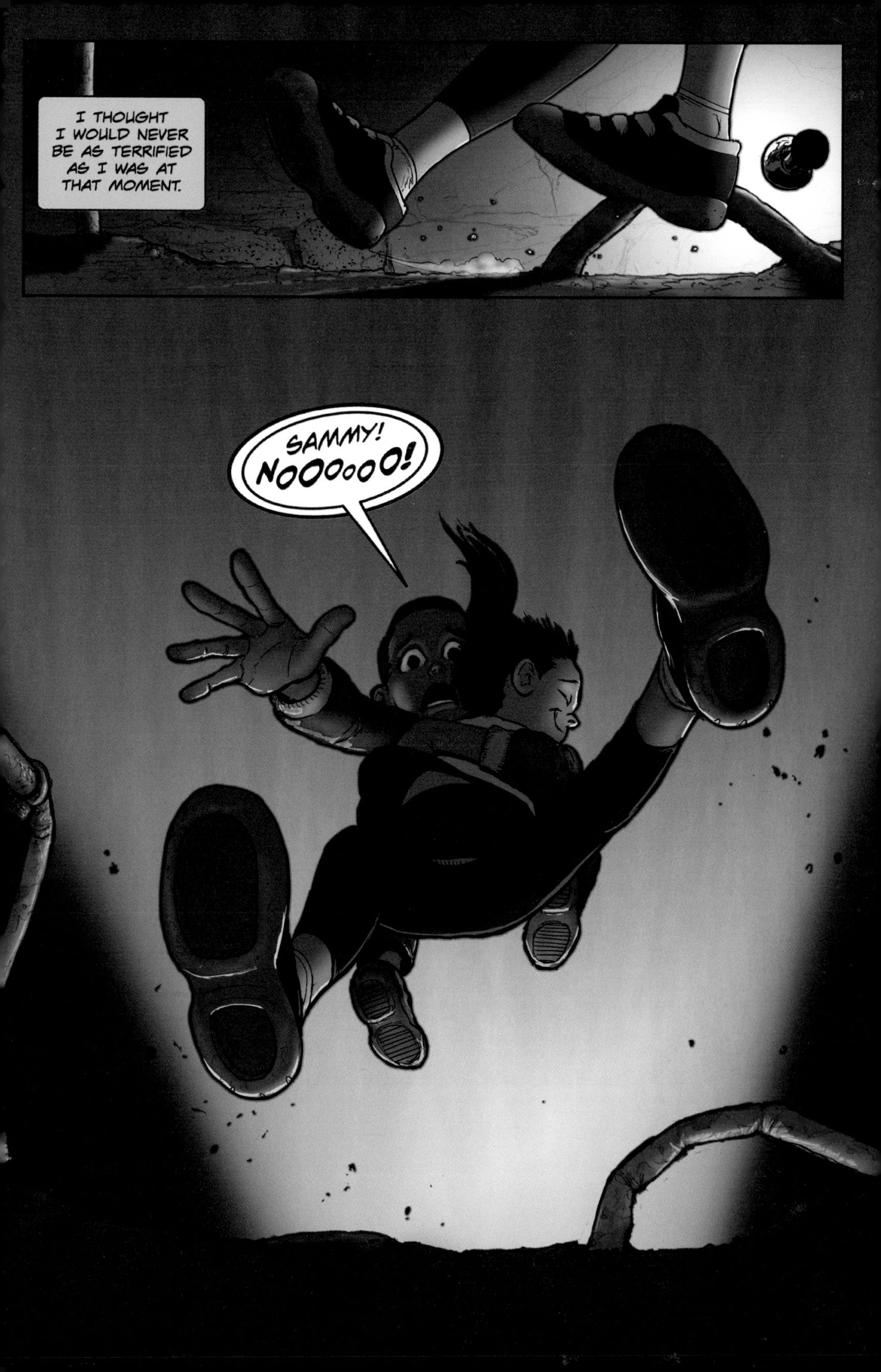
I THOUGHT I WOULD NEVER BE AS TERRIFIED AS I WAS AT THAT MOMENT.
SAMMY! NOOOoOO!

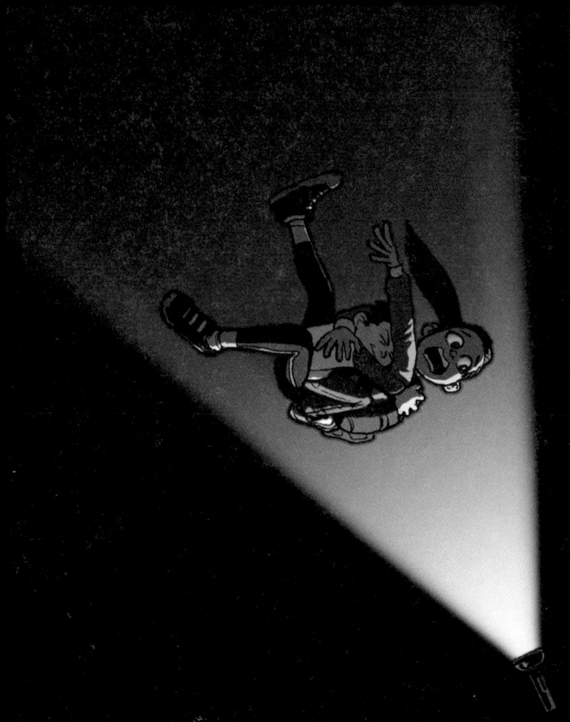

FETCH

Verb 1. Go for and then bring back
2. Bring forth blood or tears

Noun 1. The distance traveled by wind or waves across open water.
2. A strategem or trick.

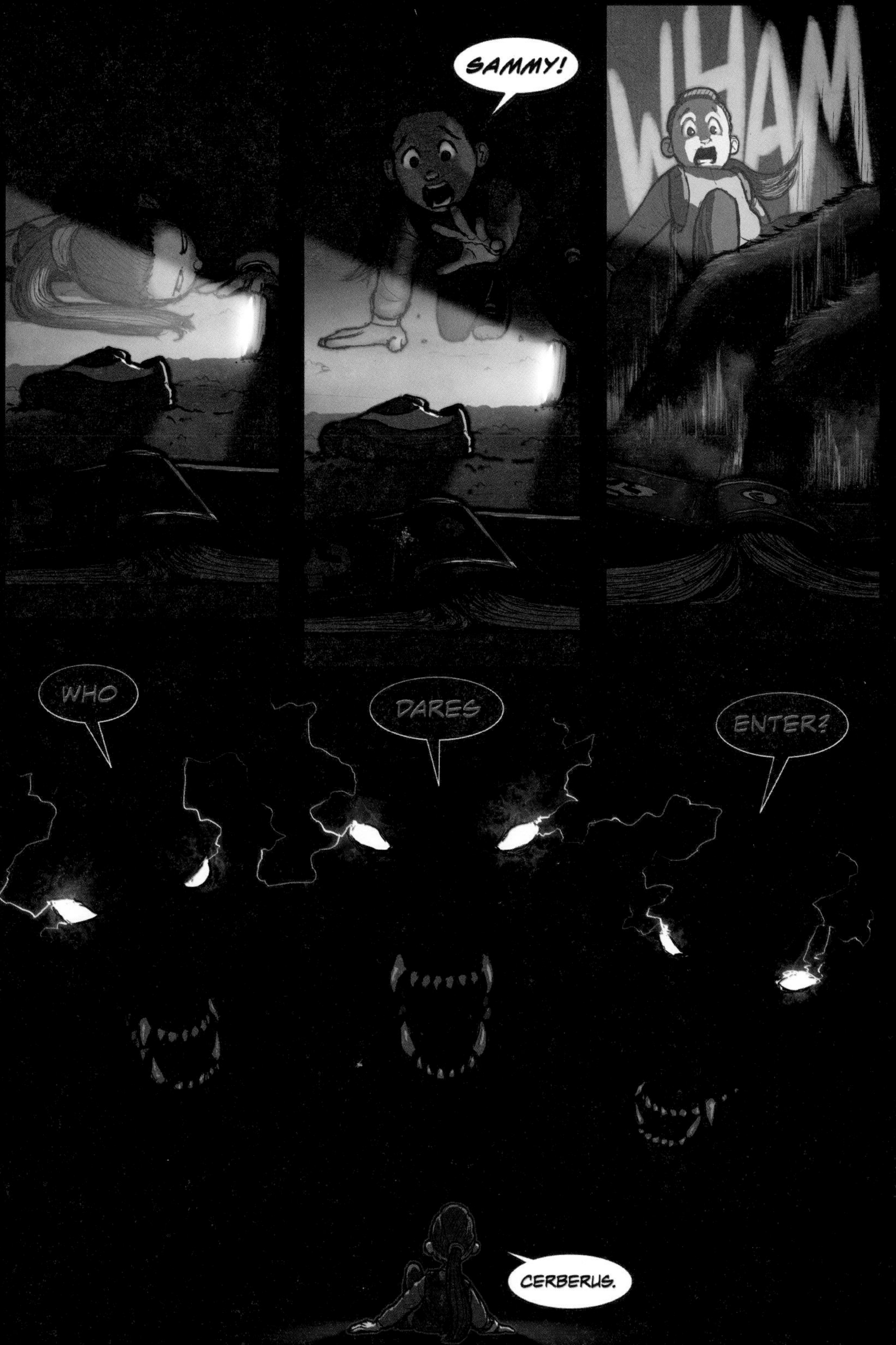
SAMMY!
WHAM
WHO
DARES
ENTER?
CERBERUS.

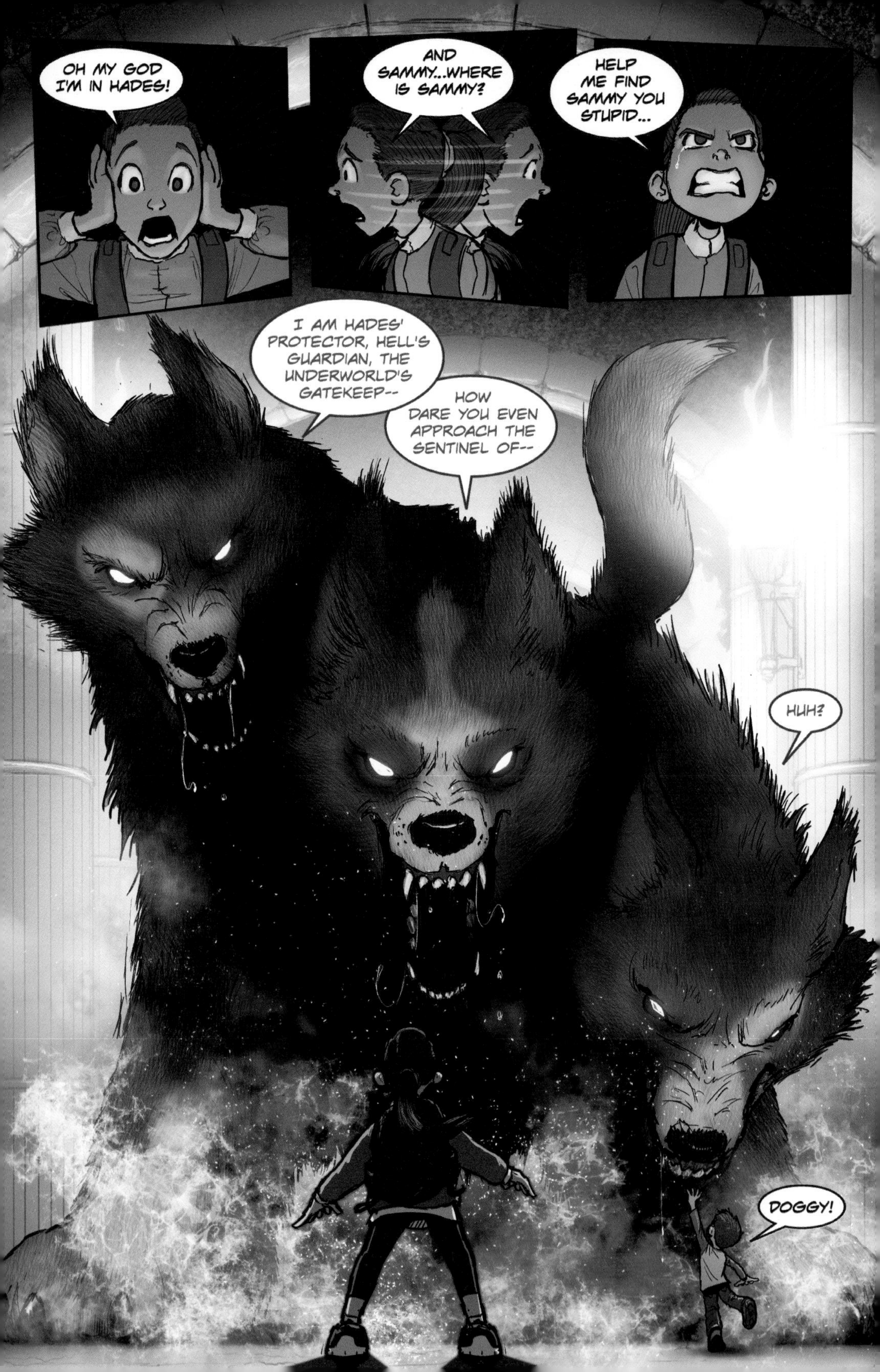
OH MY GOD I'M IN HADES!
AND SAMMY...WHERE IS SAMMY?
HELP ME FIND SAMMY YOU STUPID...
I AM HADES' PROTECTOR, HELL'S GUARDIAN, THE UNDERWORLD'S GATEKEEP--
HOW DARE YOU EVEN APPROACH THE SENTINEL OF--
HUH?
DOGGY!

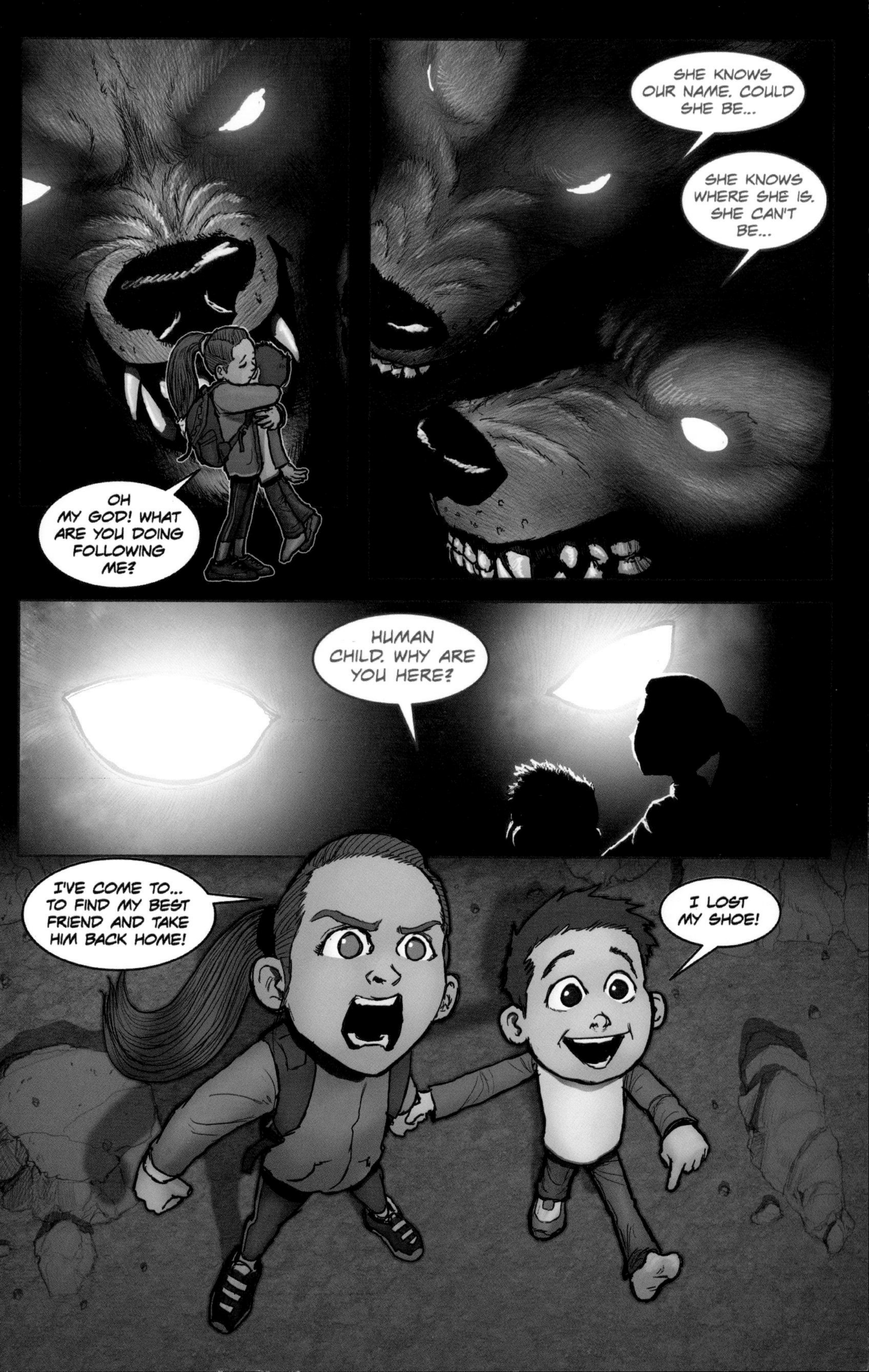
OH MY GOD! WHAT ARE YOU DOING FOLLOWING ME?
SHE KNOWS OUR NAME. COULD SHE BE...
SHE KNOWS WHERE SHE IS. SHE CAN'T BE...
HUMAN CHILD. WHY ARE YOU HERE?
I'VE COME TO... TO FIND MY BEST FRIEND AND TAKE HIM BACK HOME!
I LOST MY SHOE!

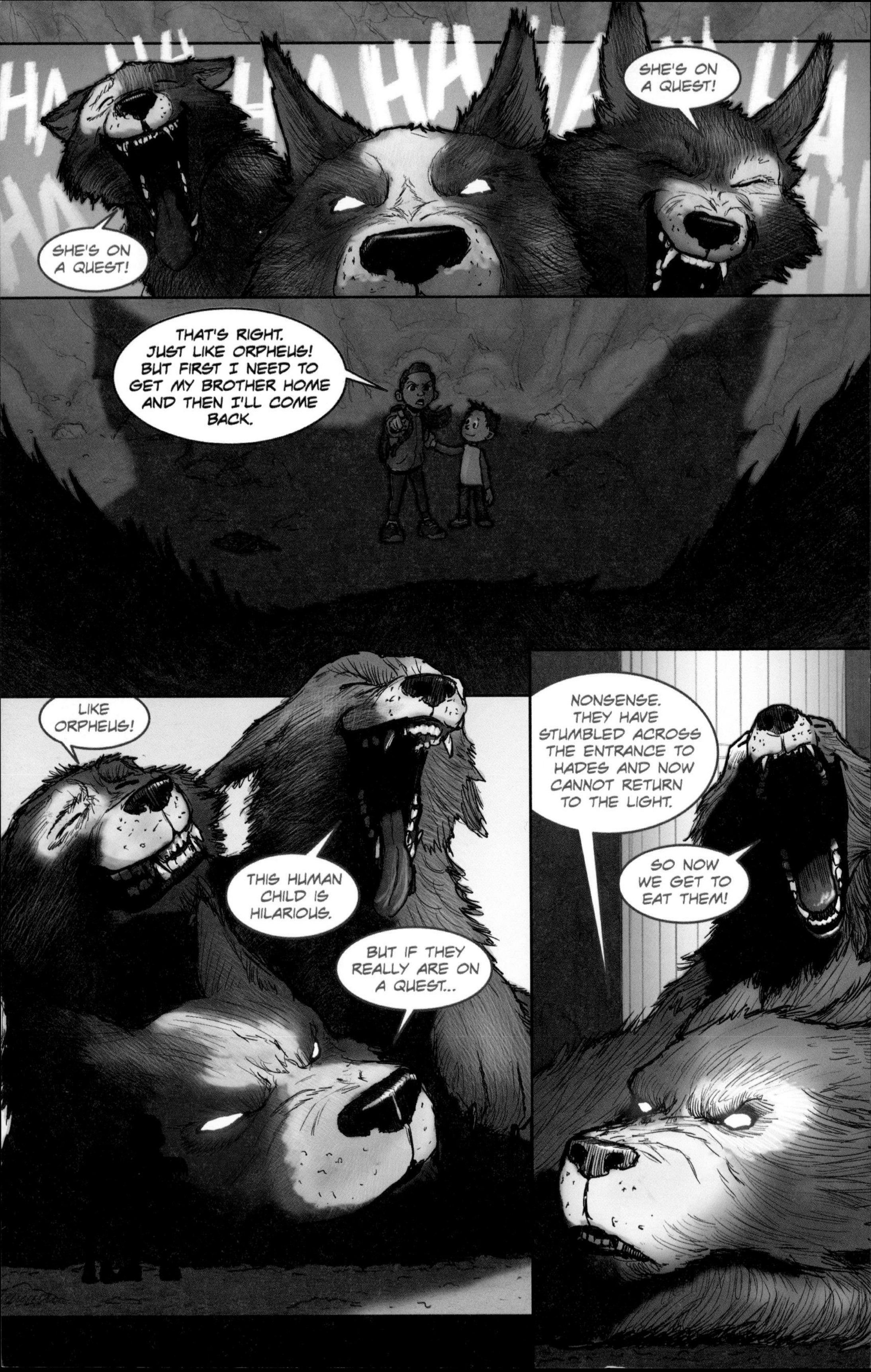
HA HA HA HA HA HA
SHE'S ON A QUEST!
SHE'S ON A QUEST!
THAT'S RIGHT. JUST LIKE ORPHEUS! BUT FIRST I NEED TO GET MY BROTHER HOME AND THEN I'LL COME BACK.
LIKE ORPHEUS!
THIS HUMAN CHILD IS HILARIOUS.
BUT IF THEY REALLY ARE ON A QUEST...
NONSENSE. THEY HAVE STUMBLED ACROSS THE ENTRANCE TO HADES AND NOW CANNOT RETURN TO THE LIGHT.
SO NOW WE GET TO EAT THEM!

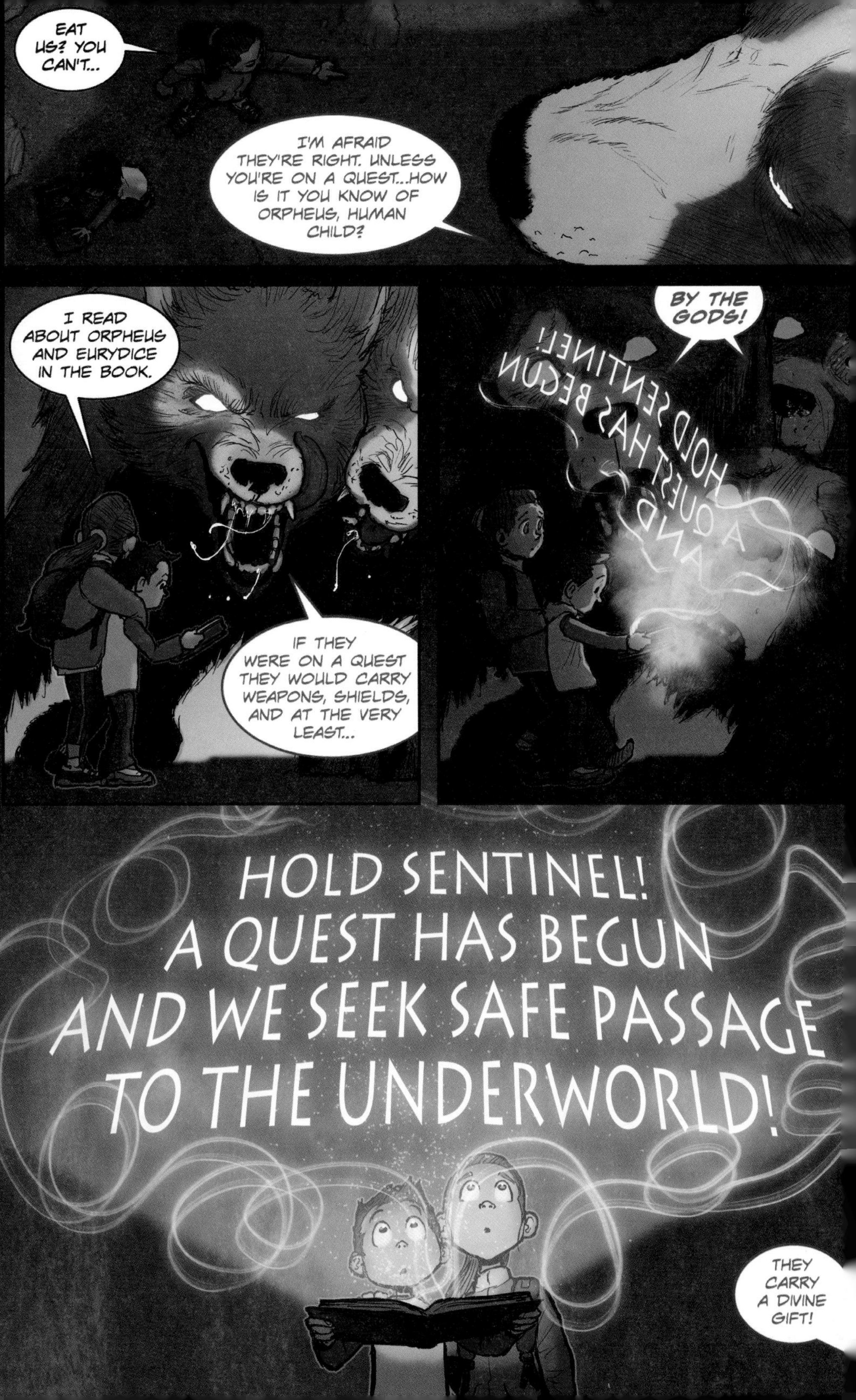

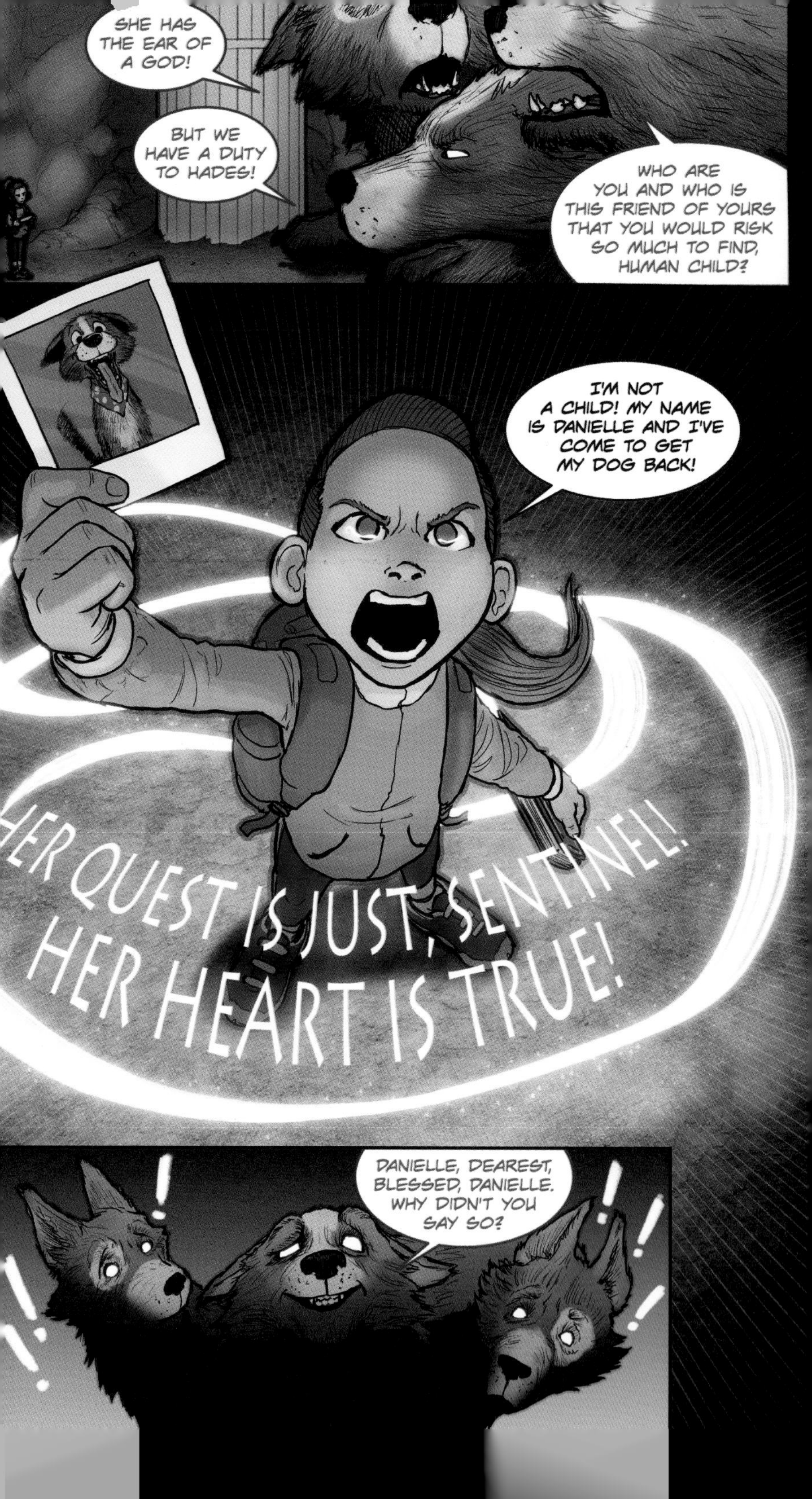
SHE HAS THE EAR OF A GOD!
BUT WE HAVE A DUTY TO HADES!
WHO ARE YOU AND WHO IS THIS FRIEND OF YOURS THAT YOU WOULD RISK SO MUCH TO FIND, HUMAN CHILD?
I'M NOT A CHILD! MY NAME IS DANIELLE AND I'VE COME TO GET MY DOG BACK!
HER QUEST IS JUST, SENTINEL! HER HEART IS TRUE!
DANIELLE, DEAREST, BLESSED, DANIELLE. WHY DIDN'T YOU SAY SO?
!
!
!
!
!

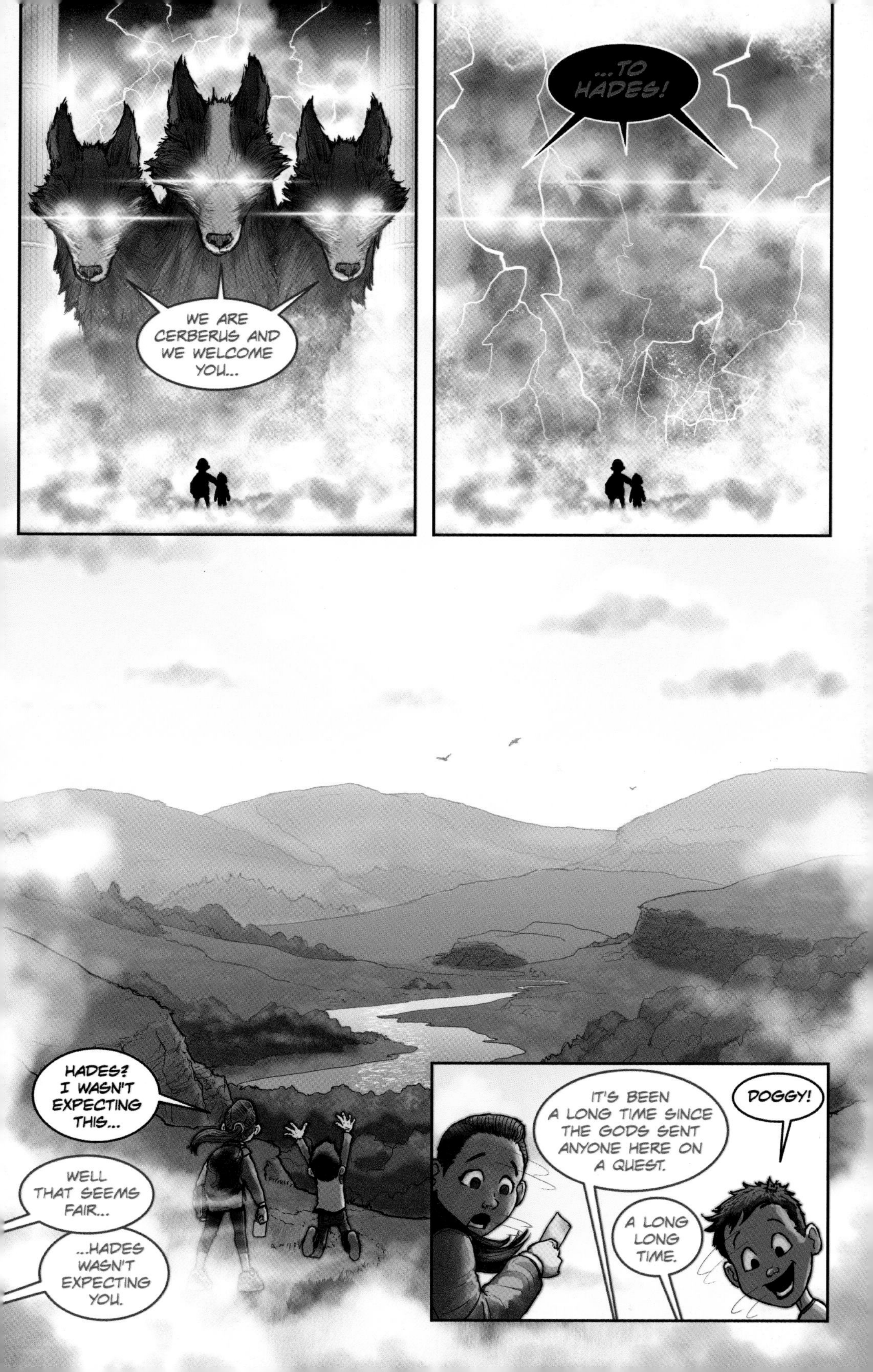
WE ARE CERBERUS AND WE WELCOME YOU...
...TO HADES!
HADES? I WASN'T EXPECTING THIS...
WELL THAT SEEMS FAIR...
...HADES WASN'T EXPECTING YOU.
IT'S BEEN A LONG TIME SINCE THE GODS SENT ANYONE HERE ON A QUEST.
DOGGY!
A LONG LONG TIME.

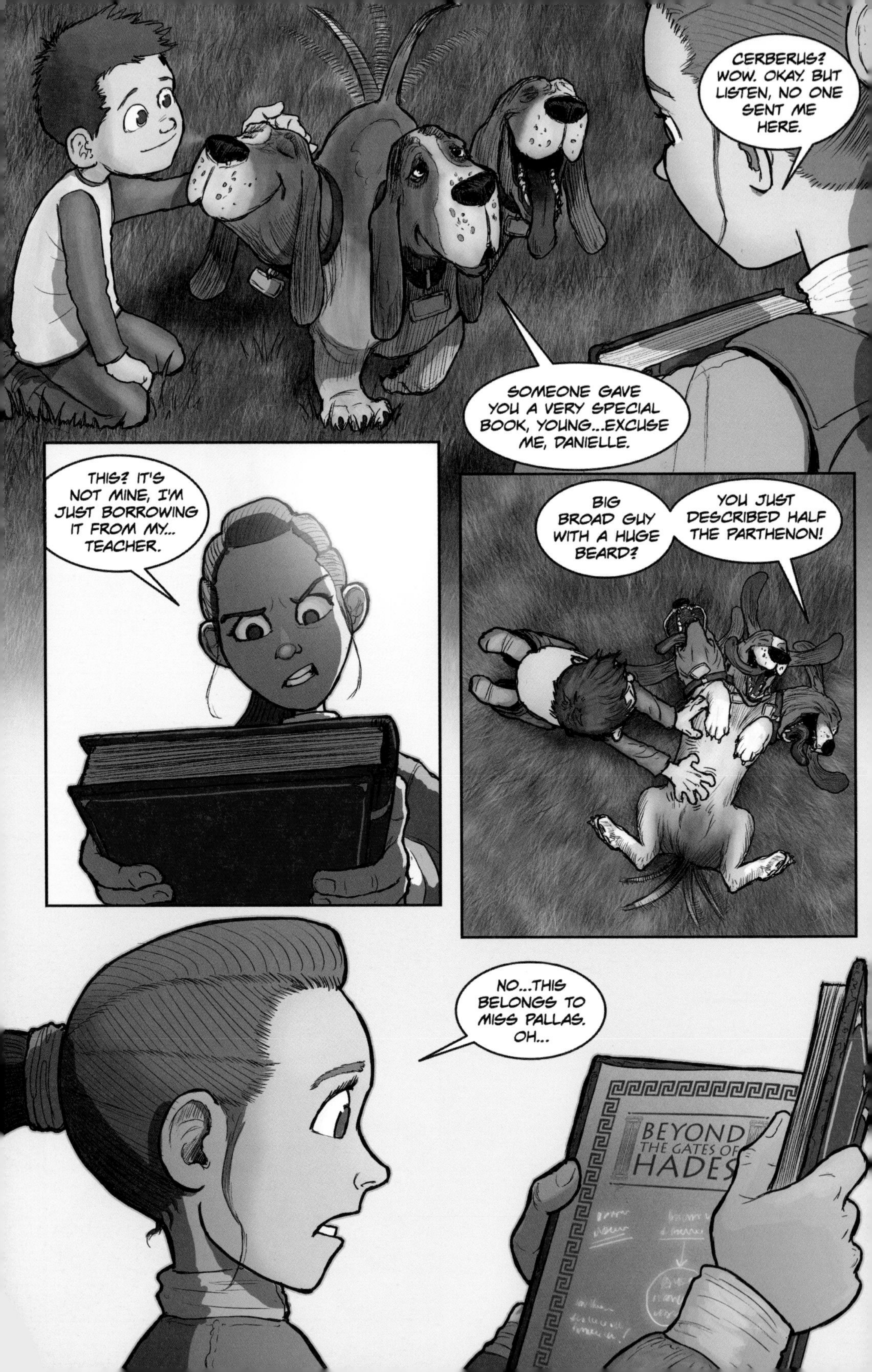
CERBERUS? WOW. OKAY. BUT LISTEN, NO ONE SENT ME HERE.
SOMEONE GAVE YOU A VERY SPECIAL BOOK, YOUNG...EXCUSE ME, DANIELLE.
THIS? IT'S NOT MINE, I'M JUST BORROWING IT FROM MY... TEACHER.
BIG BROAD GUY WITH A HUGE BEARD?
YOU JUST DESCRIBED HALF THE PARTHENON!
NO...THIS BELONGS TO MISS PALLAS. OH...
BEYOND THE GATES OF HADES

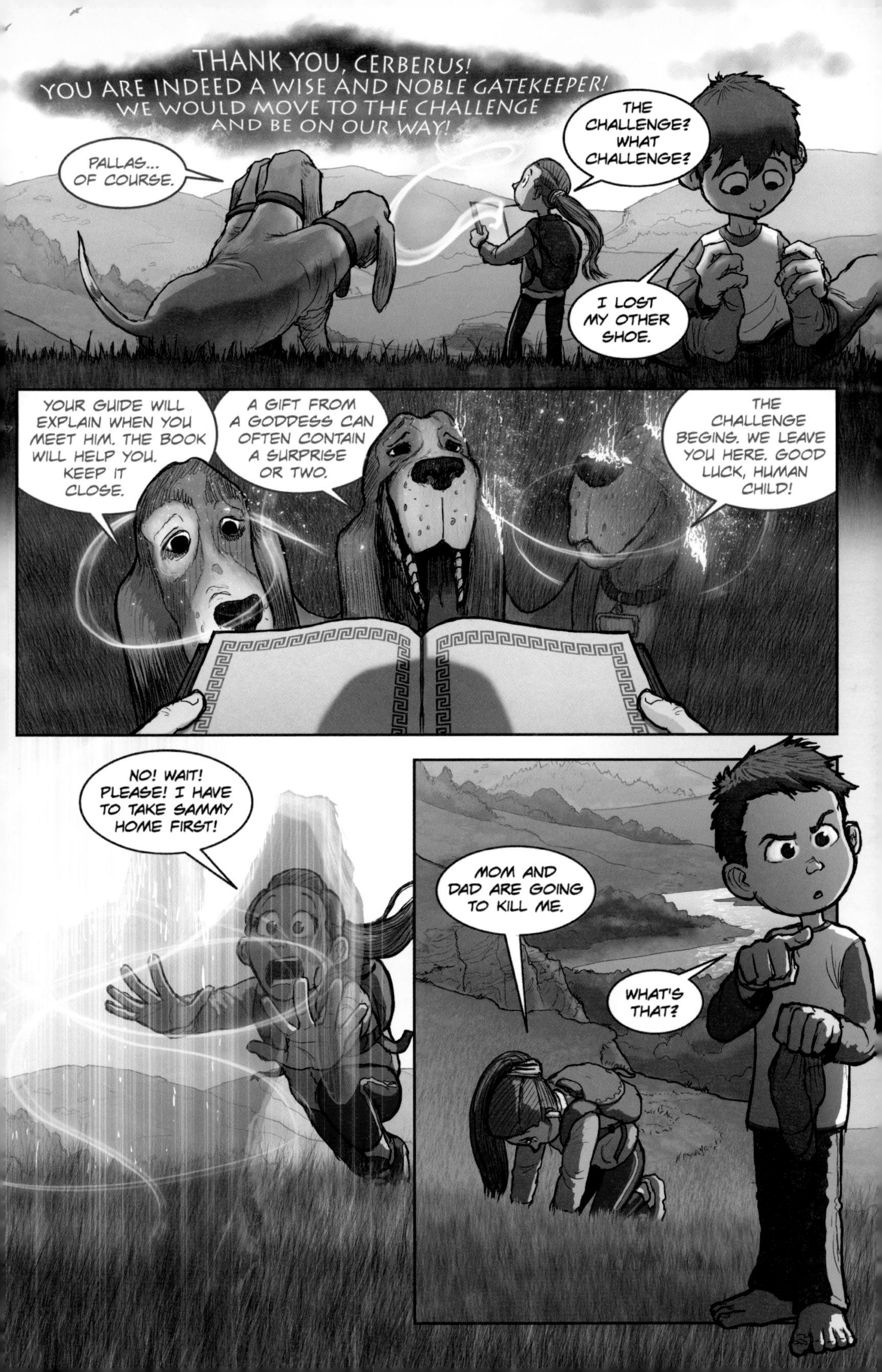
THANK YOU, CERBERUS! YOU ARE INDEED A WISE AND NOBLE GATEKEEPER! WE WOULD MOVE TO THE CHALLENGE AND BE ON OUR WAY!
PALLAS... OF COURSE.
THE CHALLENGE? WHAT CHALLENGE?
I LOST MY OTHER SHOE.
YOUR GUIDE WILL EXPLAIN WHEN YOU MEET HIM. THE BOOK WILL HELP YOU. KEEP IT CLOSE.
A GIFT FROM A GODDESS CAN OFTEN CONTAIN A SURPRISE OR TWO.
THE CHALLENGE BEGINS. WE LEAVE YOU HERE. GOOD LUCK, HUMAN CHILD!
NO! WAIT! PLEASE! I HAVE TO TAKE SAMMY HOME FIRST!
MOM AND DAD ARE GOING TO KILL ME.
WHAT'S THAT?

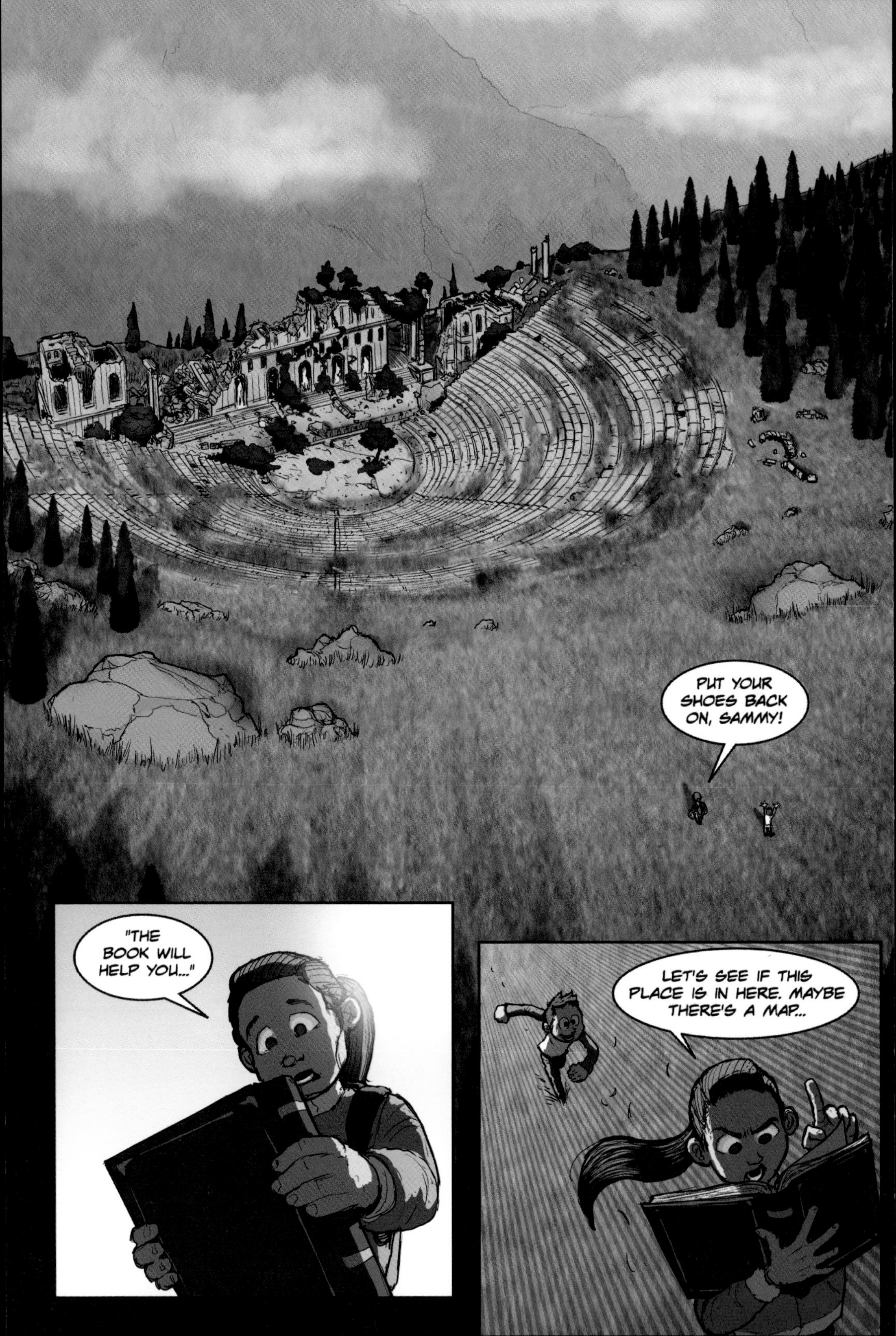
PUT YOUR SHOES BACK ON, SAMMY!
"THE BOOK WILL HELP YOU..."
LET'S SEE IF THIS PLACE IS IN HERE. MAYBE THERE'S A MAP...

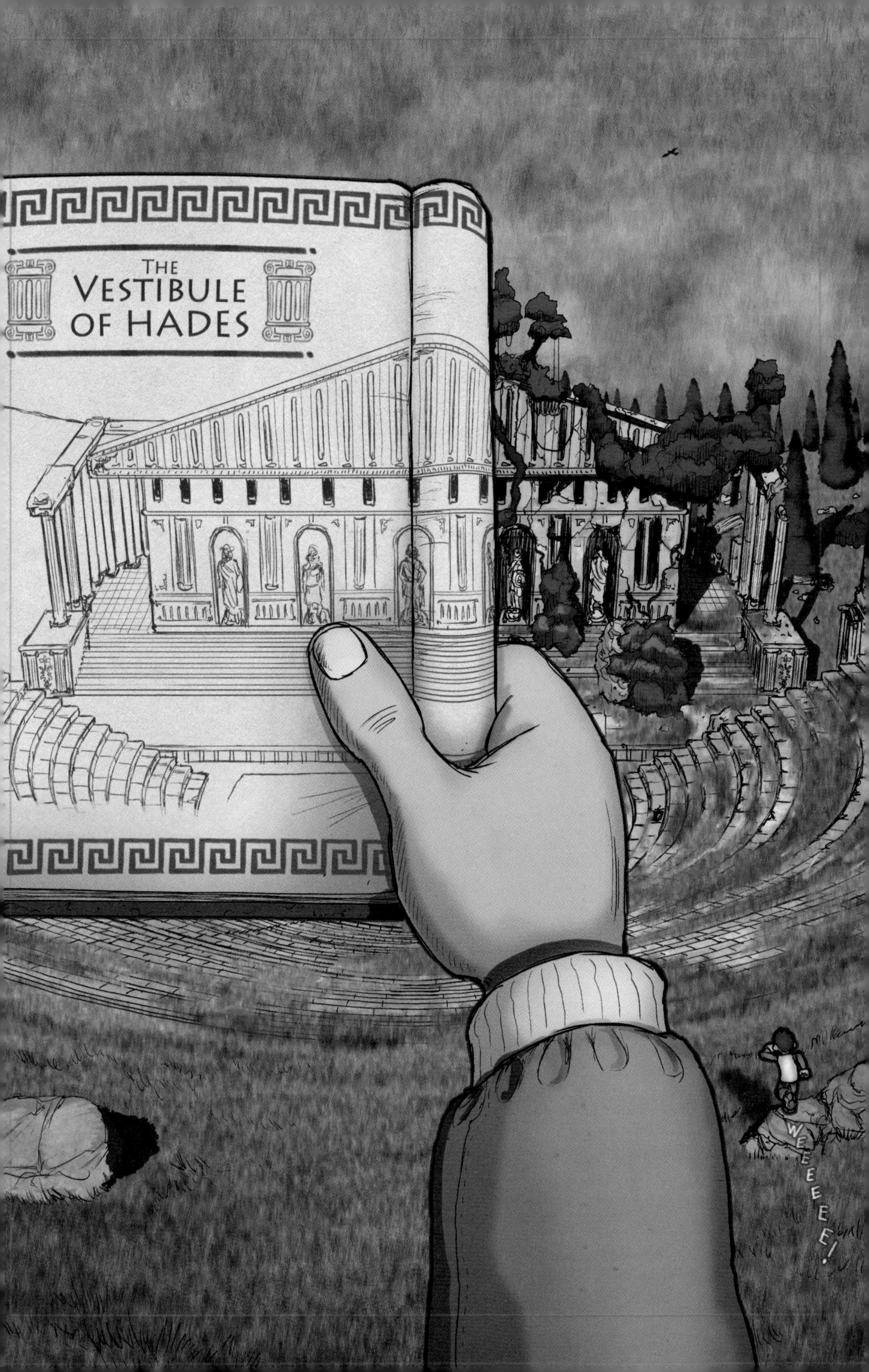
THE VESTIBULE OF HADES
WEEEEEE!

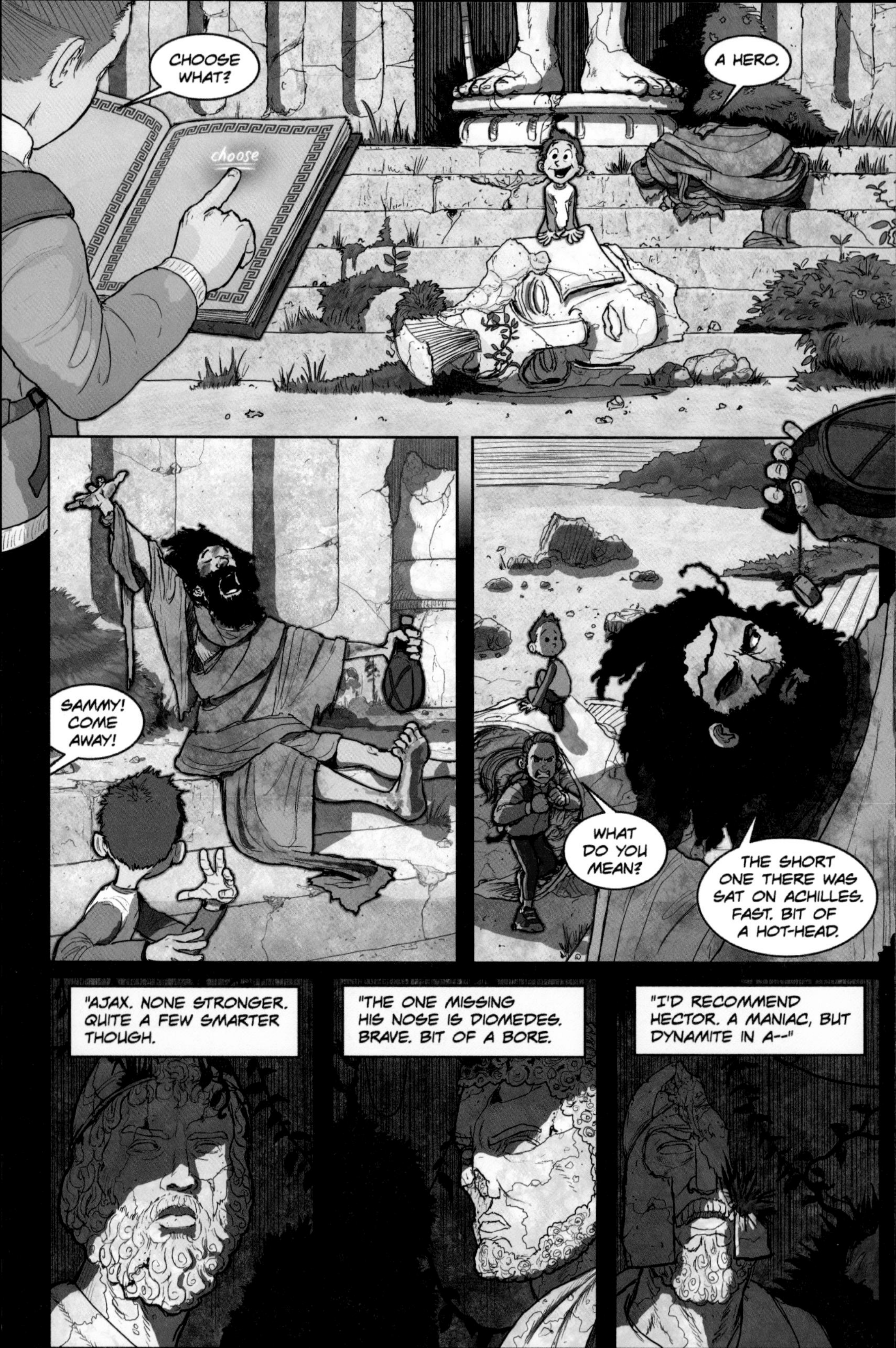
CHOOSE WHAT?
choose
A HERO.
SAMMY! COME AWAY!
WHAT DO YOU MEAN?
THE SHORT ONE THERE WAS SAT ON ACHILLES. FAST. BIT OF A HOT-HEAD.
"AJAX. NONE STRONGER. QUITE A FEW SMARTER THOUGH.
"THE ONE MISSING HIS NOSE IS DIOMEDES. BRAVE. BIT OF A BORE.
"I'D RECOMMEND HECTOR. A MANIAC, BUT DYNAMITE IN A--"

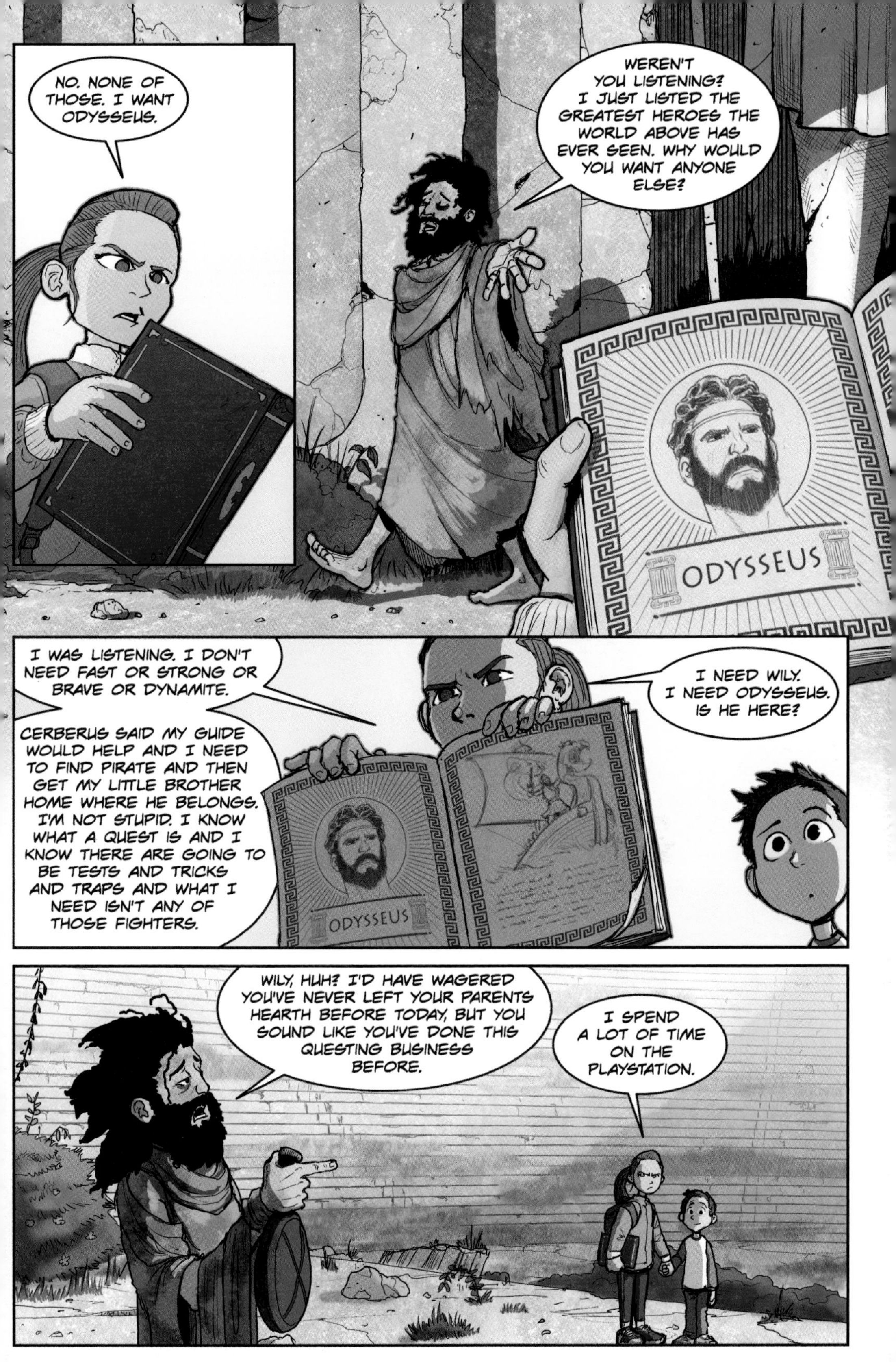
NO. NONE OF THOSE. I WANT ODYSSEUS.
WEREN'T YOU LISTENING? I JUST LISTED THE GREATEST HEROES THE WORLD ABOVE HAS EVER SEEN. WHY WOULD YOU WANT ANYONE ELSE?
ODYSSEUS
I WAS LISTENING. I DON'T NEED FAST OR STRONG OR BRAVE OR DYNAMITE.
CERBERUS SAID MY GUIDE WOULD HELP AND I NEED TO FIND PIRATE AND THEN GET MY LITTLE BROTHER HOME WHERE HE BELONGS. I'M NOT STUPID. I KNOW WHAT A QUEST IS AND I KNOW THERE ARE GOING TO BE TESTS AND TRICKS AND TRAPS AND WHAT I NEED ISN'T ANY OF THOSE FIGHTERS.
I NEED WILY. I NEED ODYSSEUS. IS HE HERE?
ODYSSEUS
WILY, HUH? I'D HAVE WAGERED YOU'VE NEVER LEFT YOUR PARENTS HEARTH BEFORE TODAY, BUT YOU SOUND LIKE YOU'VE DONE THIS QUESTING BUSINESS BEFORE.
I SPEND A LOT OF TIME ON THE PLAYSTATION.

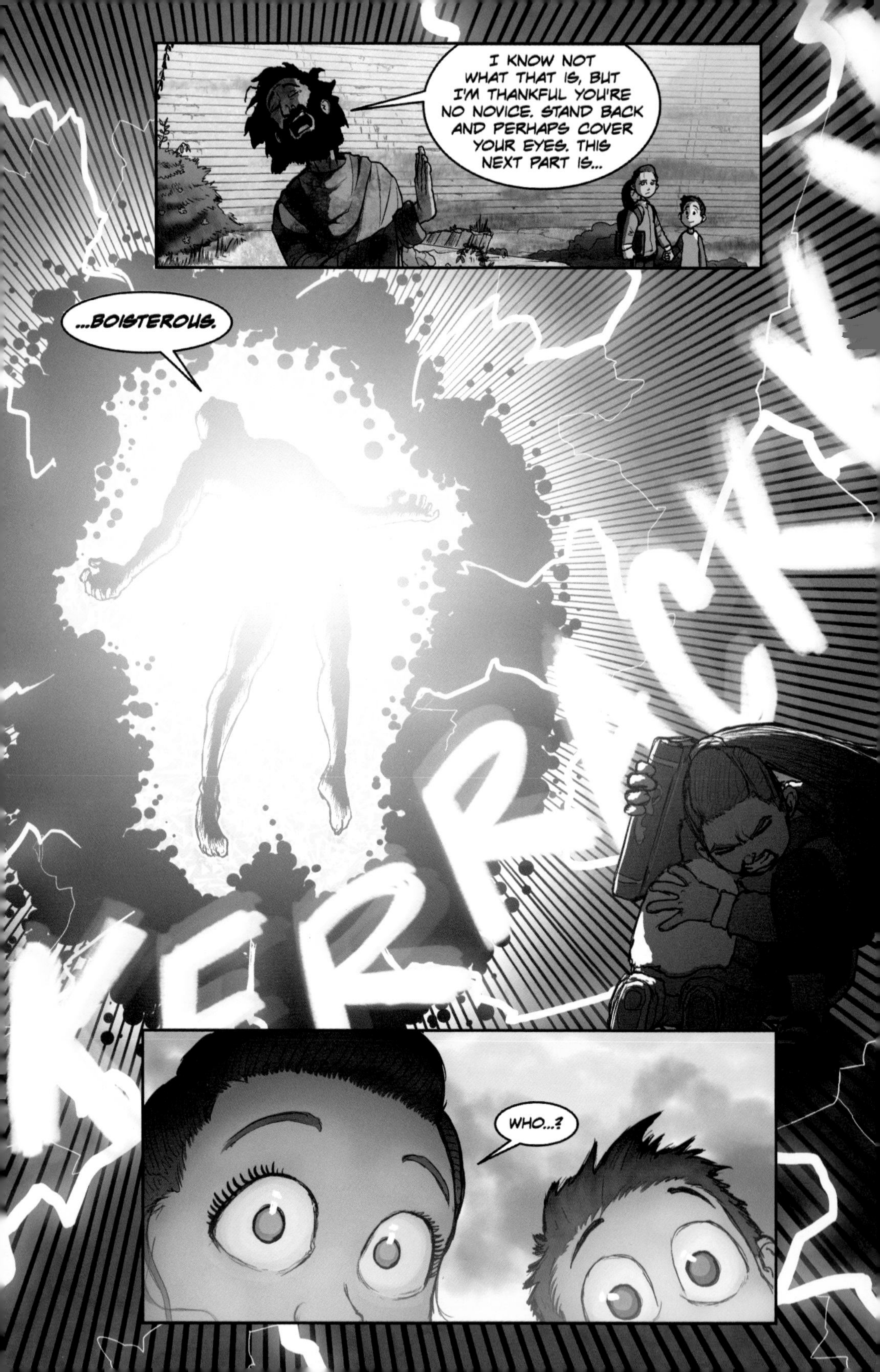
I KNOW NOT WHAT THAT IS, BUT I'M THANKFUL YOU'RE NO NOVICE. STAND BACK AND PERHAPS COVER YOUR EYES. THIS NEXT PART IS...
...BOISTEROUS.
WHO...?

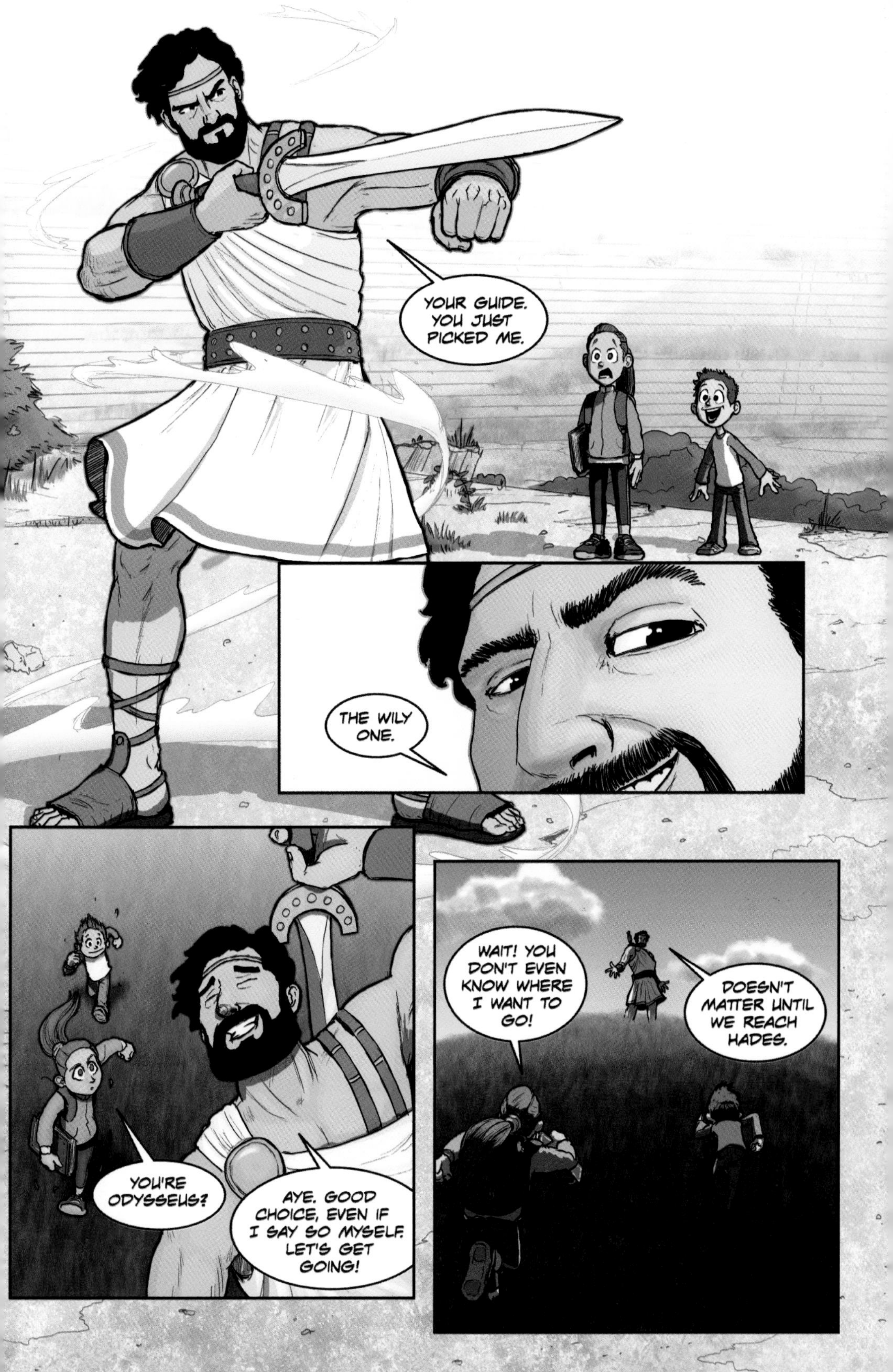
YOUR GUIDE. YOU JUST PICKED ME.
THE WILY ONE.
YOU'RE ODYSSEUS?
AYE. GOOD CHOICE, EVEN IF I SAY SO MYSELF. LET'S GET GOING!
WAIT! YOU DON'T EVEN KNOW WHERE I WANT TO GO!
DOESN'T MATTER UNTIL WE REACH HADES.

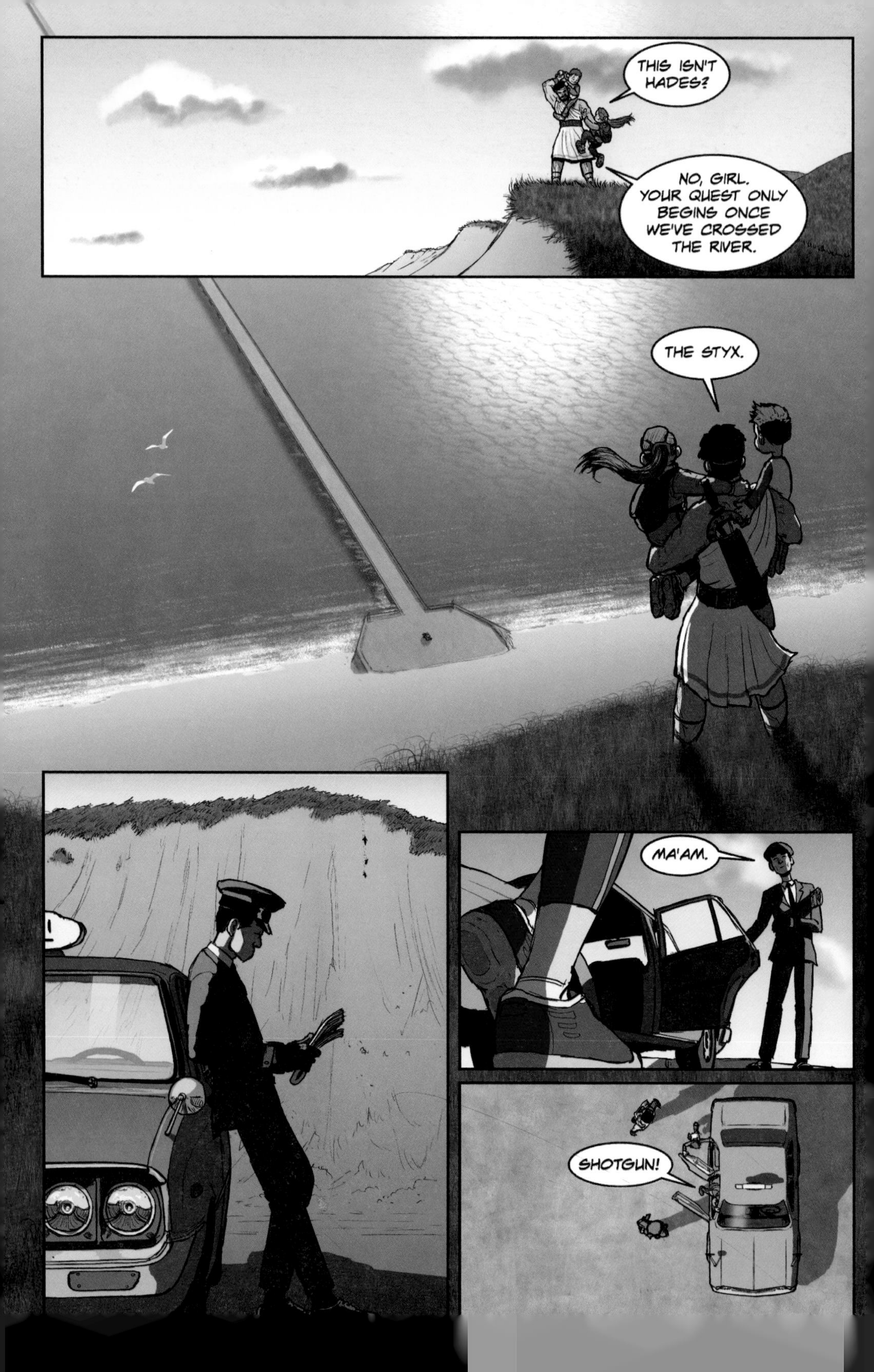
THIS ISN'T HADES?
NO, GIRL. YOUR QUEST ONLY BEGINS ONCE WE'VE CROSSED THE RIVER.
THE STYX.
MA'AM.
SHOTGUN!

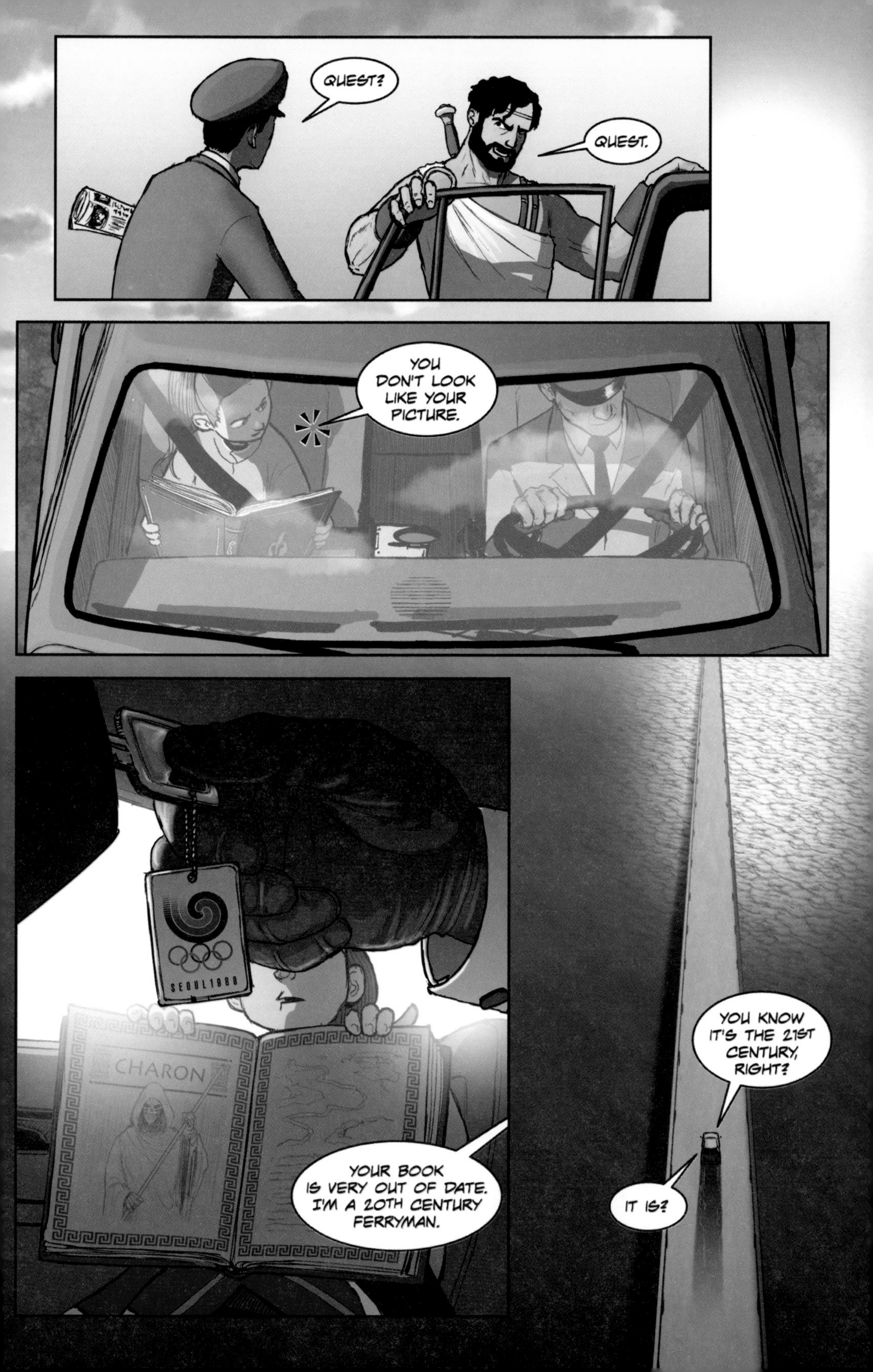
QUEST?
QUEST.
YOU DON'T LOOK LIKE YOUR PICTURE.
SEOUL1988
CHARON
YOUR BOOK IS VERY OUT OF DATE. I'M A 20TH CENTURY FERRYMAN.
YOU KNOW IT'S THE 21ST CENTURY, RIGHT?
IT IS?

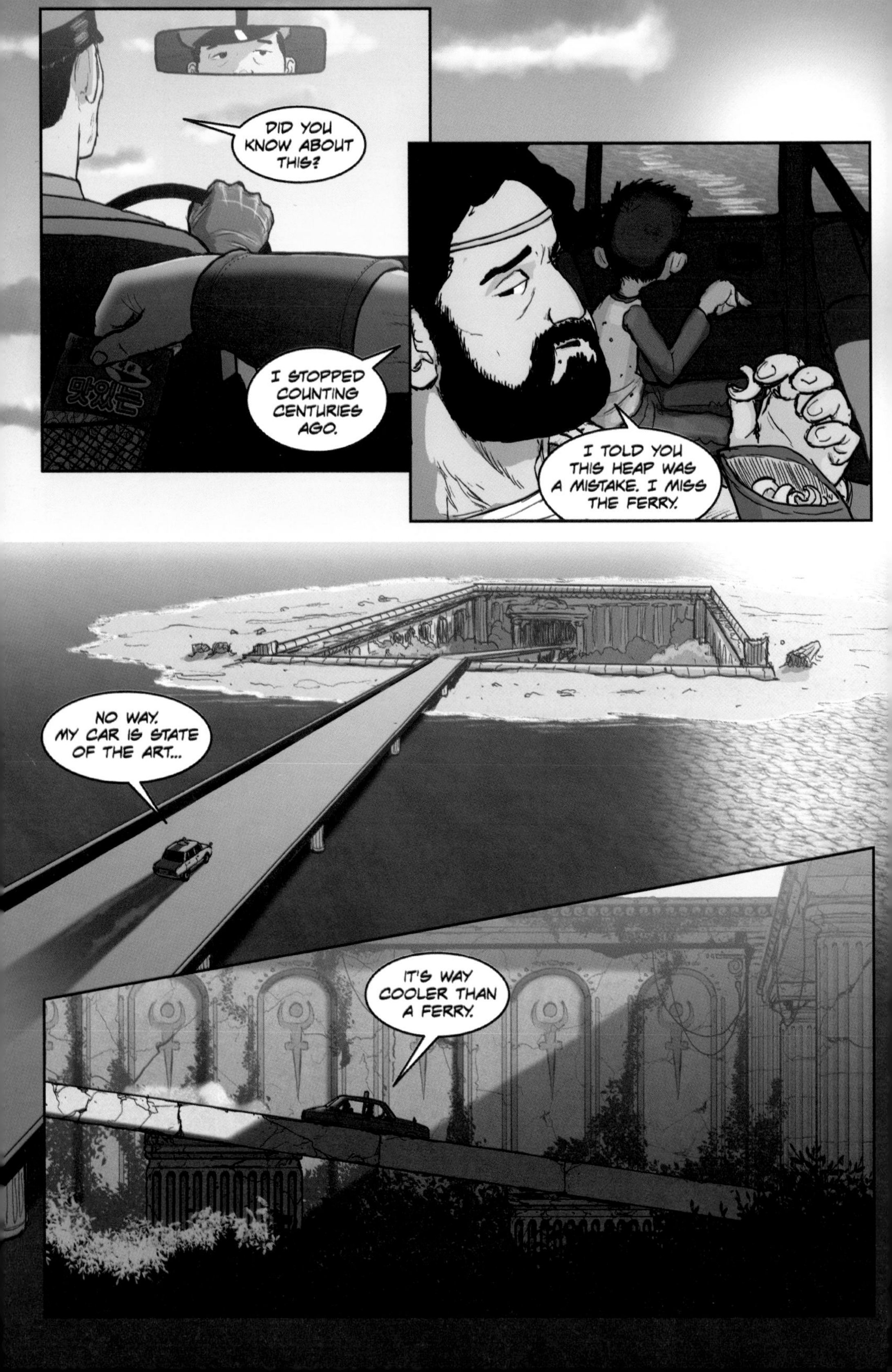
DID YOU KNOW ABOUT THIS?
I STOPPED COUNTING CENTURIES AGO.
I TOLD YOU THIS HEAP WAS A MISTAKE. I MISS THE FERRY.
NO WAY. MY CAR IS STATE OF THE ART...
IT'S WAY COOLER THAN A FERRY.

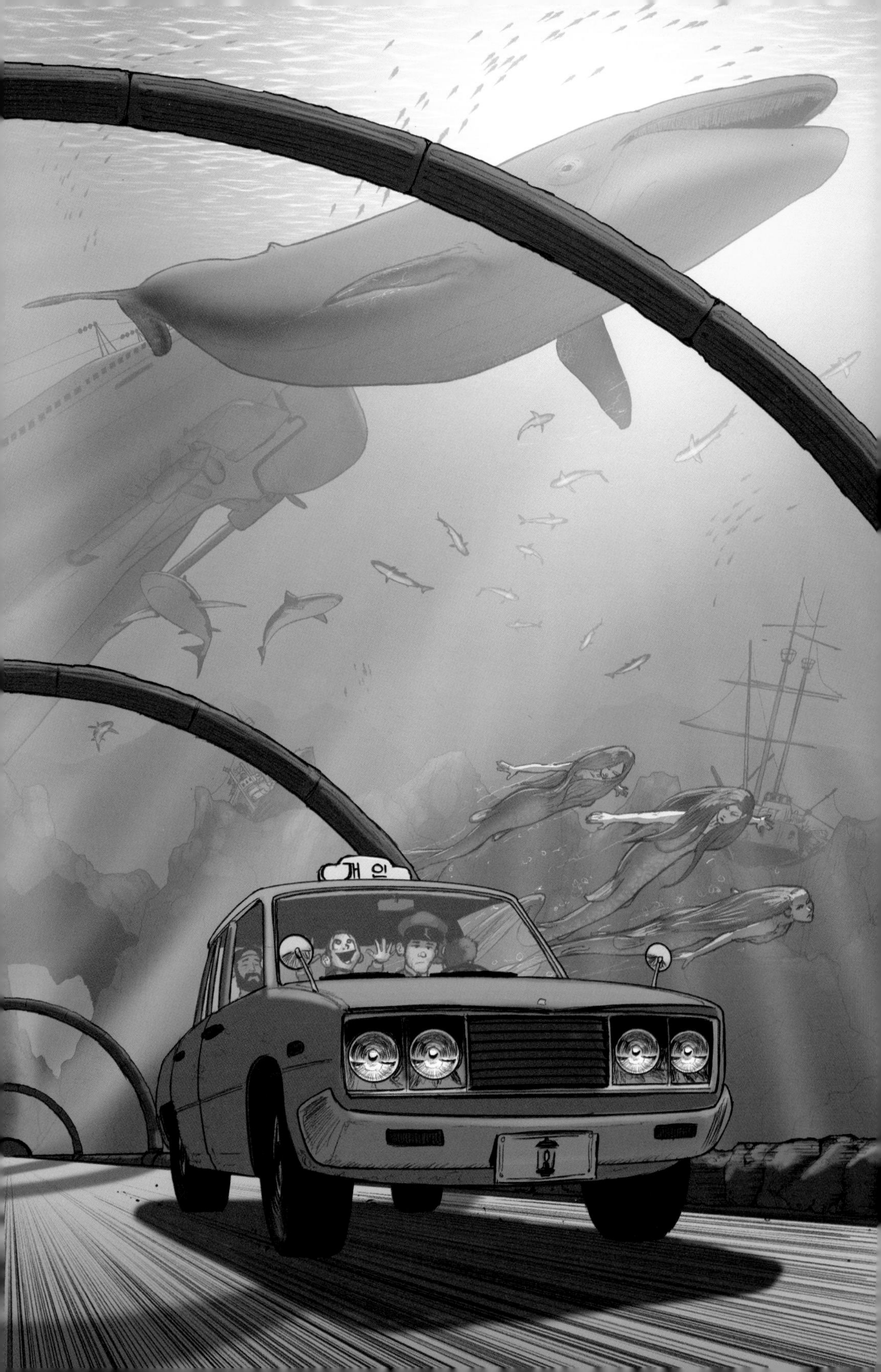
개 의

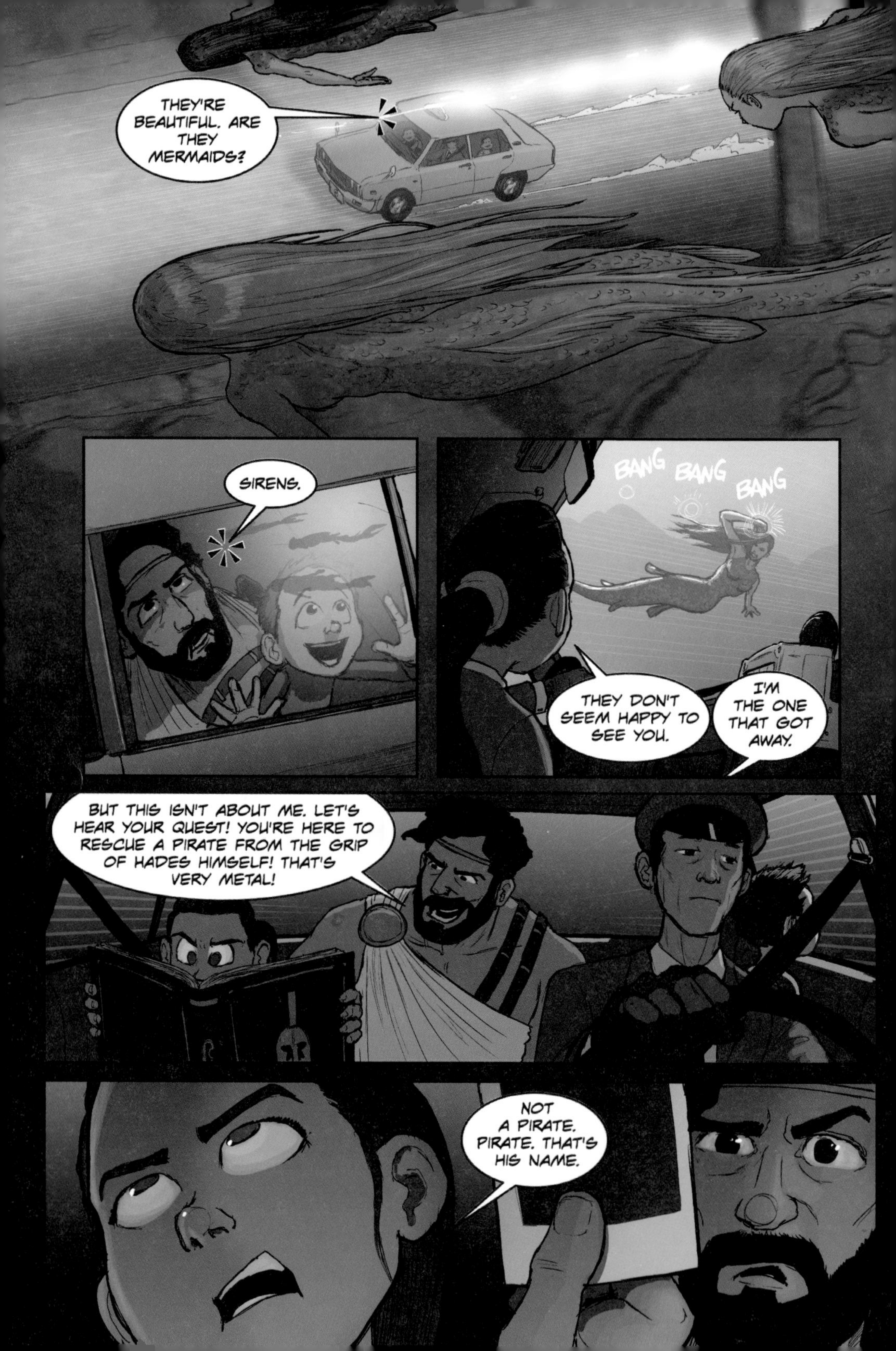
THEY'RE BEAUTIFUL. ARE THEY MERMAIDS?
SIRENS.
BANG
BANG
BANG
THEY DON'T SEEM HAPPY TO SEE YOU.
I'M THE ONE THAT GOT AWAY.
BUT THIS ISN'T ABOUT ME. LET'S HEAR YOUR QUEST! YOU'RE HERE TO RESCUE A PIRATE FROM THE GRIP OF HADES HIMSELF! THAT'S VERY METAL!
NOT A PIRATE. PIRATE. THAT'S HIS NAME.

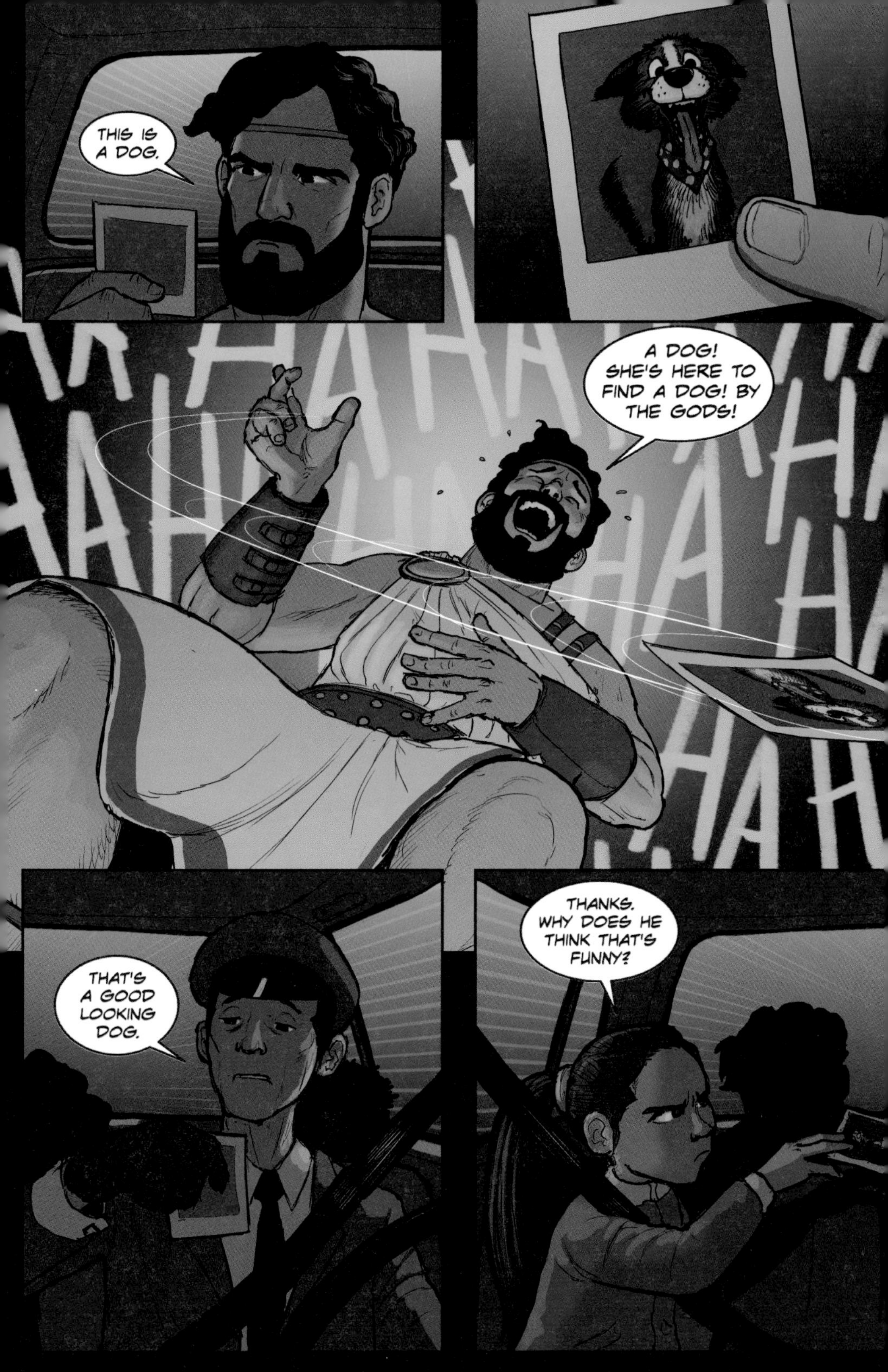
THIS IS A DOG.
A DOG! SHE'S HERE TO FIND A DOG! BY THE GODS!
HAHAHAHA
THAT'S A GOOD LOOKING DOG.
THANKS. WHY DOES HE THINK THAT'S FUNNY?

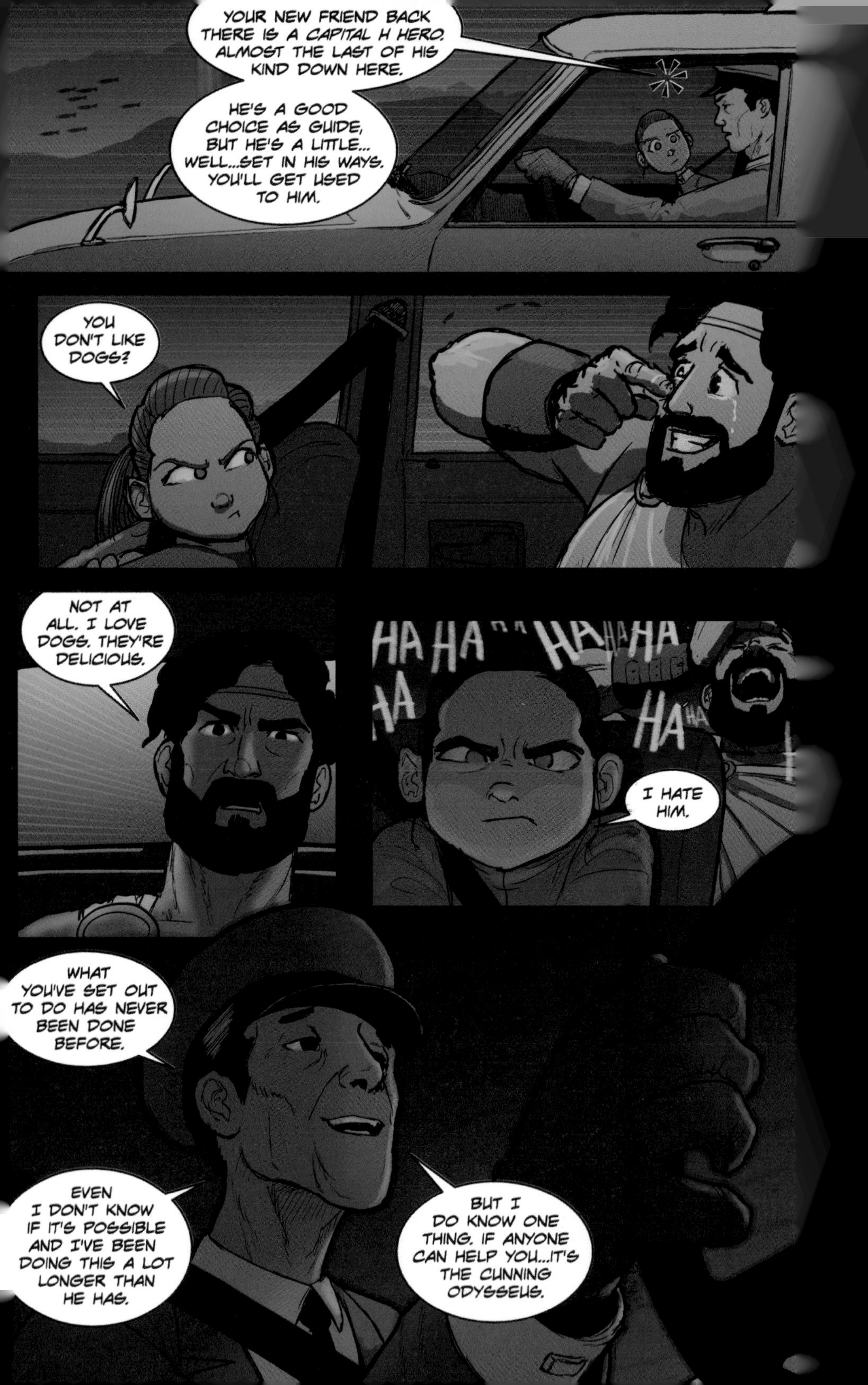
YOUR NEW FRIEND BACK THERE IS A CAPITAL H HERO. ALMOST THE LAST OF HIS KIND DOWN HERE.
HE'S A GOOD CHOICE AS GUIDE, BUT HE'S A LITTLE... WELL...SET IN HIS WAYS. YOU'LL GET USED TO HIM.
YOU DON'T LIKE DOGS?
NOT AT ALL. I LOVE DOGS. THEY'RE DELICIOUS.
HA HA HA HA HA HA HA HA
I HATE HIM.
WHAT YOU'VE SET OUT TO DO HAS NEVER BEEN DONE BEFORE.
EVEN I DON'T KNOW IF IT'S POSSIBLE AND I'VE BEEN DOING THIS A LOT LONGER THAN HE HAS.
BUT I DO KNOW ONE THING. IF ANYONE CAN HELP YOU...IT'S THE CUNNING ODYSSEUS.

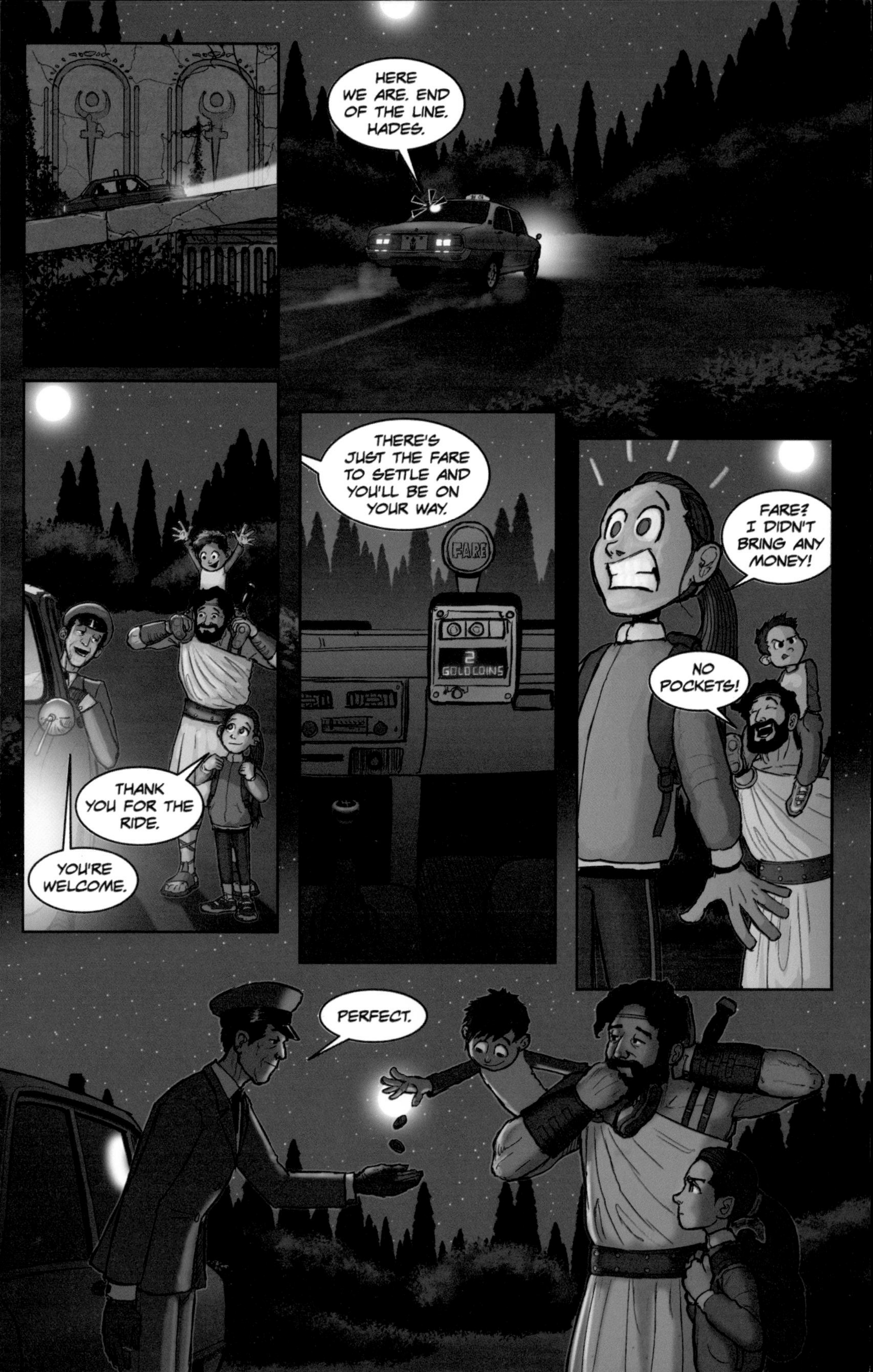
HERE WE ARE. END OF THE LINE. HADES.
THANK YOU FOR THE RIDE.
YOU'RE WELCOME.
THERE'S JUST THE FARE TO SETTLE AND YOU'LL BE ON YOUR WAY.
FARE
2 GOLD COINS
FARE? I DIDN'T BRING ANY MONEY!
NO POCKETS!
PERFECT.

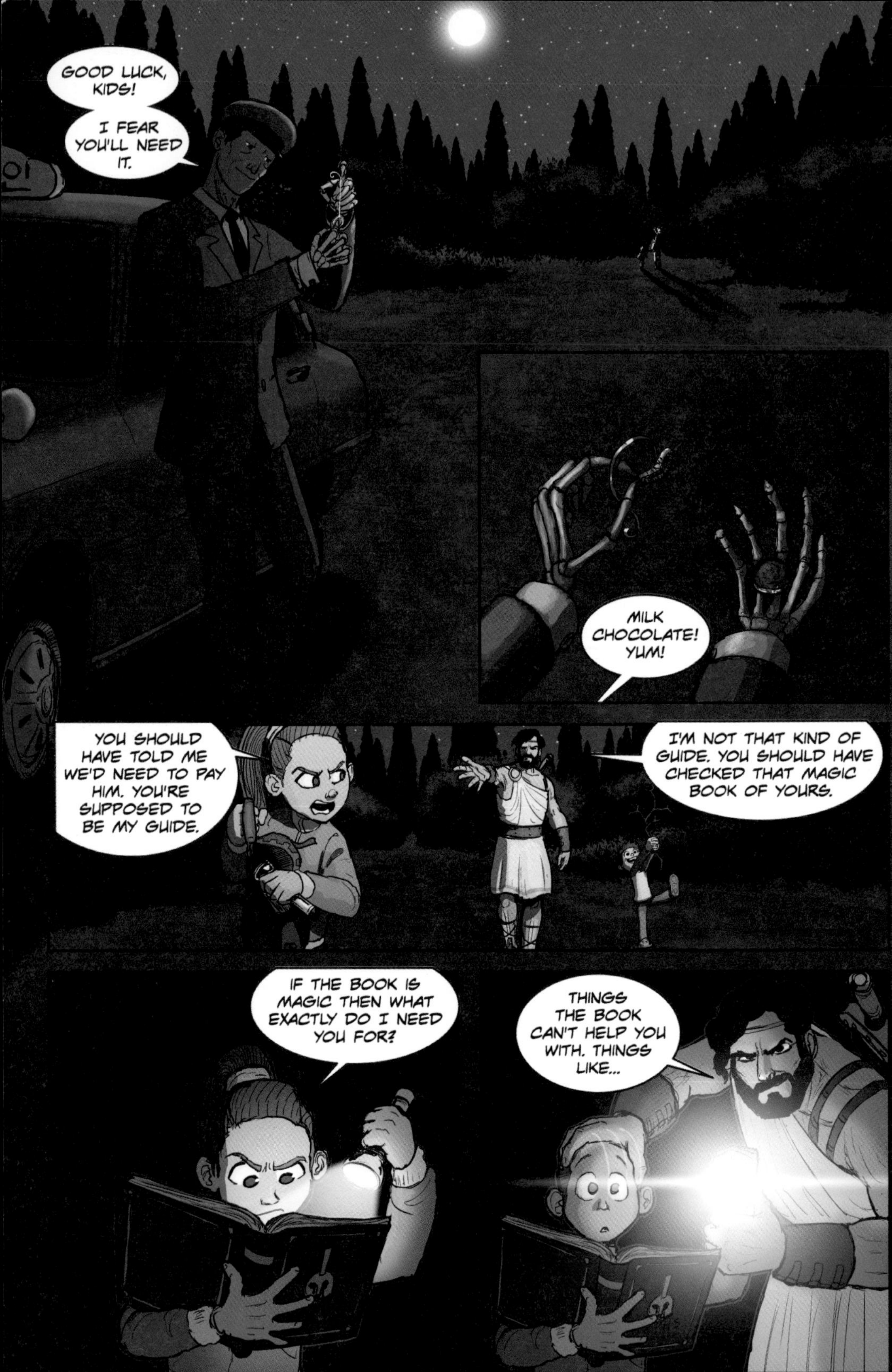
GOOD LUCK, KIDS!
I FEAR YOU'LL NEED IT.
MILK CHOCOLATE! YUM!
YOU SHOULD HAVE TOLD ME WE'D NEED TO PAY HIM. YOU'RE SUPPOSED TO BE MY GUIDE.
I'M NOT THAT KIND OF GUIDE. YOU SHOULD HAVE CHECKED THAT MAGIC BOOK OF YOURS.
IF THE BOOK IS MAGIC THEN WHAT EXACTLY DO I NEED YOU FOR?
THINGS THE BOOK CAN'T HELP YOU WITH. THINGS LIKE...

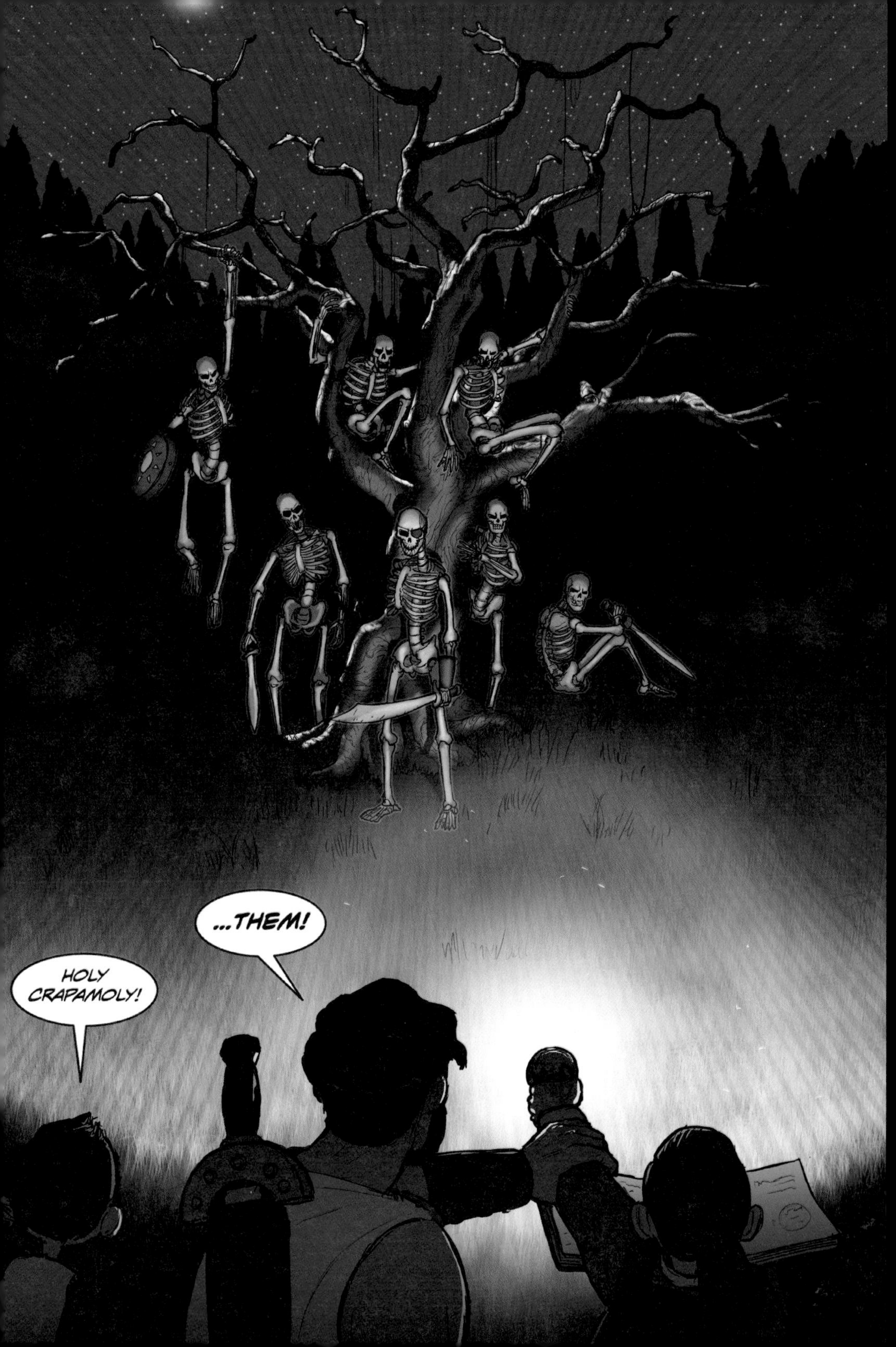
HOLY CRAPAMOLY!
...THEM!

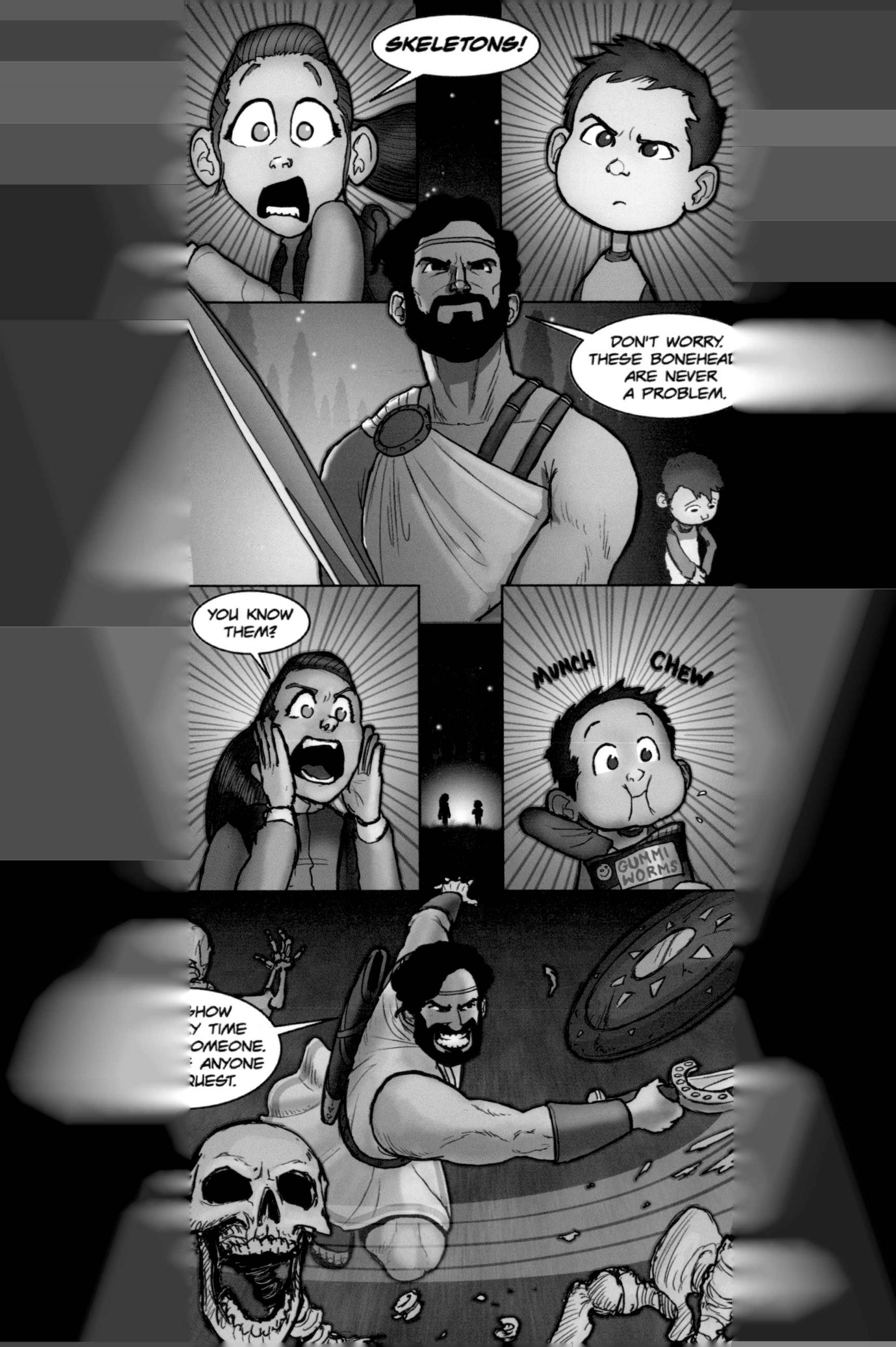
SKELETONS!
DON'T WORRY. THESE BONEHEA ARE NEVER A PROBLEM.
YOU KNOW THEM?
MUNCH
CHEW
GUMMI WORMS
SHOW Y TIME OMEONE. ANYONE QUEST.

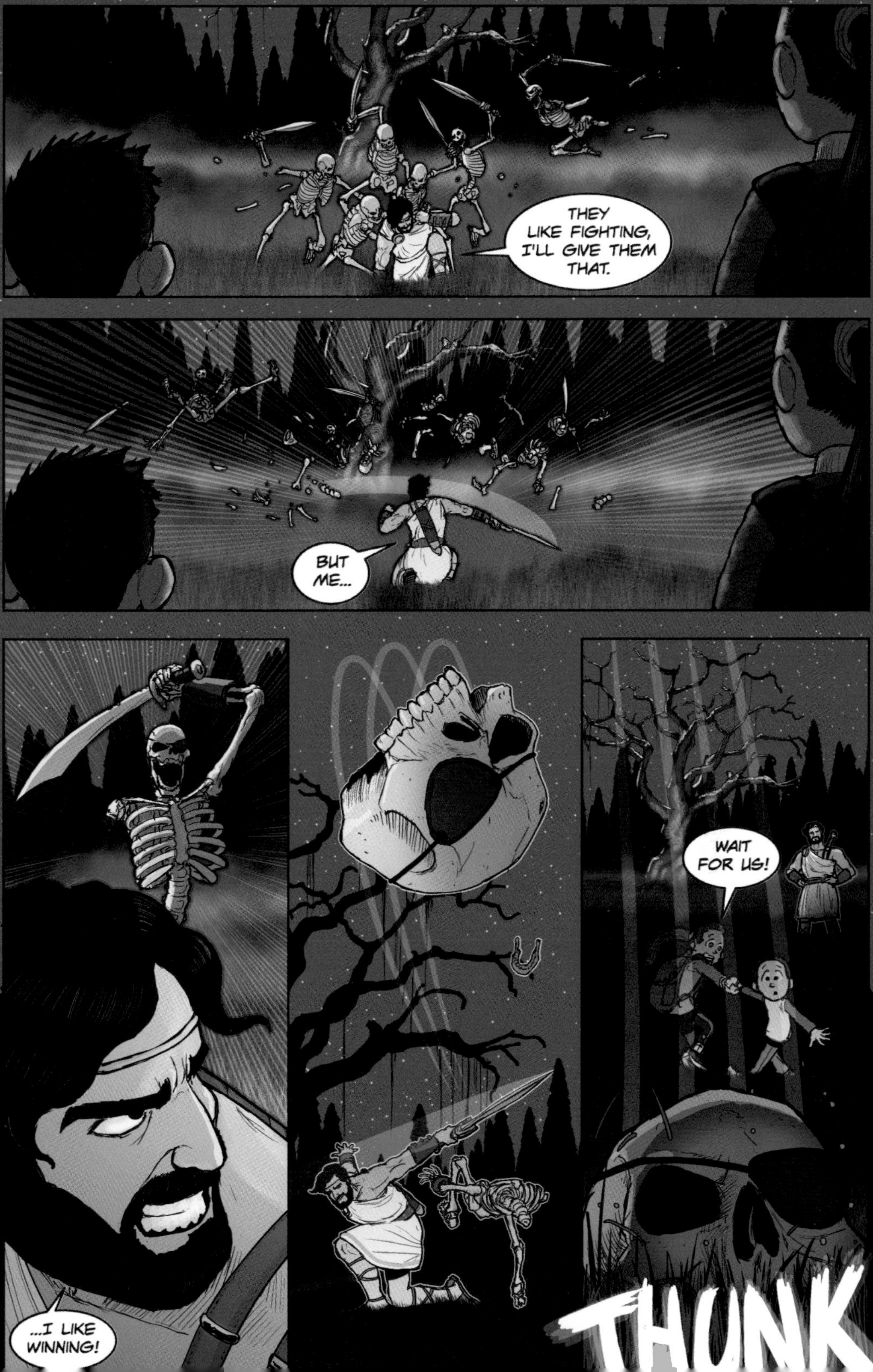
THEY LIKE FIGHTING, I'LL GIVE THEM THAT.
BUT ME...
...I LIKE WINNING!
WAIT FOR US!
THUNK

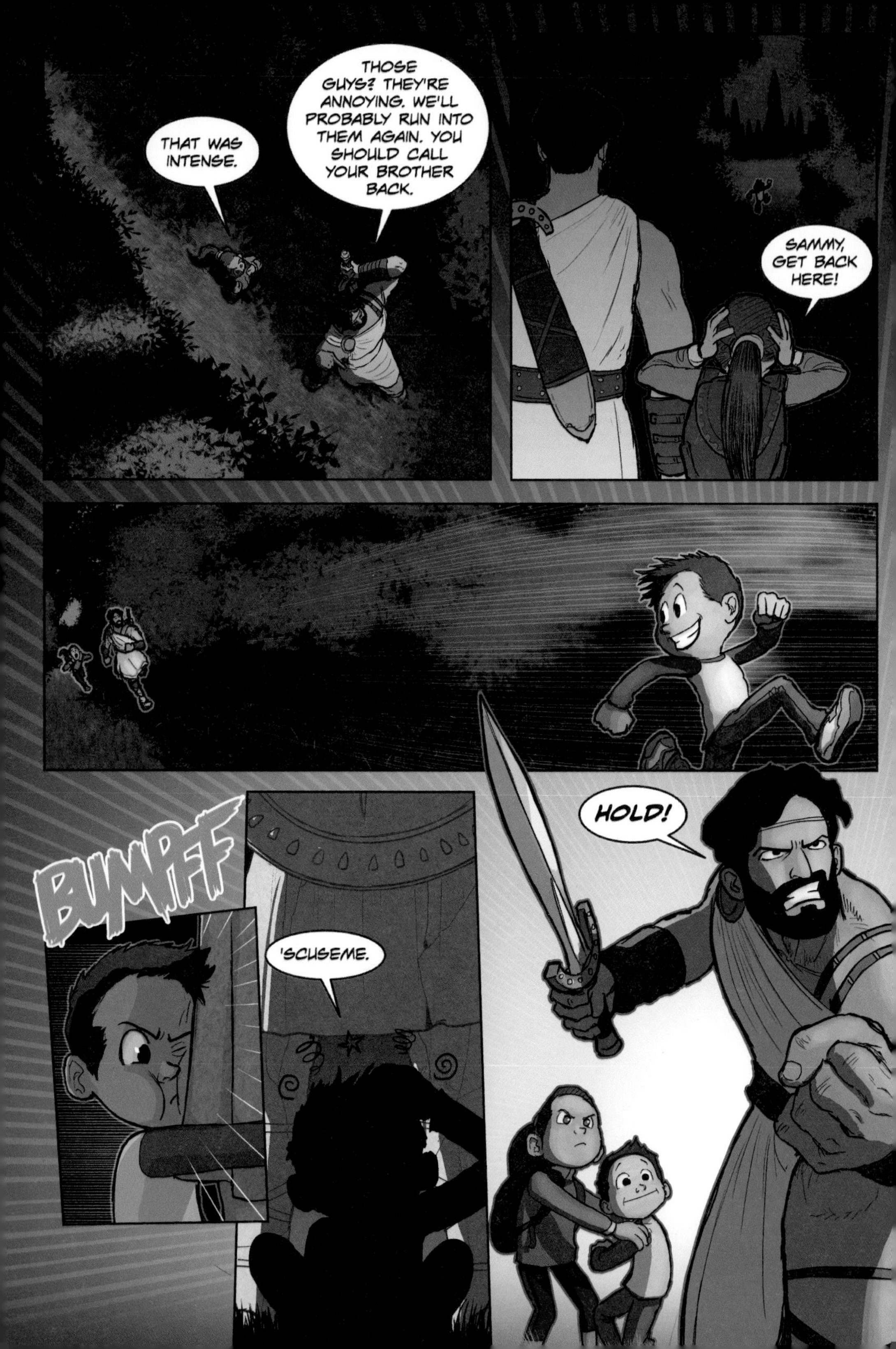
THAT WAS INTENSE.
THOSE GUYS? THEY'RE ANNOYING. WE'LL PROBABLY RUN INTO THEM AGAIN. YOU SHOULD CALL YOUR BROTHER BACK.
SAMMY, GET BACK HERE!
BUMPFF
'SCUSEME.
HOLD!

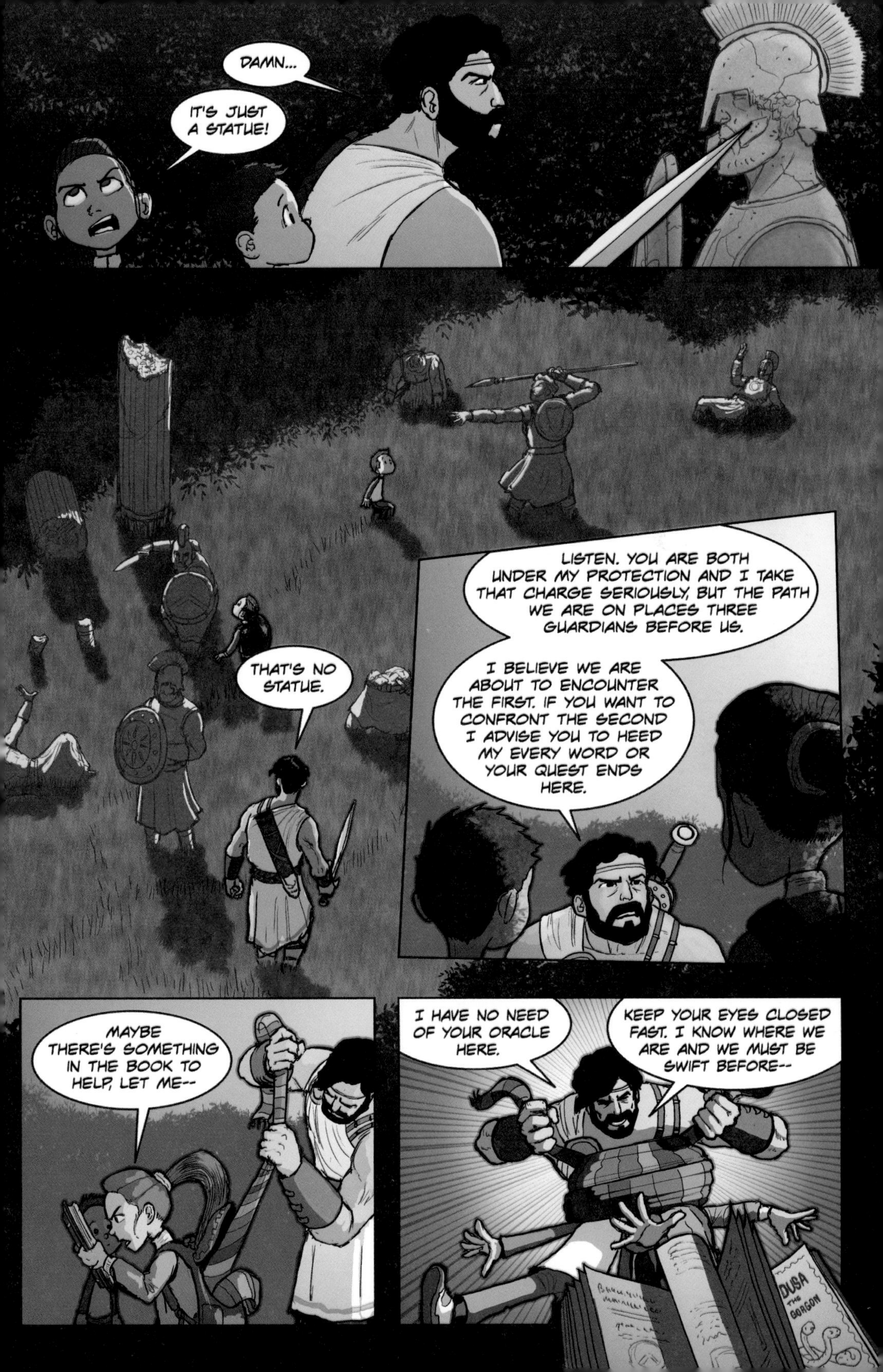
DAMN...
IT'S JUST A STATUE!
THAT'S NO STATUE.
LISTEN. YOU ARE BOTH UNDER MY PROTECTION AND I TAKE THAT CHARGE SERIOUSLY, BUT THE PATH WE ARE ON PLACES THREE GUARDIANS BEFORE US.
I BELIEVE WE ARE ABOUT TO ENCOUNTER THE FIRST. IF YOU WANT TO CONFRONT THE SECOND I ADVISE YOU TO HEED MY EVERY WORD OR YOUR QUEST ENDS HERE.
MAYBE THERE'S SOMETHING IN THE BOOK TO HELP, LET ME--
I HAVE NO NEED OF YOUR ORACLE HERE.
KEEP YOUR EYES CLOSED FAST. I KNOW WHERE WE ARE AND WE MUST BE SWIFT BEFORE--
DUSA THE GORGON

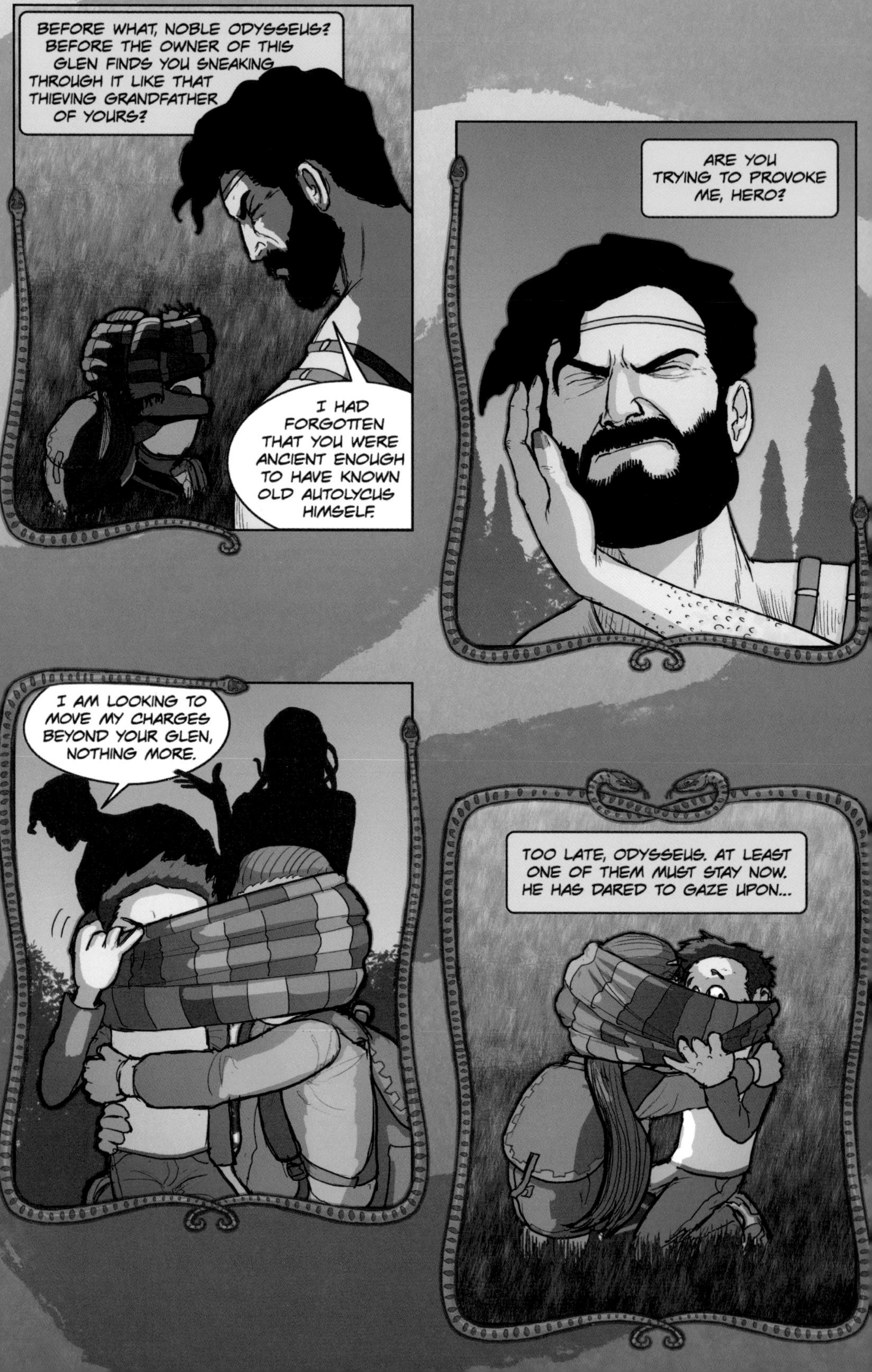
BEFORE WHAT, NOBLE ODYSSEUS? BEFORE THE OWNER OF THIS GLEN FINDS YOU SNEAKING THROUGH IT LIKE THAT THIEVING GRANDFATHER OF YOURS?
I HAD FORGOTTEN THAT YOU WERE ANCIENT ENOUGH TO HAVE KNOWN OLD AUTOLYCUS HIMSELF.
ARE YOU TRYING TO PROVOKE ME, HERO?
I AM LOOKING TO MOVE MY CHARGES BEYOND YOUR GLEN, NOTHING MORE.
TOO LATE, ODYSSEUS. AT LEAST ONE OF THEM MUST STAY NOW. HE HAS DARED TO GAZE UPON...

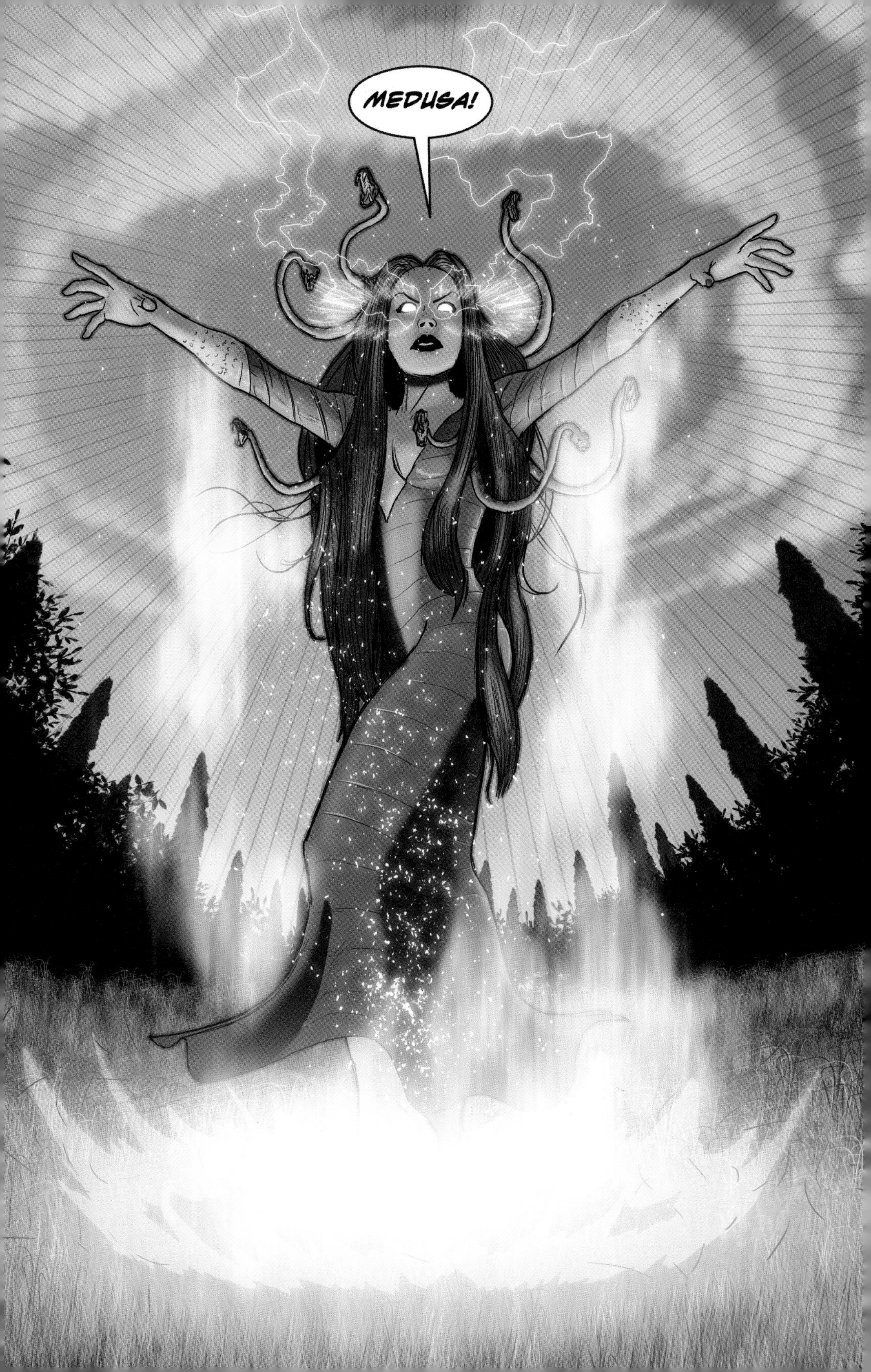
MEDUSA!

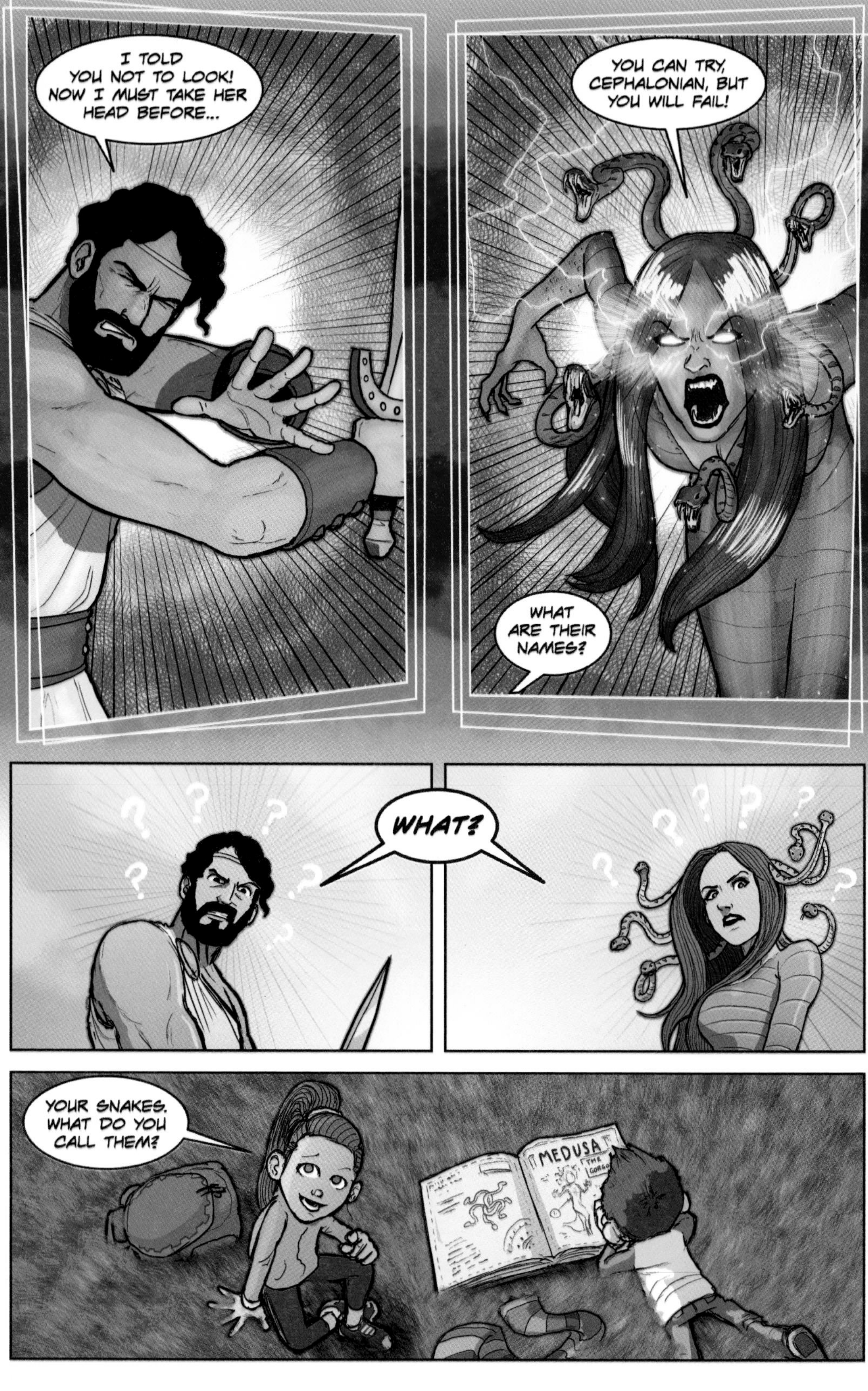
I TOLD YOU NOT TO LOOK! NOW I MUST TAKE HER HEAD BEFORE...
YOU CAN TRY, CEPHALONIAN, BUT YOU WILL FAIL!
WHAT ARE THEIR NAMES?
WHAT?
YOUR SNAKES. WHAT DO YOU CALL THEM?
MEDUSA
THE GORGO

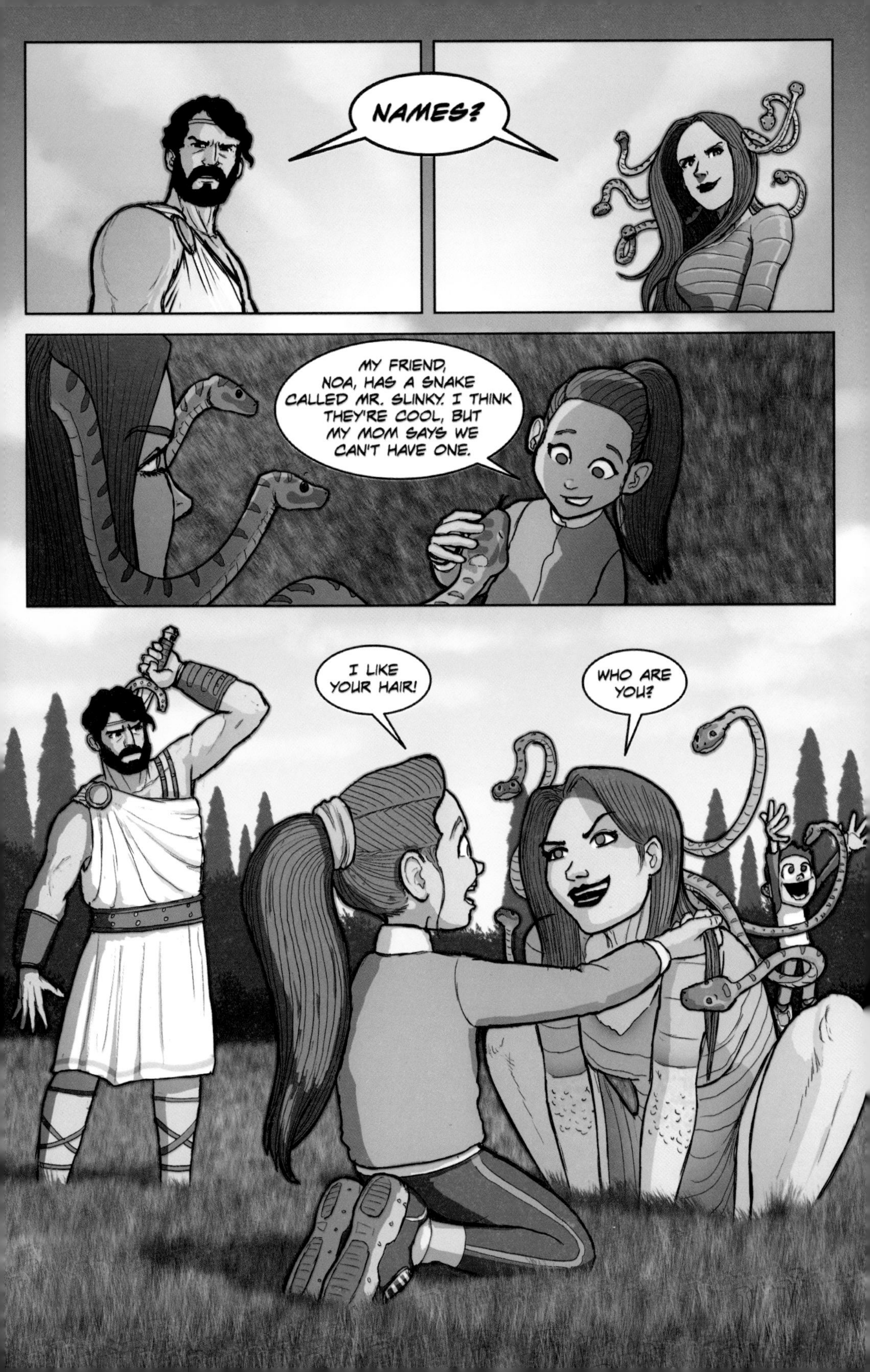
NAMES?
MY FRIEND, NOA, HAS A SNAKE CALLED MR. SLINKY. I THINK THEY'RE COOL, BUT MY MOM SAYS WE CAN'T HAVE ONE.
I LIKE YOUR HAIR!
WHO ARE YOU?

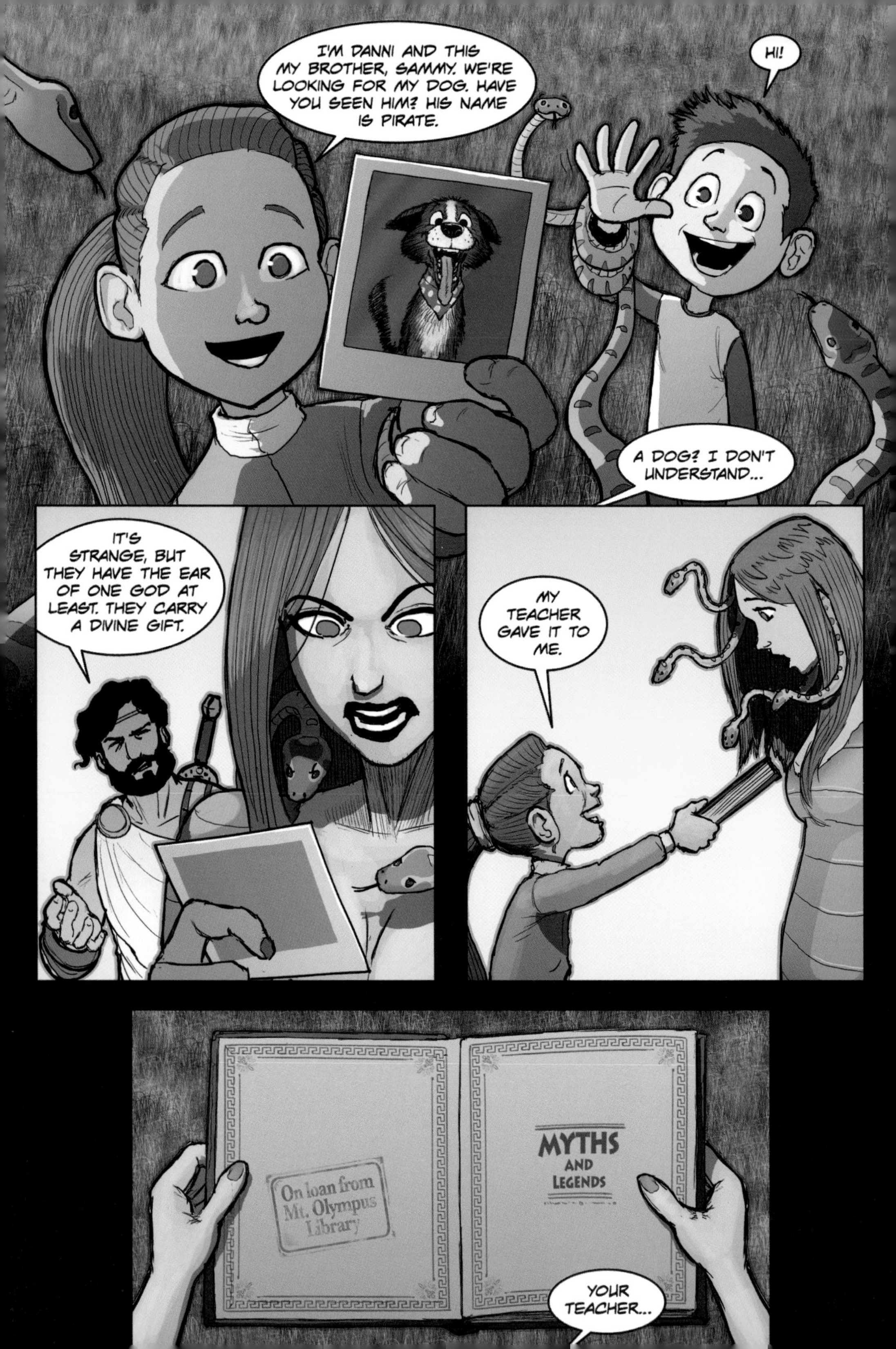
I'M DANNI AND THIS MY BROTHER, SAMMY. WE'RE LOOKING FOR MY DOG. HAVE YOU SEEN HIM? HIS NAME IS PIRATE.
HI!
A DOG? I DON'T UNDERSTAND...
IT'S STRANGE, BUT THEY HAVE THE EAR OF ONE GOD AT LEAST. THEY CARRY A DIVINE GIFT.
MY TEACHER GAVE IT TO ME.
On loan from Mt. Olympus Library
MYTHS AND LEGENDS
YOUR TEACHER...

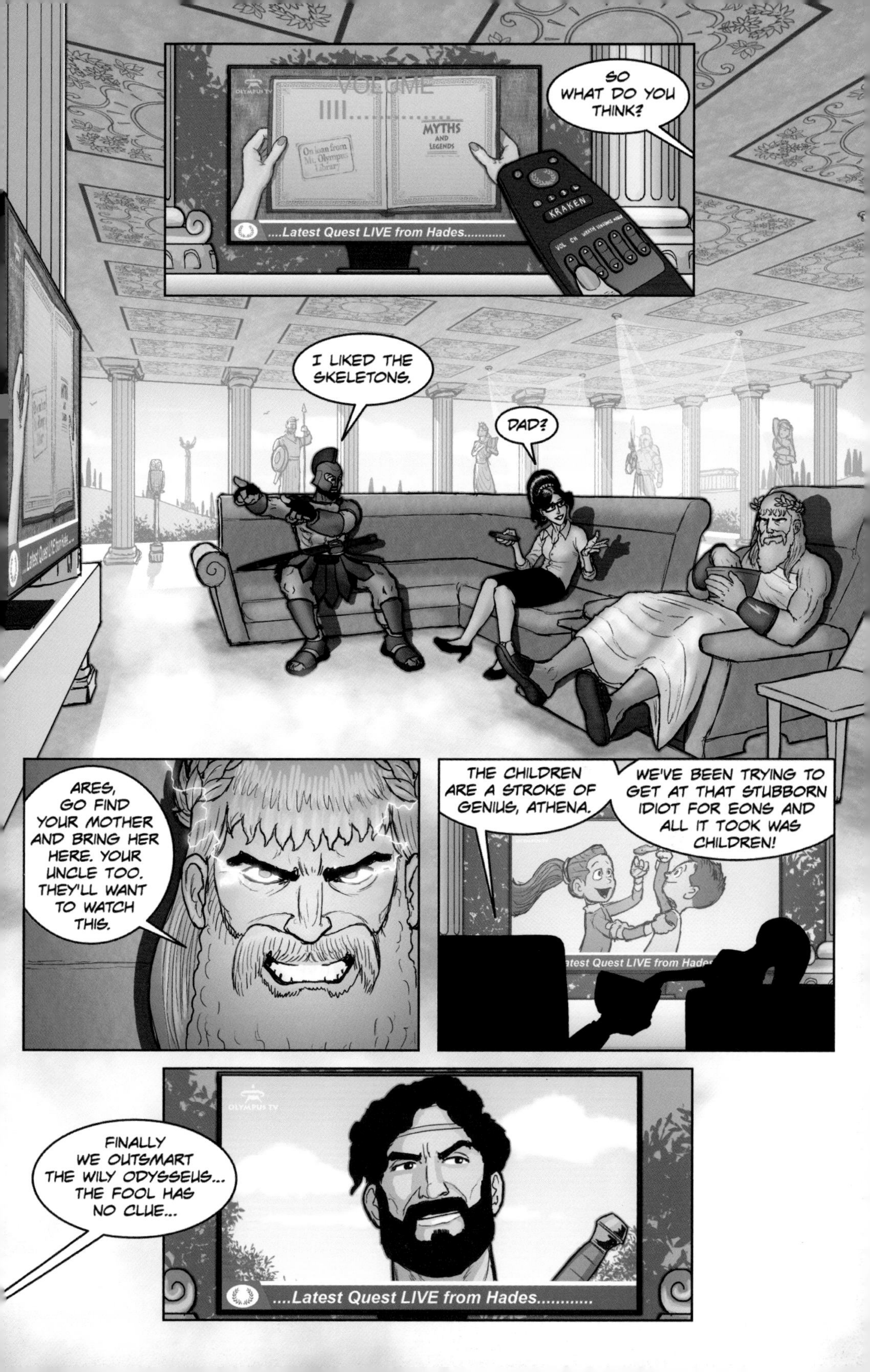
VOLUME
IIII............
On loan from Mt. Olympus Library
MYTHS AND LEGENDS
OLYMPUS TV
....Latest Quest LIVE from Hades............
KRAKEN
SO WHAT DO YOU THINK?
I LIKED THE SKELETONS.
DAD?
ARES, GO FIND YOUR MOTHER AND BRING HER HERE. YOUR UNCLE TOO. THEY'LL WANT TO WATCH THIS.
THE CHILDREN ARE A STROKE OF GENIUS, ATHENA.
WE'VE BEEN TRYING TO GET AT THAT STUBBORN IDIOT FOR EONS AND ALL IT TOOK WAS CHILDREN!
atest Quest LIVE from Hade
OLYMPUS TV
FINALLY WE OUTSMART THE WILY ODYSSEUS... THE FOOL HAS NO CLUE...
....Latest Quest LIVE from Hades............

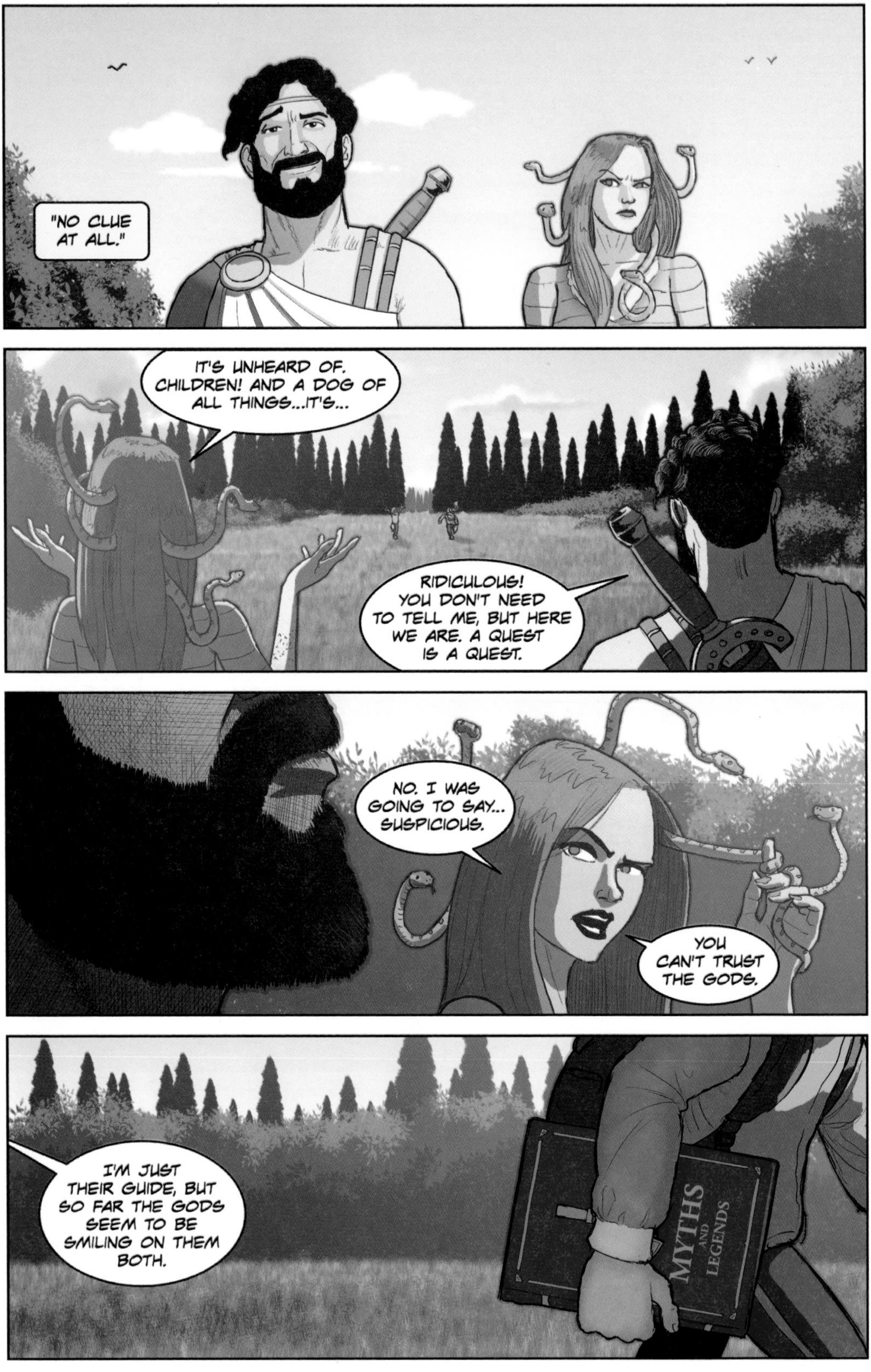
"NO CLUE AT ALL."
IT'S UNHEARD OF. CHILDREN! AND A DOG OF ALL THINGS...IT'S...
RIDICULOUS! YOU DON'T NEED TO TELL ME, BUT HERE WE ARE. A QUEST IS A QUEST.
NO. I WAS GOING TO SAY... SUSPICIOUS.
YOU CAN'T TRUST THE GODS.
I'M JUST THEIR GUIDE, BUT SO FAR THE GODS SEEM TO BE SMILING ON THEM BOTH.
MYTHS AND LEGENDS

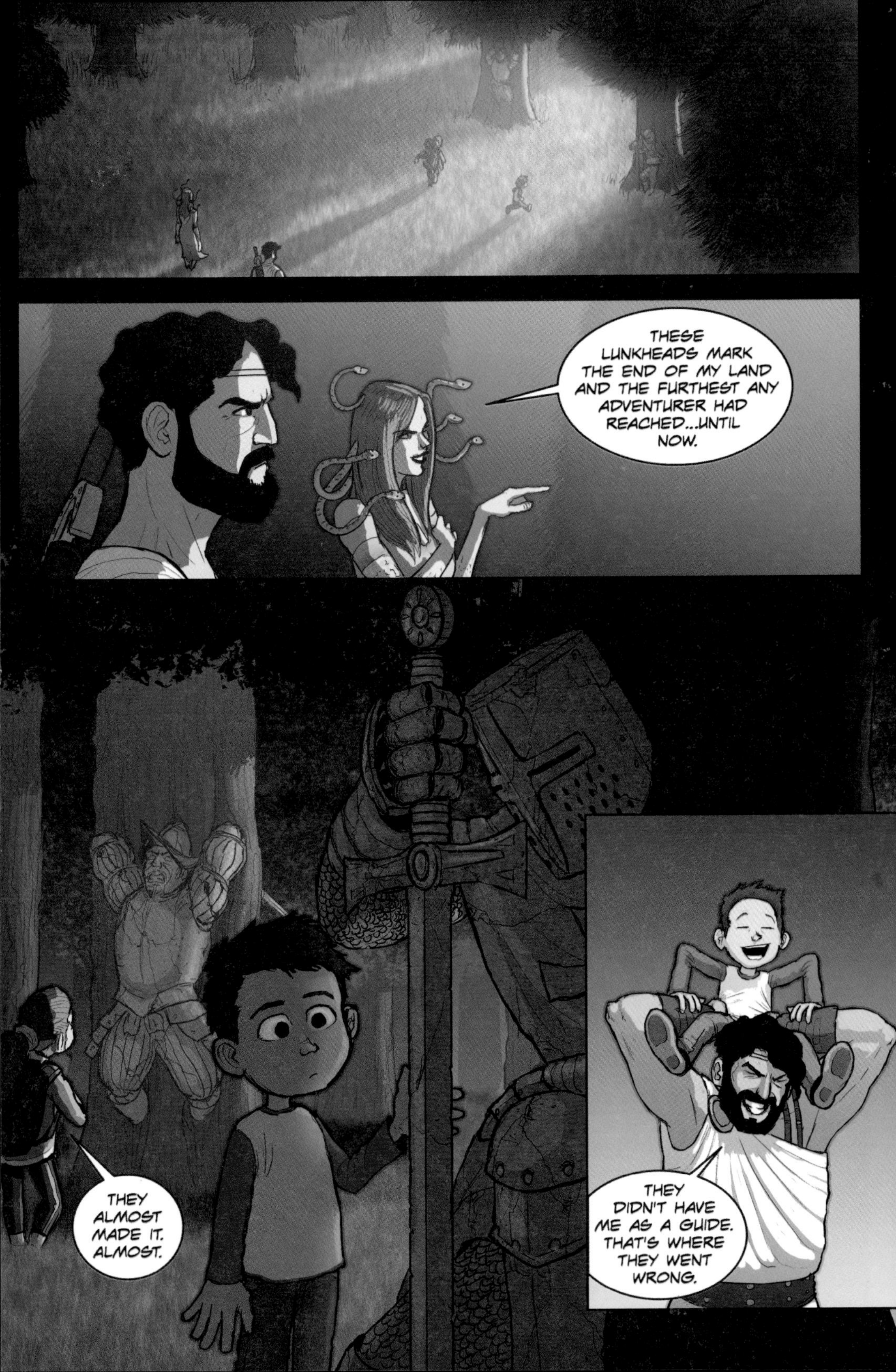
THESE LUNKHEADS MARK THE END OF MY LAND AND THE FURTHEST ANY ADVENTURER HAD REACHED...UNTIL NOW.
THEY ALMOST MADE IT. ALMOST.
THEY DIDN'T HAVE ME AS A GUIDE. THAT'S WHERE THEY WENT WRONG.

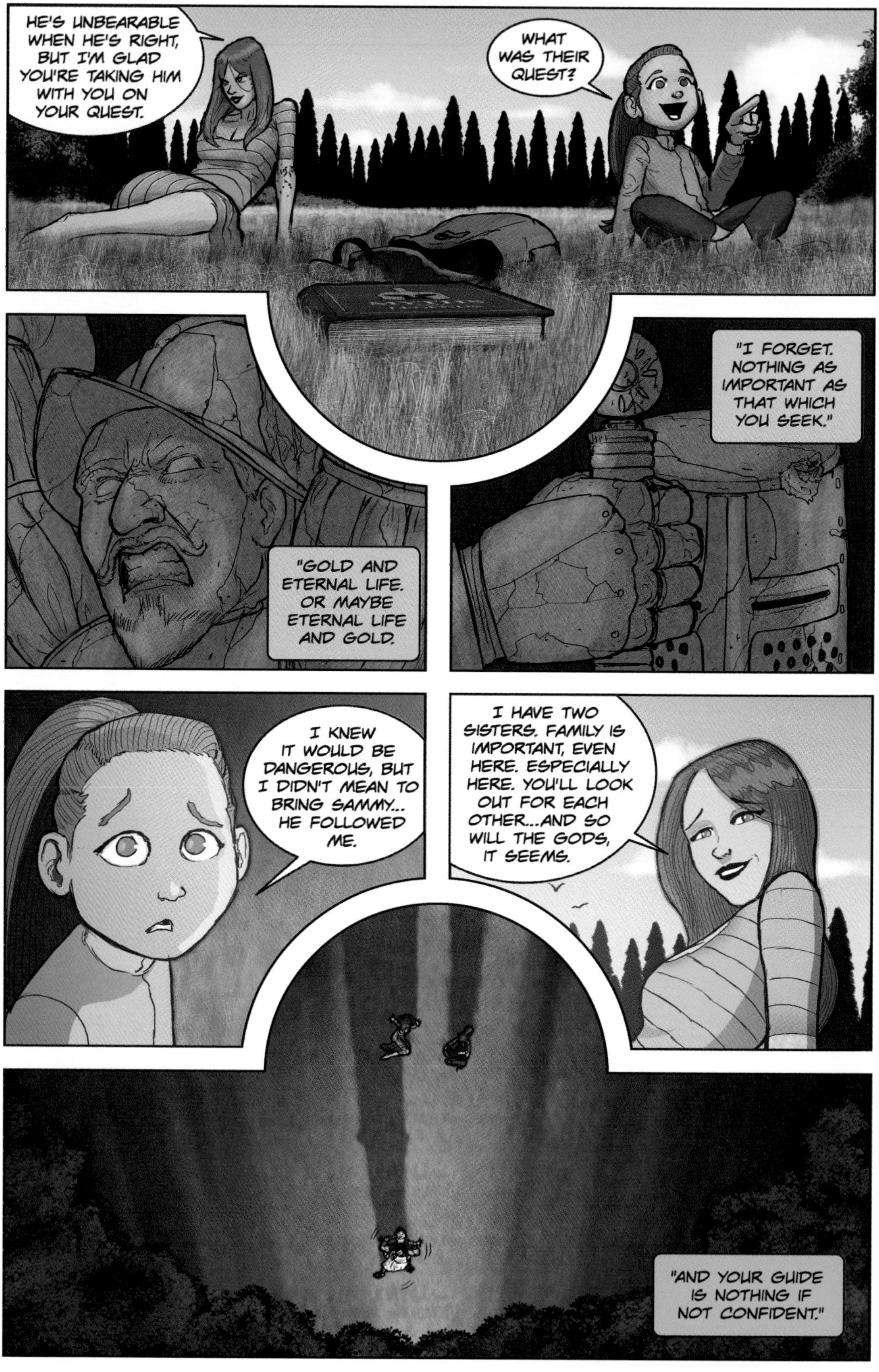
HE'S UNBEARABLE WHEN HE'S RIGHT, BUT I'M GLAD YOU'RE TAKING HIM WITH YOU ON YOUR QUEST.
WHAT WAS THEIR QUEST?
"GOLD AND ETERNAL LIFE. OR MAYBE ETERNAL LIFE AND GOLD.
"I FORGET. NOTHING AS IMPORTANT AS THAT WHICH YOU SEEK."
I KNEW IT WOULD BE DANGEROUS, BUT I DIDN'T MEAN TO BRING SAMMY... HE FOLLOWED ME.
I HAVE TWO SISTERS. FAMILY IS IMPORTANT, EVEN HERE. ESPECIALLY HERE. YOU'LL LOOK OUT FOR EACH OTHER...AND SO WILL THE GODS, IT SEEMS.
"AND YOUR GUIDE IS NOTHING IF NOT CONFIDENT."

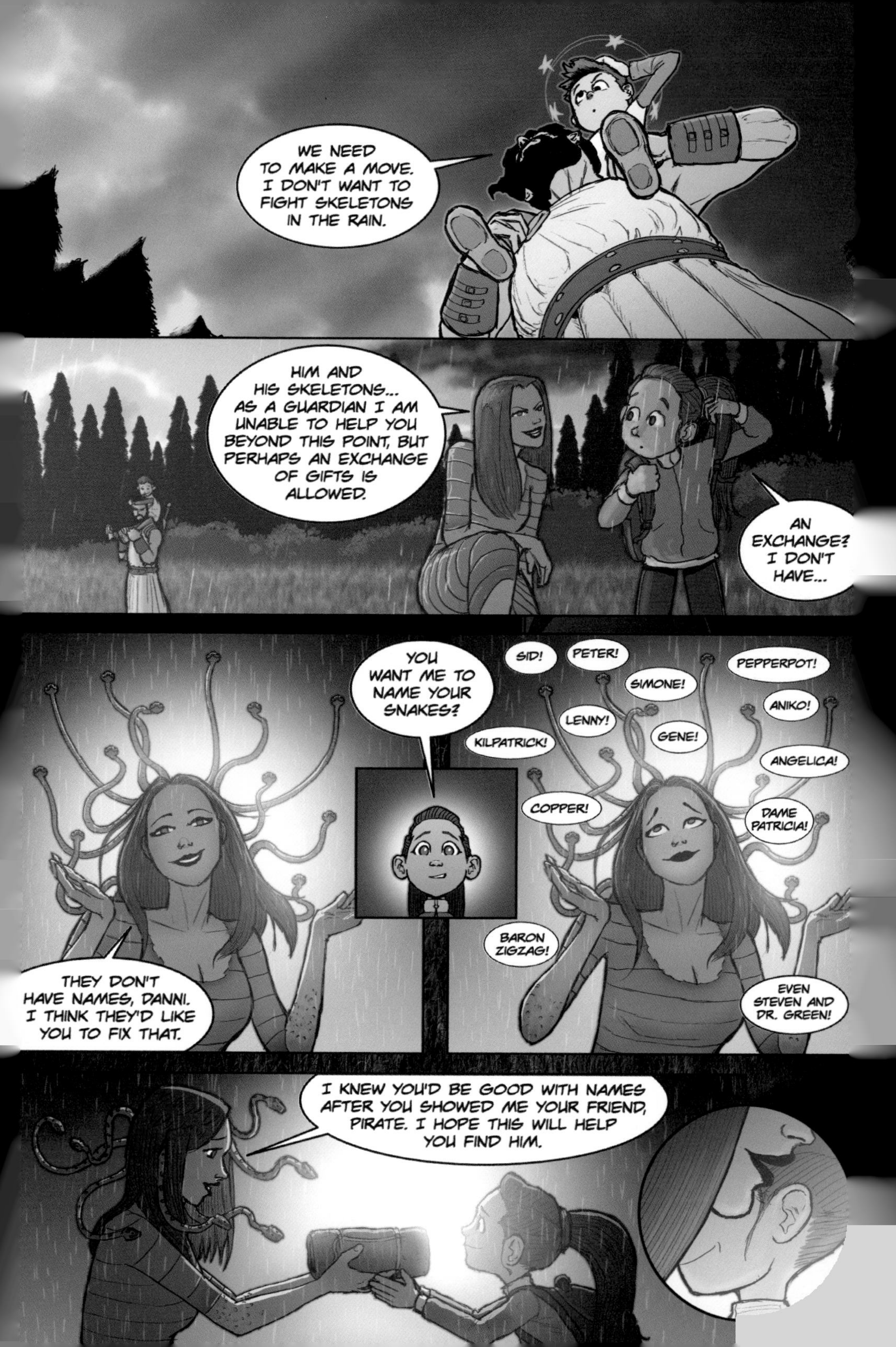
WE NEED TO MAKE A MOVE. I DON'T WANT TO FIGHT SKELETONS IN THE RAIN.
HIM AND HIS SKELETONS... AS A GUARDIAN I AM UNABLE TO HELP YOU BEYOND THIS POINT, BUT PERHAPS AN EXCHANGE OF GIFTS IS ALLOWED.
AN EXCHANGE? I DON'T HAVE...
THEY DON'T HAVE NAMES, DANNI. I THINK THEY'D LIKE YOU TO FIX THAT.
YOU WANT ME TO NAME YOUR SNAKES?
SID!
PETER!
PEPPERPOT!
SIMONE!
ANIKO!
LENNY!
KILPATRICK!
GENE!
ANGELICA!
COPPER!
DAME PATRICIA!
BARON ZIGZAG!
EVEN STEVEN AND DR. GREEN!
I KNEW YOU'D BE GOOD WITH NAMES AFTER YOU SHOWED ME YOUR FRIEND, PIRATE. I HOPE THIS WILL HELP YOU FIND HIM.

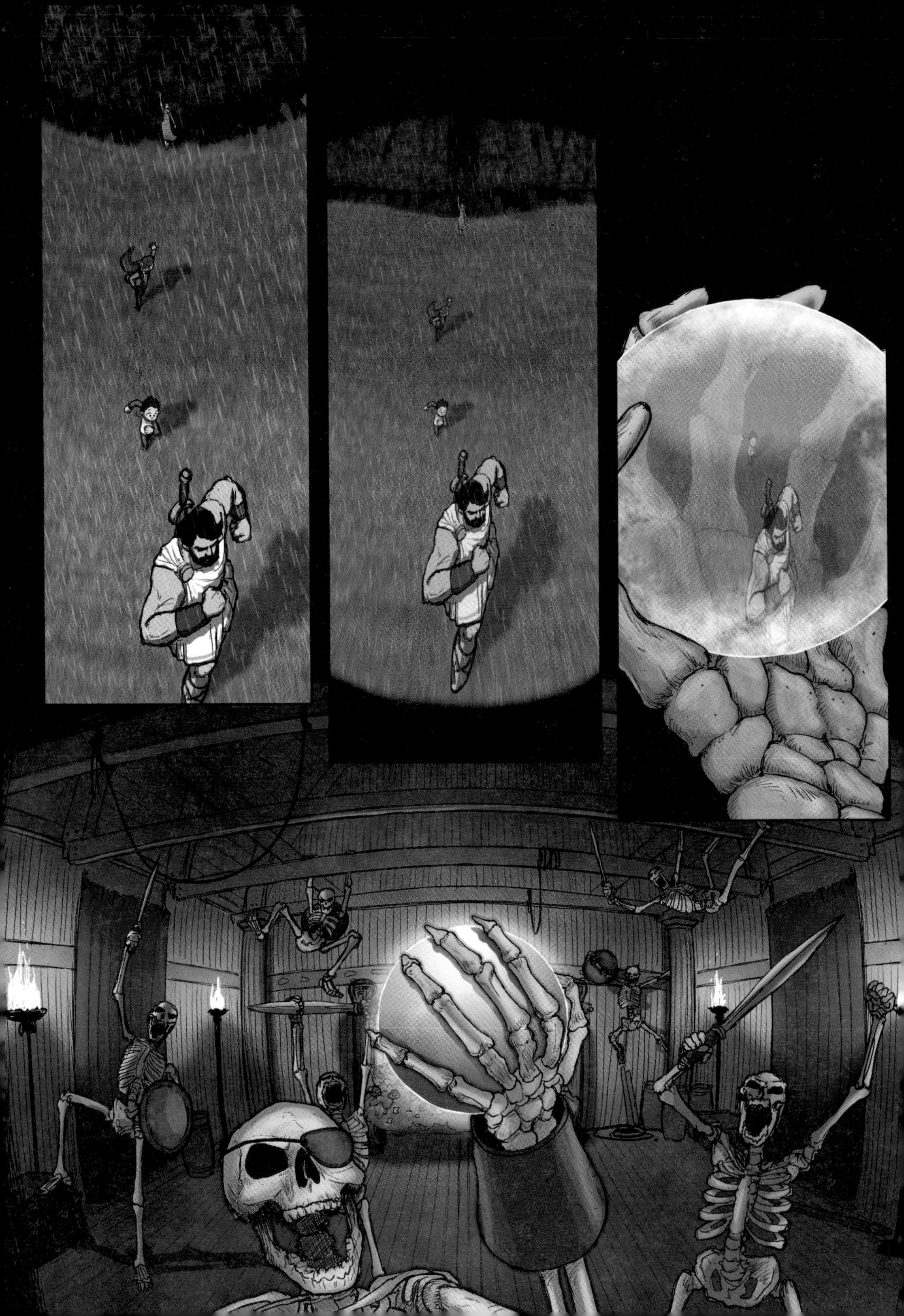

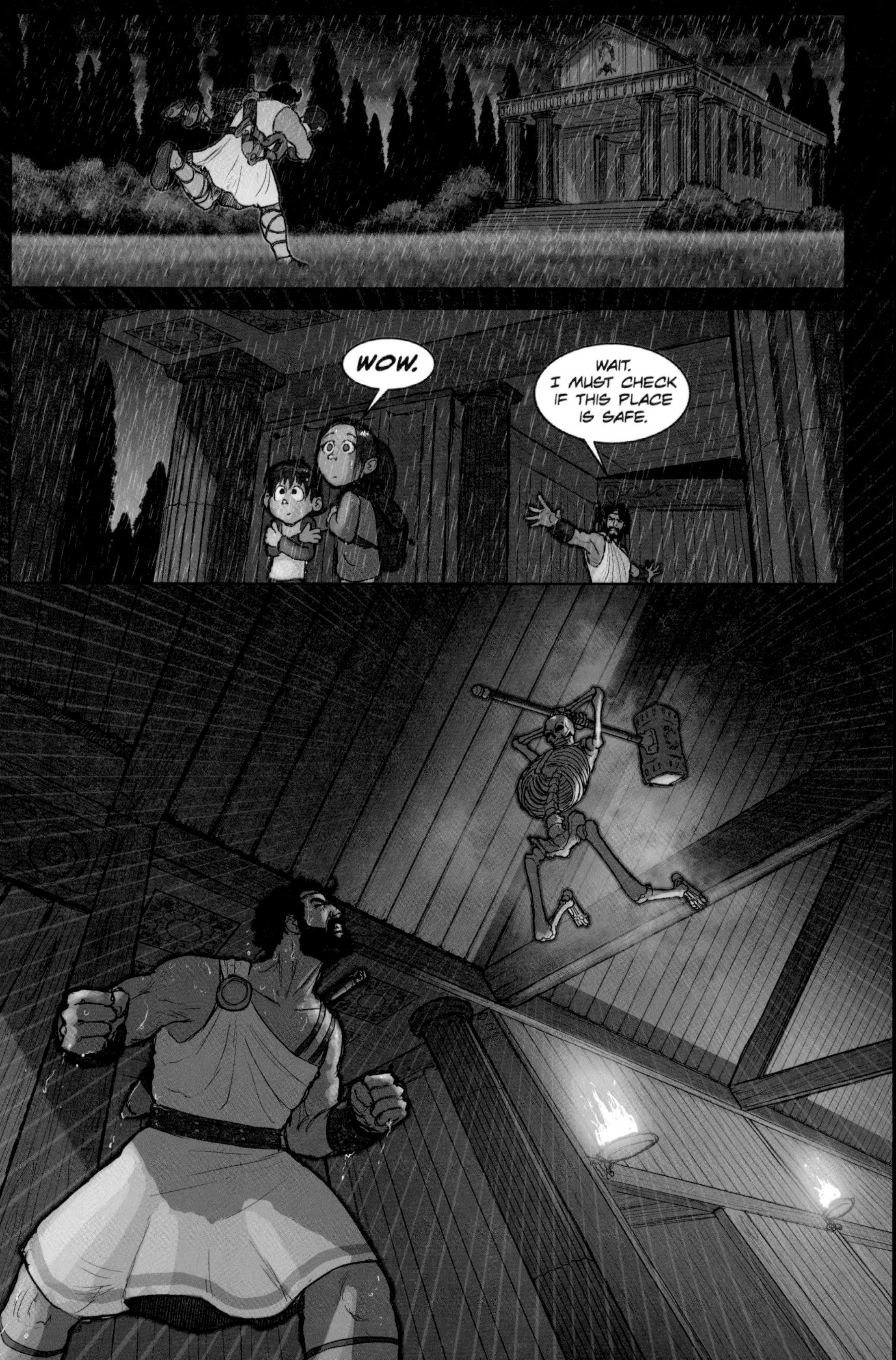
WOW.
WAIT. I MUST CHECK IF THIS PLACE IS SAFE.

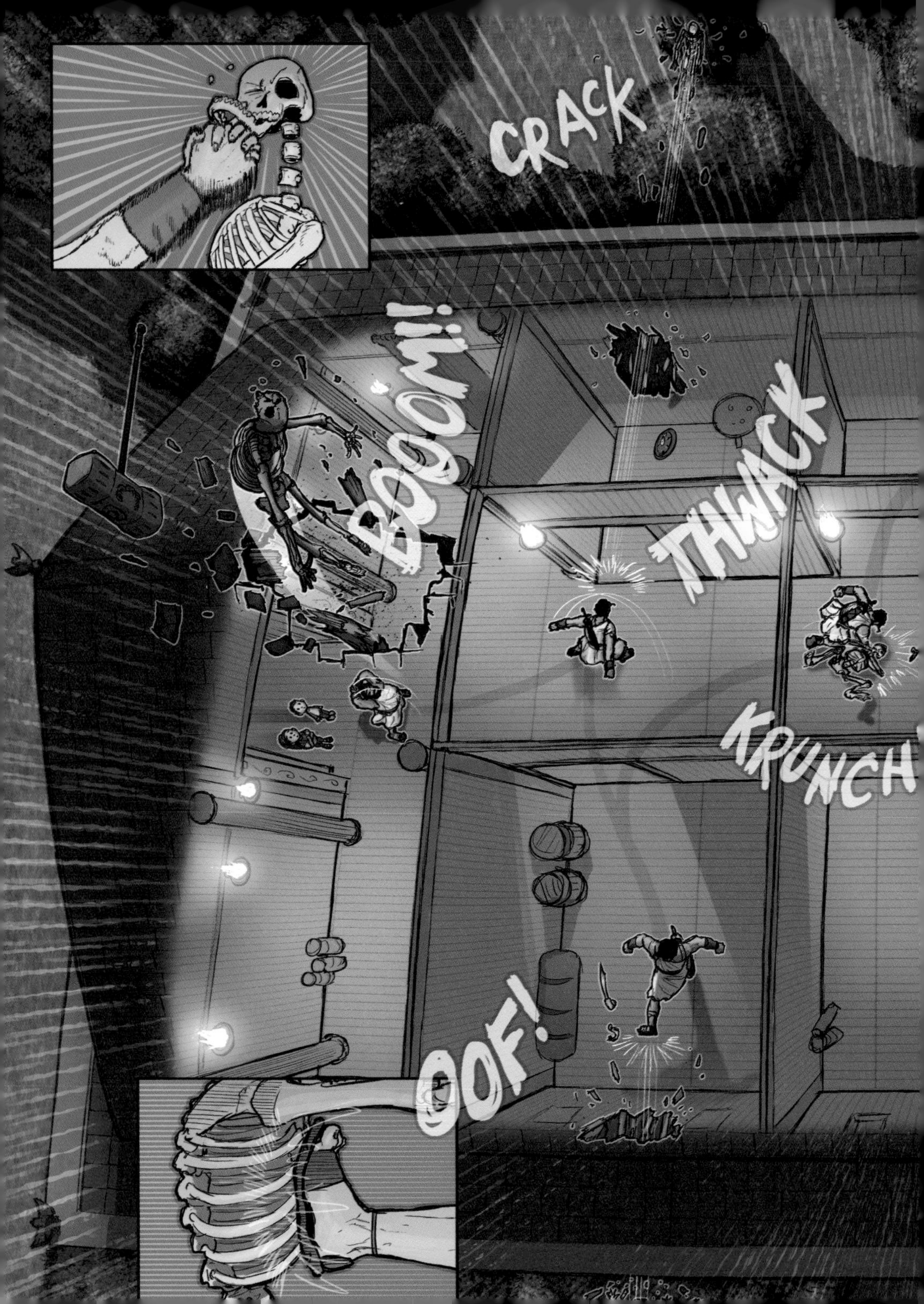
CRACK
BOOOM!!!
THWACK
KRUNCH
OOF!

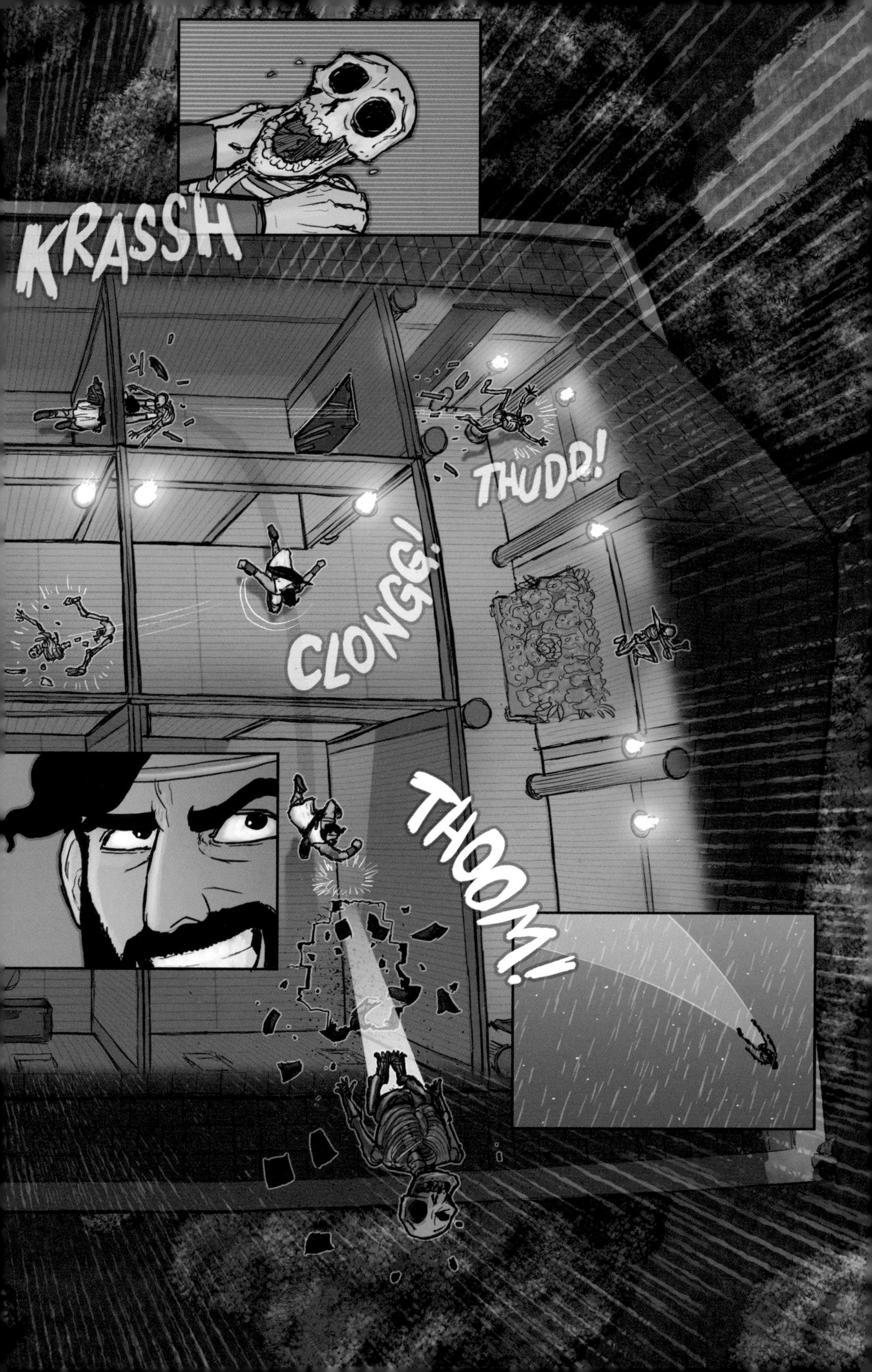
KRASSH
THUDD!
CLONGG!
THOOM!

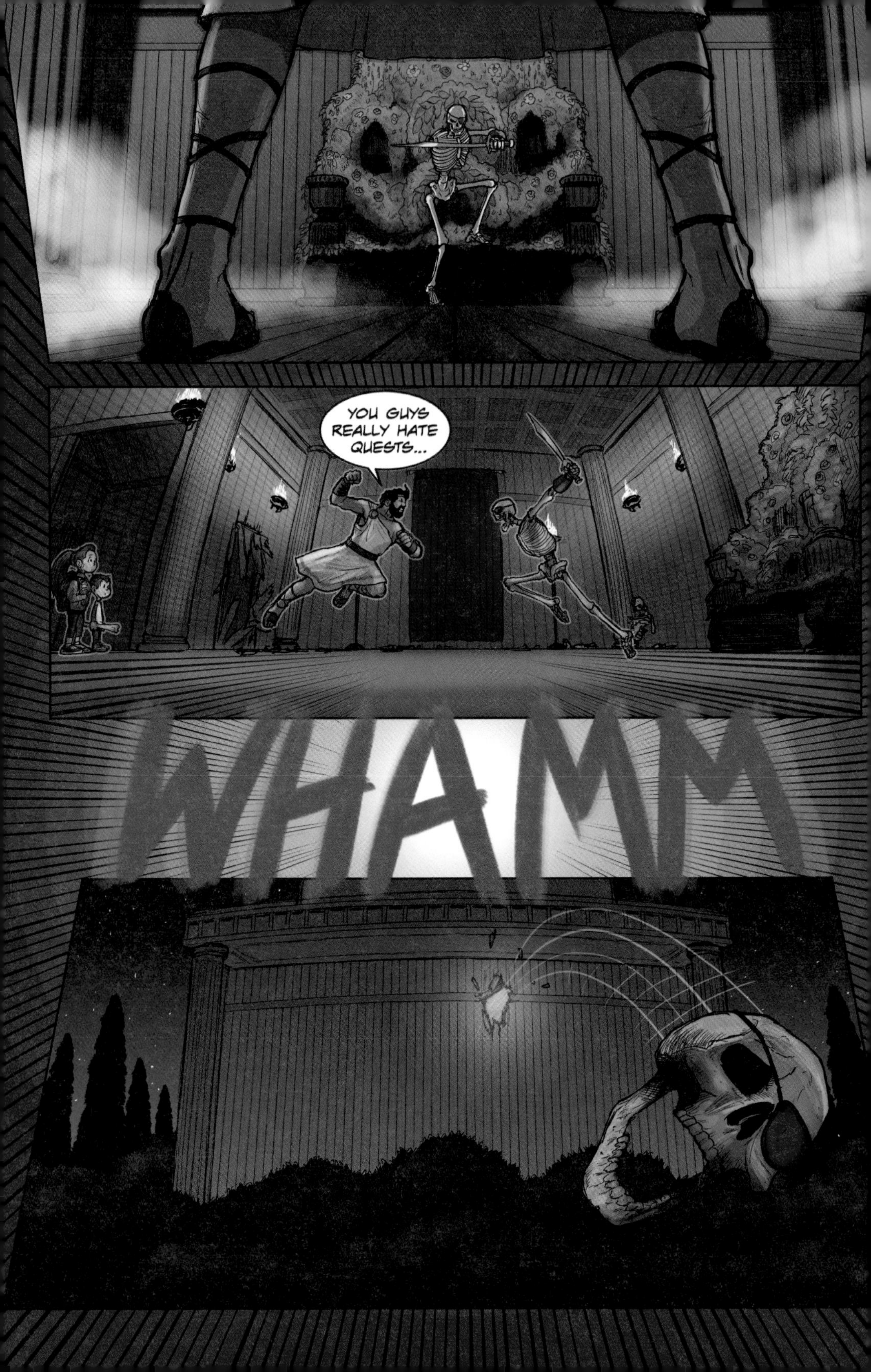
YOU GUYS
REALLY HATE
QUESTS...
WHAMM

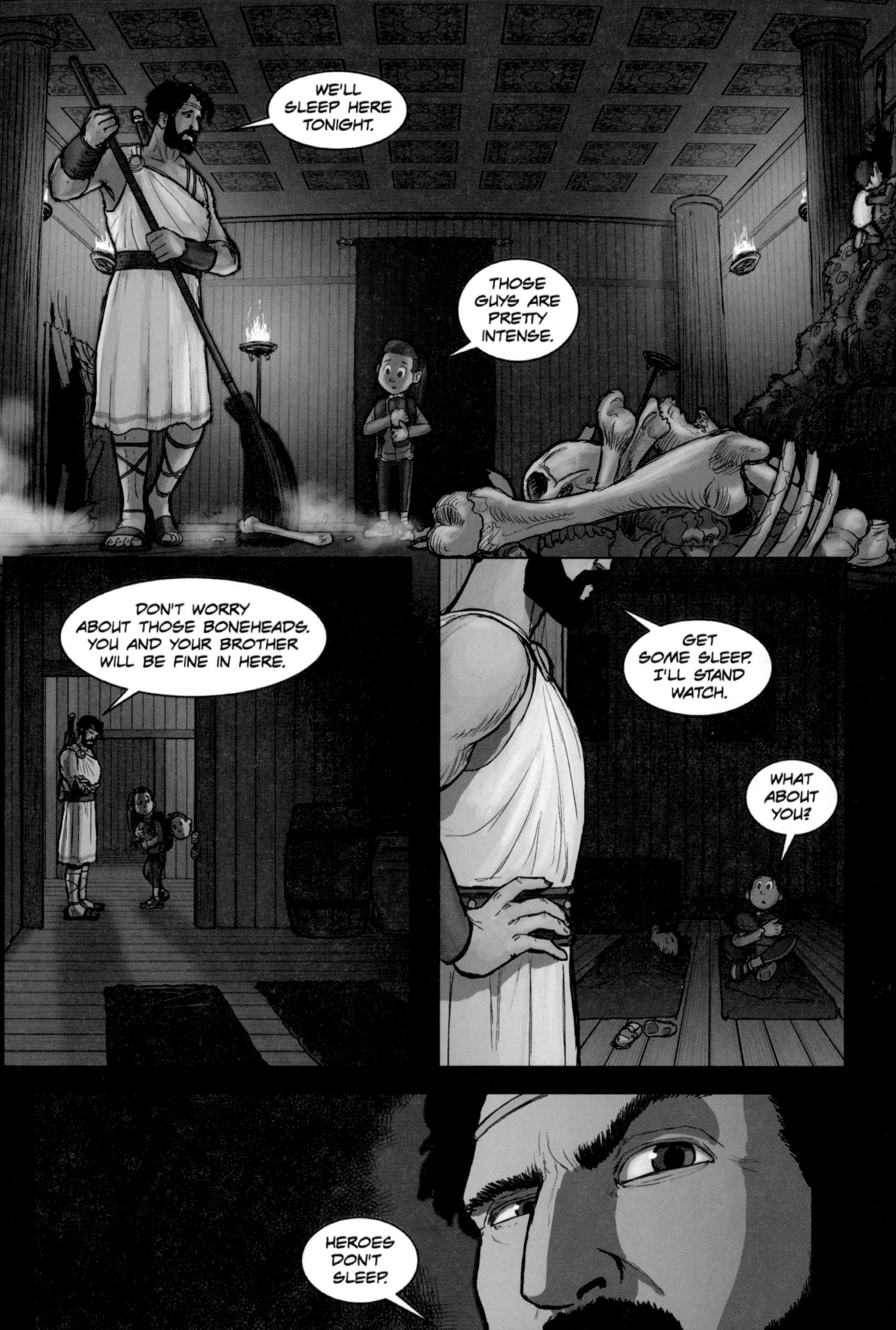
WE'LL SLEEP HERE TONIGHT.
THOSE GUYS ARE PRETTY INTENSE.
DON'T WORRY ABOUT THOSE BONEHEADS. YOU AND YOUR BROTHER WILL BE FINE IN HERE.
GET SOME SLEEP. I'LL STAND WATCH.
WHAT ABOUT YOU?
HEROES DON'T SLEEP.

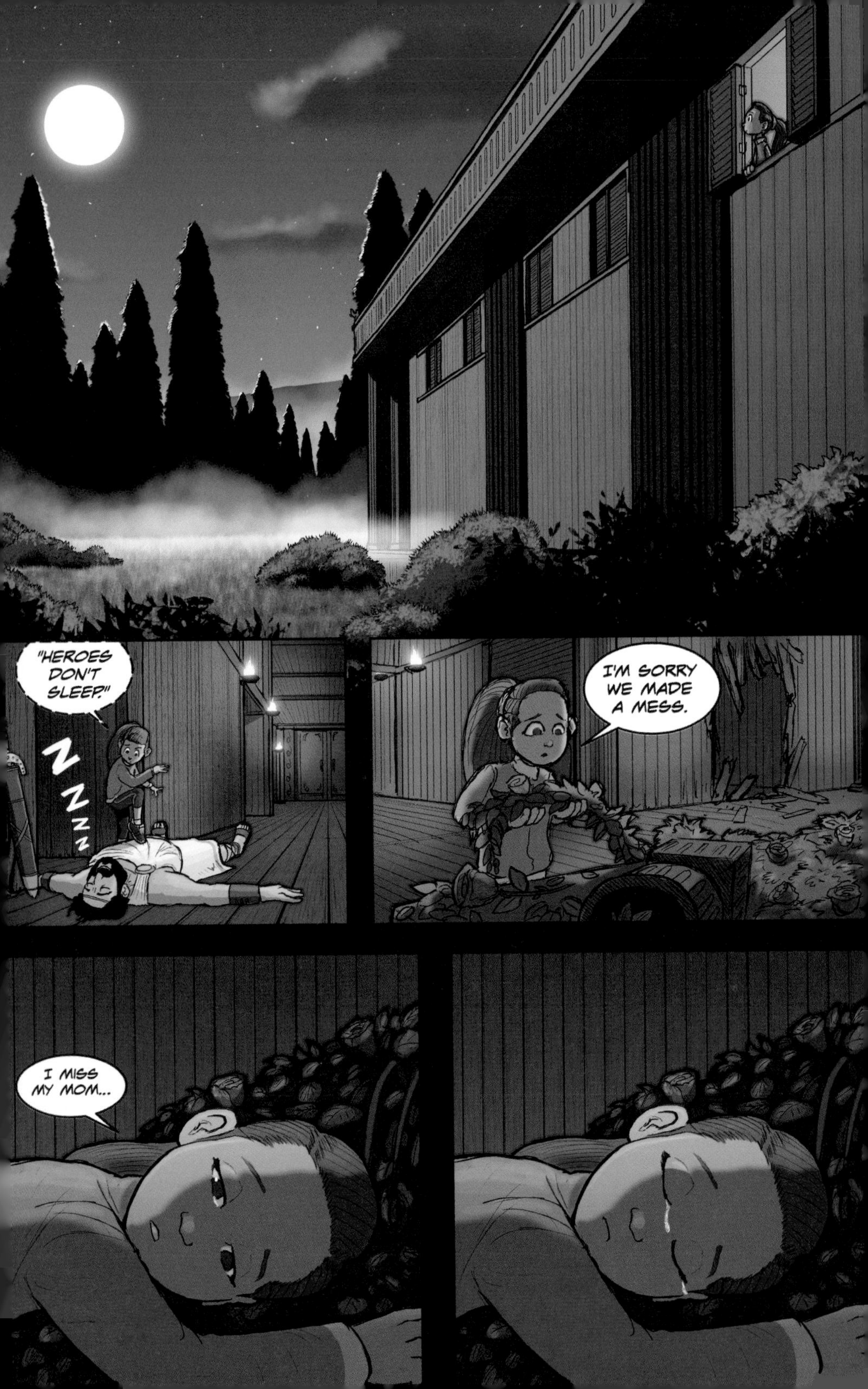
"HEROES DON'T SLEEP."
Z Z Z Z
I'M SORRY WE MADE A MESS.
I MISS MY MOM...

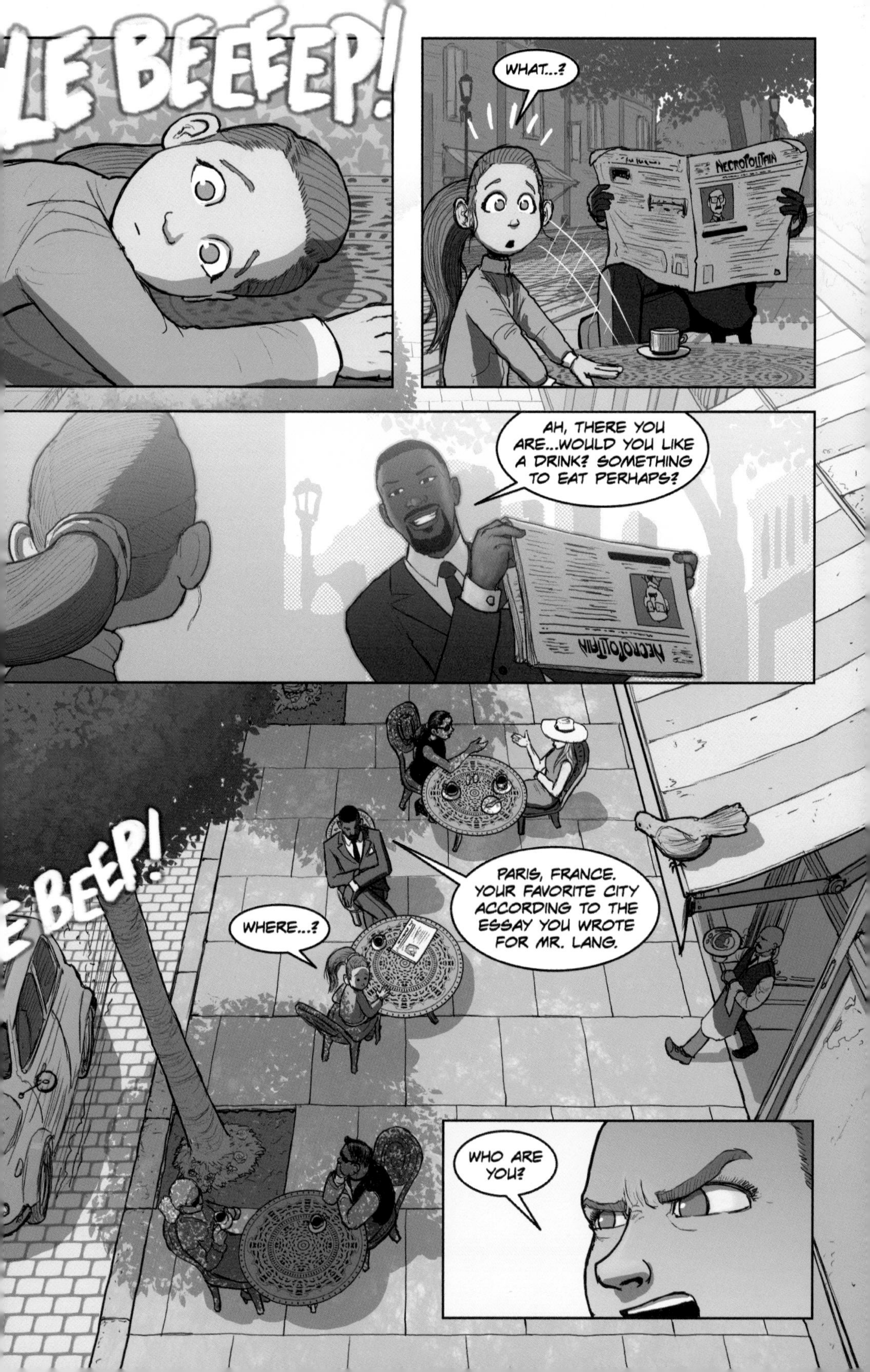
LE BEEEEP!
WHAT...?
NECROPOLITAIN
AH, THERE YOU ARE...WOULD YOU LIKE A DRINK? SOMETHING TO EAT PERHAPS?
NECROPOLITAIN
E BEEP!
WHERE...?
PARIS, FRANCE. YOUR FAVORITE CITY ACCORDING TO THE ESSAY YOU WROTE FOR MR. LANG.
WHO ARE YOU?

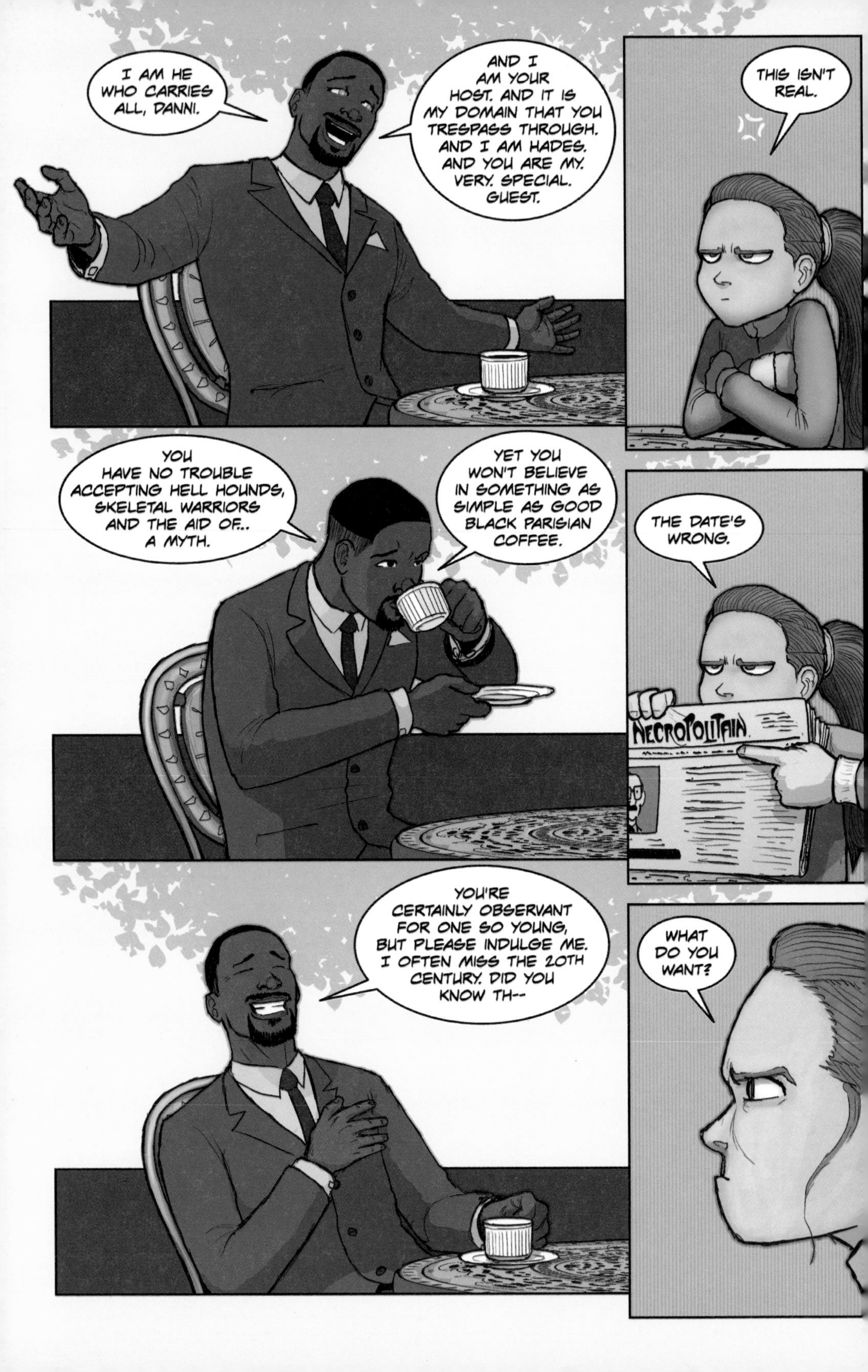
I AM HE WHO CARRIES ALL, DANNI.
AND I AM YOUR HOST. AND IT IS MY DOMAIN THAT YOU TRESPASS THROUGH. AND I AM HADES. AND YOU ARE MY. VERY. SPECIAL. GUEST.
THIS ISN'T REAL.
YOU HAVE NO TROUBLE ACCEPTING HELL HOUNDS, SKELETAL WARRIORS AND THE AID OF... A MYTH.
YET YOU WON'T BELIEVE IN SOMETHING AS SIMPLE AS GOOD BLACK PARISIAN COFFEE.
THE DATE'S WRONG.
NECROPOLITAIN
YOU'RE CERTAINLY OBSERVANT FOR ONE SO YOUNG, BUT PLEASE INDULGE ME. I OFTEN MISS THE 20TH CENTURY. DID YOU KNOW TH--
WHAT DO YOU WANT?

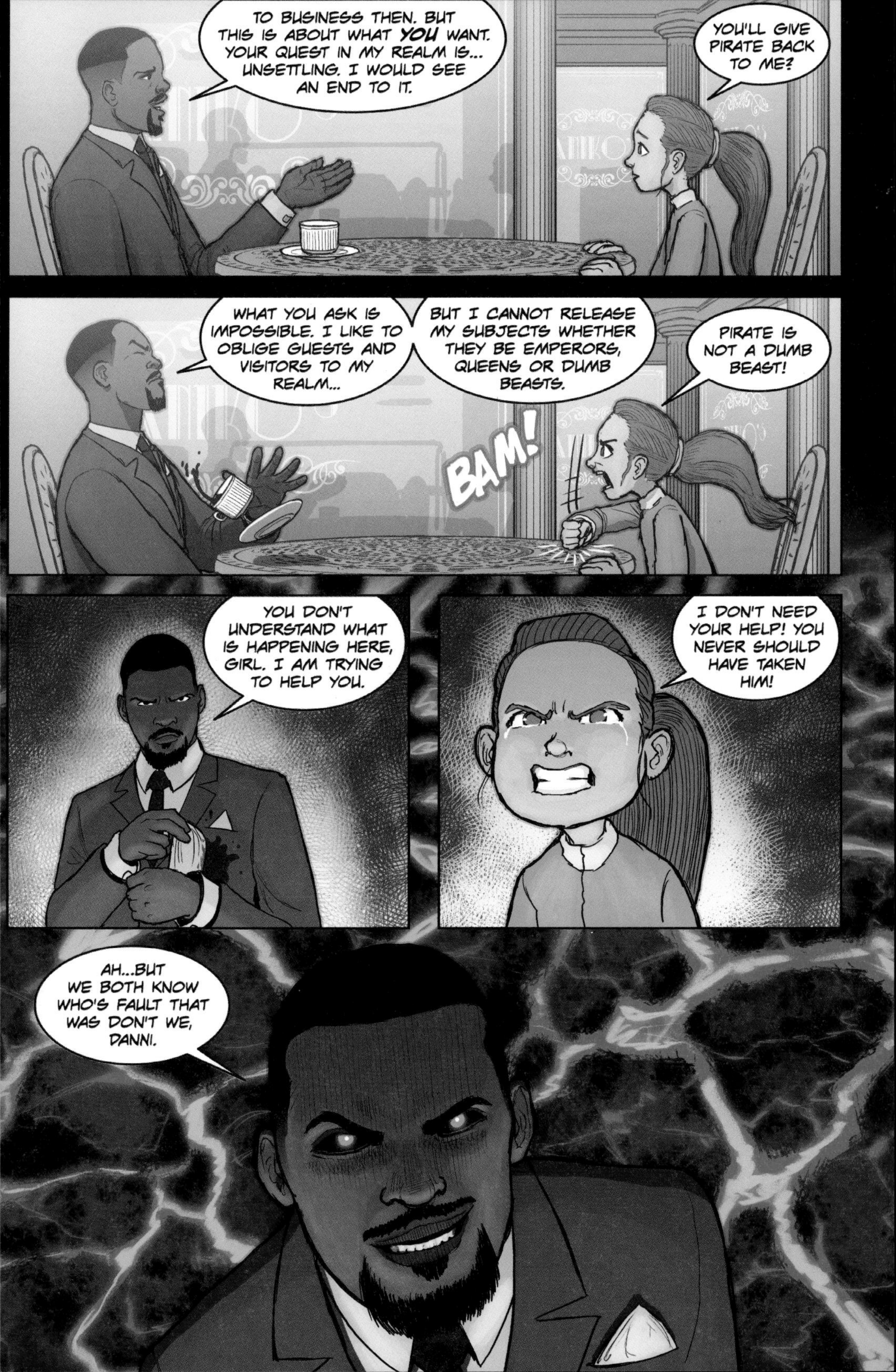
TO BUSINESS THEN. BUT THIS IS ABOUT WHAT YOU WANT. YOUR QUEST IN MY REALM IS... UNSETTLING. I WOULD SEE AN END TO IT.
YOU'LL GIVE PIRATE BACK TO ME?
WHAT YOU ASK IS IMPOSSIBLE. I LIKE TO OBLIGE GUESTS AND VISITORS TO MY REALM...
BUT I CANNOT RELEASE MY SUBJECTS WHETHER THEY BE EMPERORS, QUEENS OR DUMB BEASTS.
BAM!
PIRATE IS NOT A DUMB BEAST!
YOU DON'T UNDERSTAND WHAT IS HAPPENING HERE, GIRL. I AM TRYING TO HELP YOU.
I DON'T NEED YOUR HELP! YOU NEVER SHOULD HAVE TAKEN HIM!
AH...BUT WE BOTH KNOW WHO'S FAULT THAT WAS DON'T WE, DANNI.

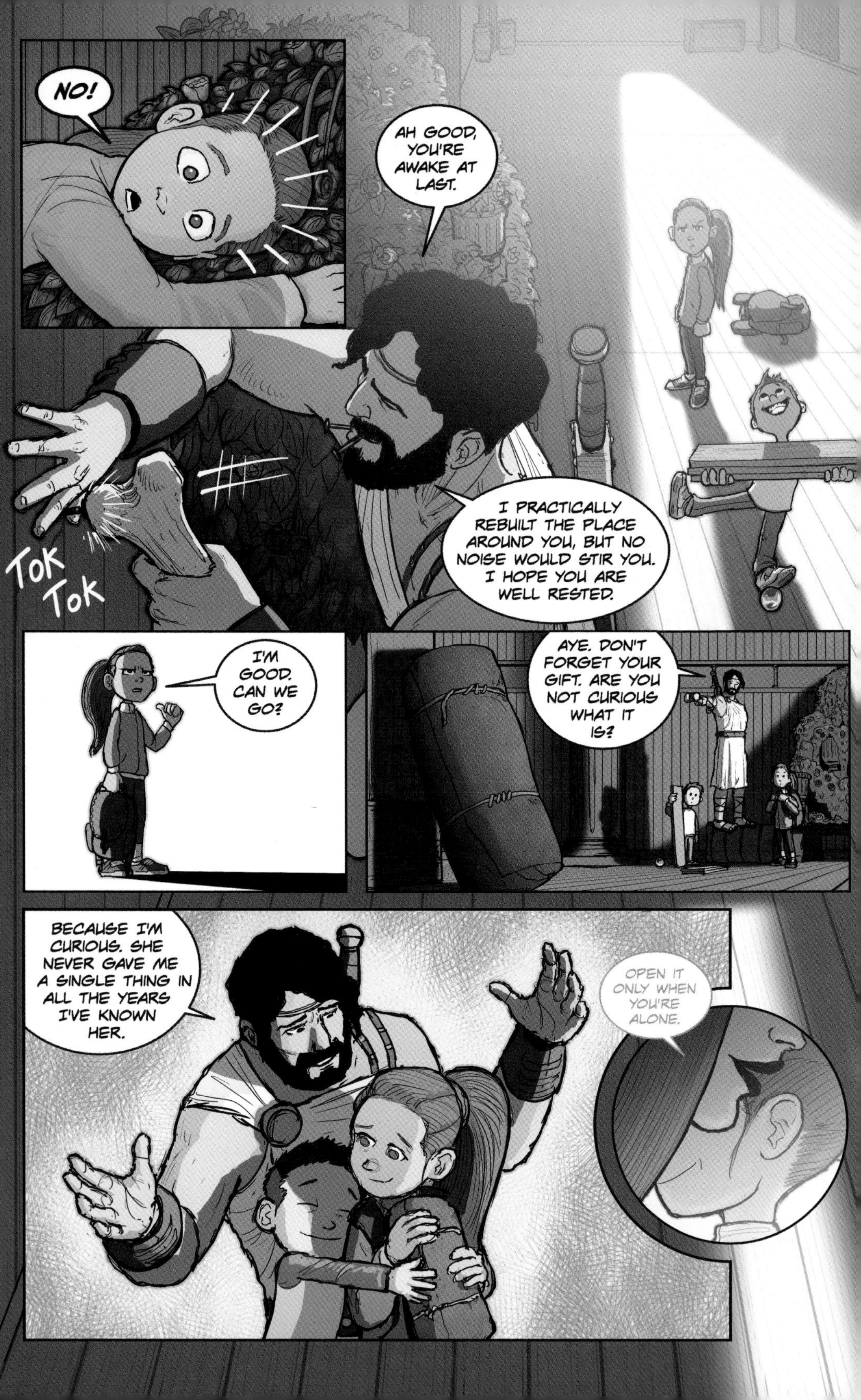
NO!
AH GOOD, YOU'RE AWAKE AT LAST.
TOK TOK
I PRACTICALLY REBUILT THE PLACE AROUND YOU, BUT NO NOISE WOULD STIR YOU. I HOPE YOU ARE WELL RESTED.
I'M GOOD. CAN WE GO?
AYE. DON'T FORGET YOUR GIFT. ARE YOU NOT CURIOUS WHAT IT IS?
BECAUSE I'M CURIOUS. SHE NEVER GAVE ME A SINGLE THING IN ALL THE YEARS I'VE KNOWN HER.
OPEN IT ONLY WHEN YOU'RE ALONE.

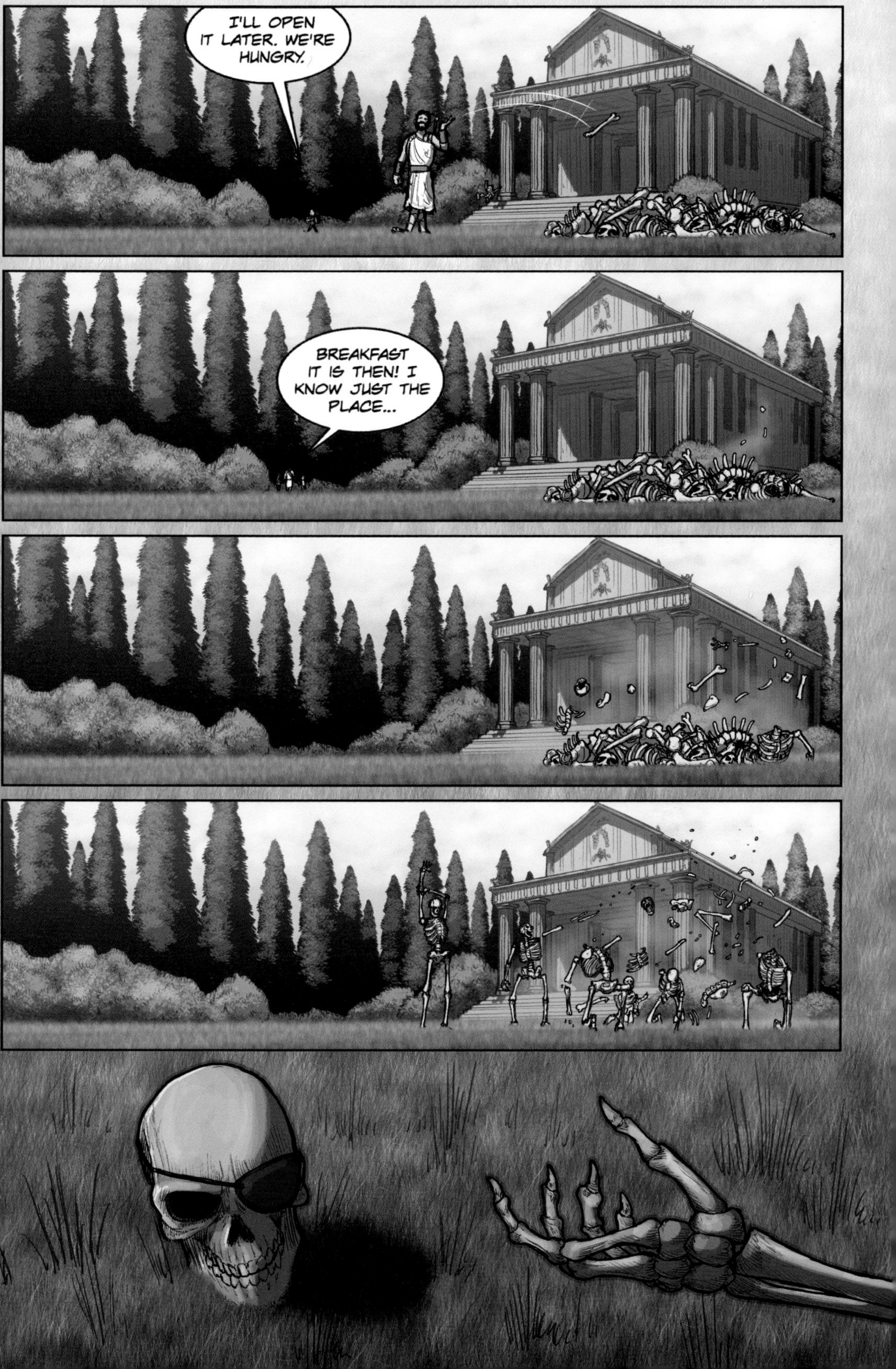
I'LL OPEN IT LATER. WE'RE HUNGRY.
BREAKFAST IT IS THEN! I KNOW JUST THE PLACE...

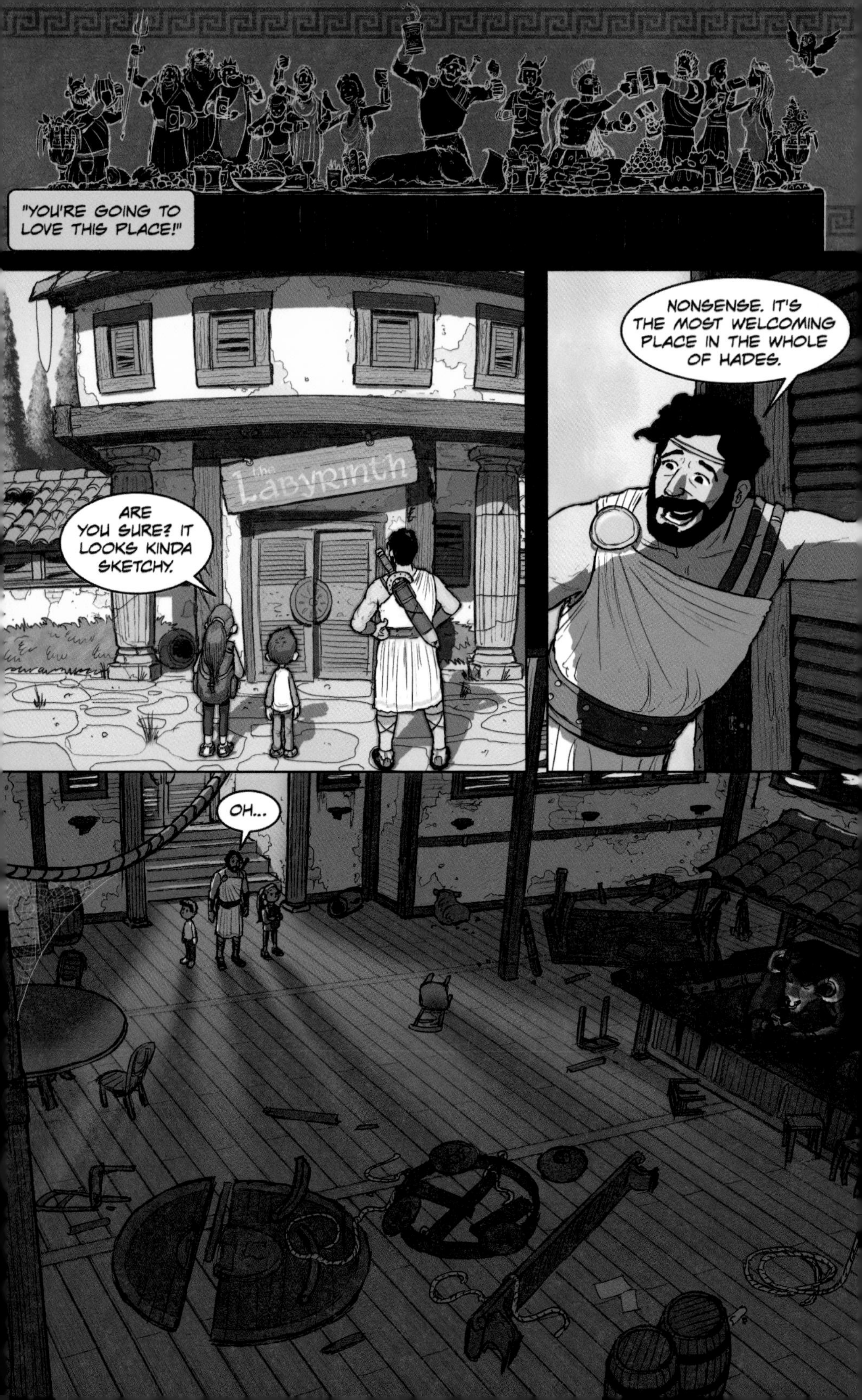
"YOU'RE GOING TO LOVE THIS PLACE!"
ARE YOU SURE? IT LOOKS KINDA SKETCHY.
The Labyrinth
NONSENSE. IT'S THE MOST WELCOMING PLACE IN THE WHOLE OF HADES.
OH...

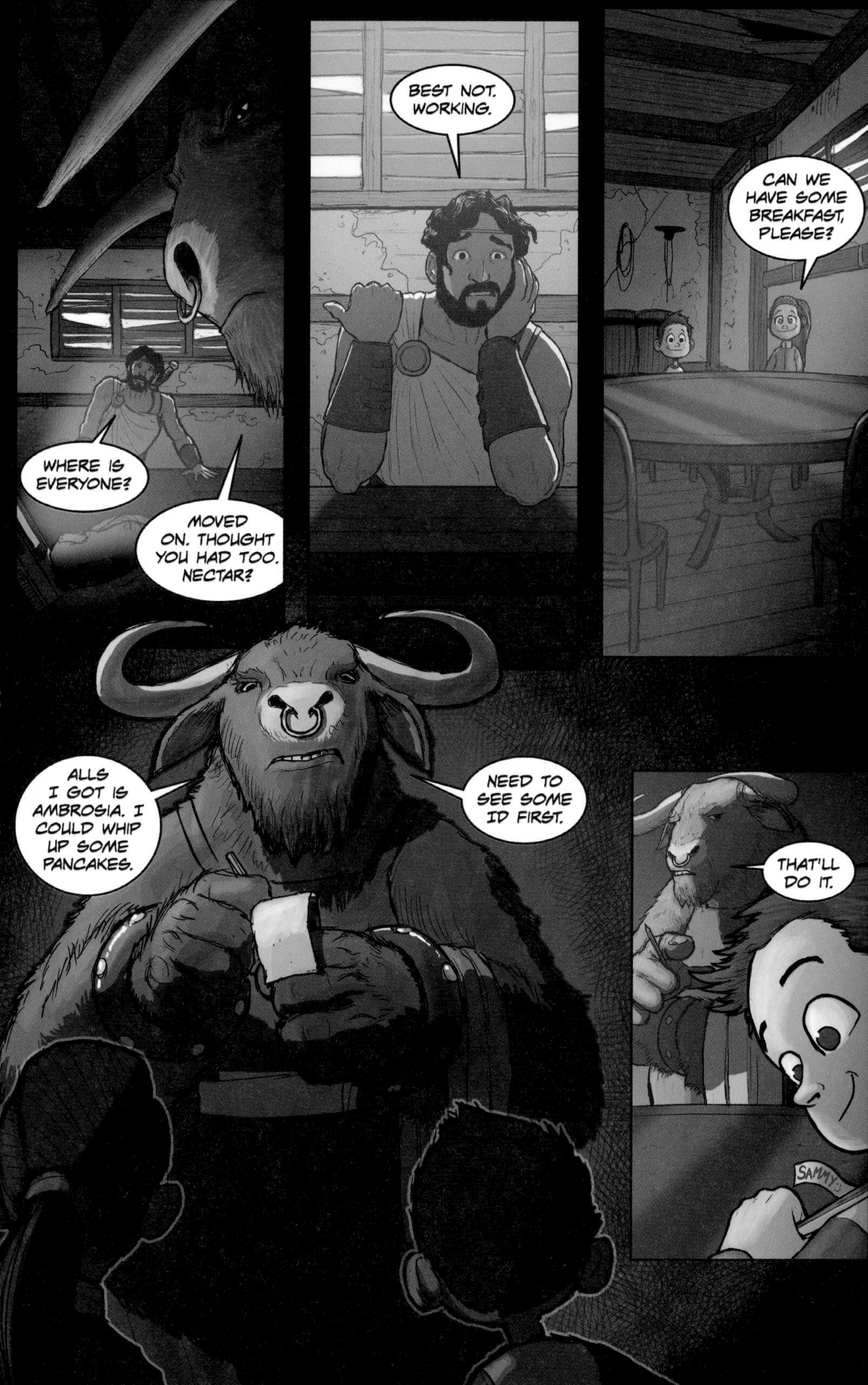
WHERE IS EVERYONE?
MOVED ON. THOUGHT YOU HAD TOO. NECTAR?
BEST NOT. WORKING.
CAN WE HAVE SOME BREAKFAST, PLEASE?
NEED TO SEE SOME ID FIRST.
ALLS I GOT IS AMBROSIA. I COULD WHIP UP SOME PANCAKES.
THAT'LL DO IT.
SAMMY

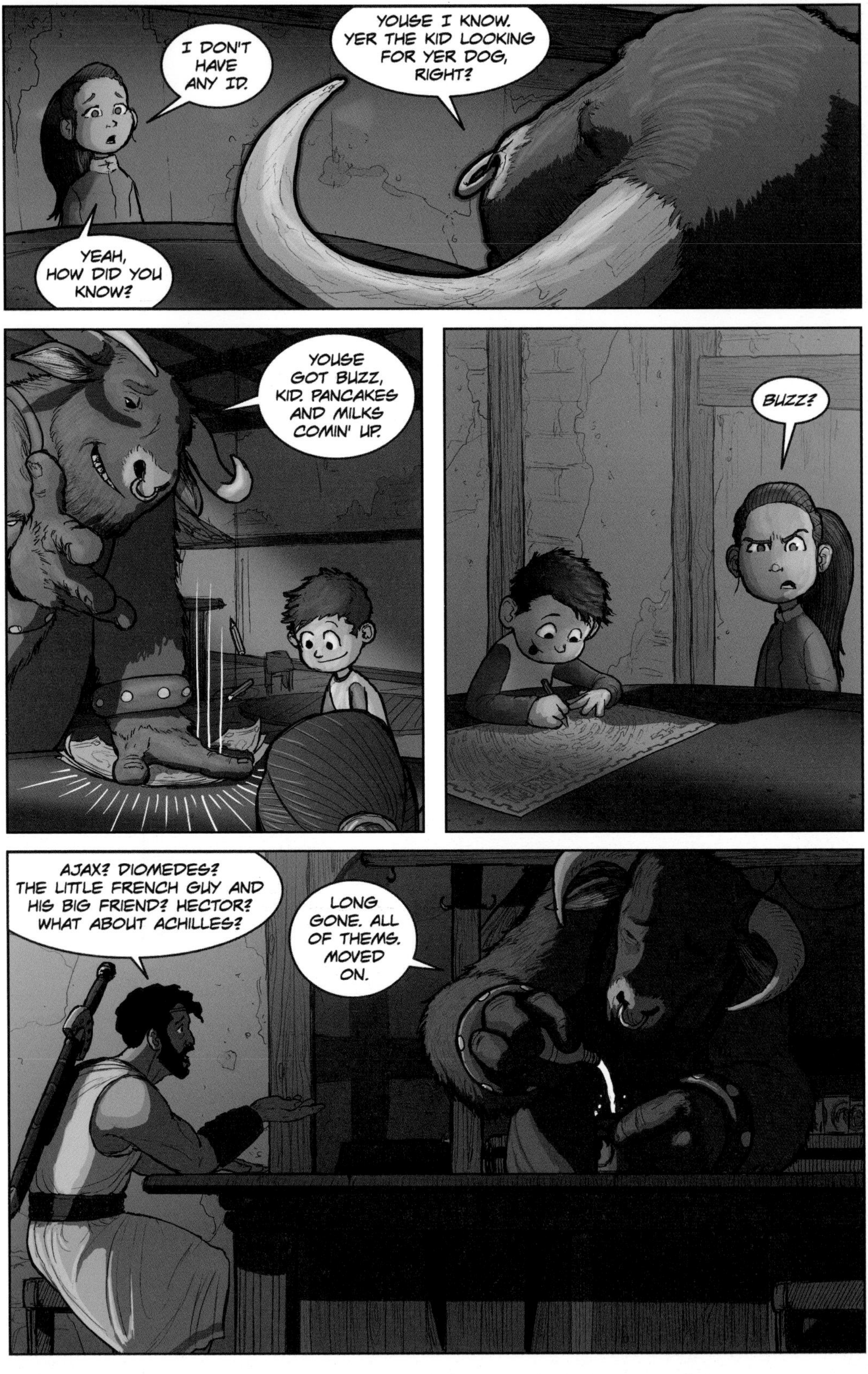
I DON'T HAVE ANY ID.
YOUSE I KNOW. YER THE KID LOOKING FOR YER DOG, RIGHT?
YEAH, HOW DID YOU KNOW?
YOUSE GOT BUZZ, KID. PANCAKES AND MILKS COMIN' UP.
BUZZ?
AJAX? DIOMEDES? THE LITTLE FRENCH GUY AND HIS BIG FRIEND? HECTOR? WHAT ABOUT ACHILLES?
LONG GONE. ALL OF THEMS. MOVED ON.

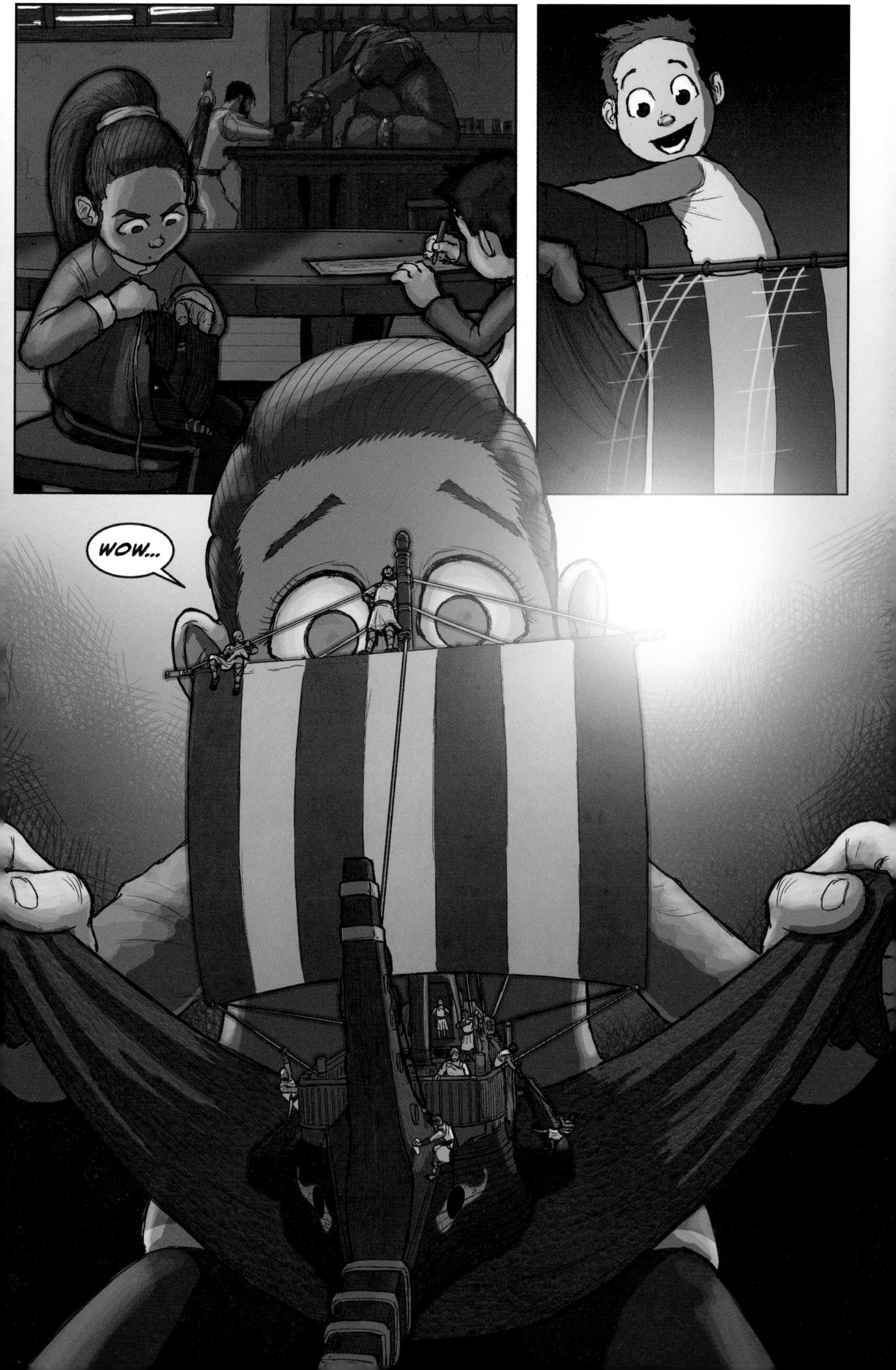
WOW...

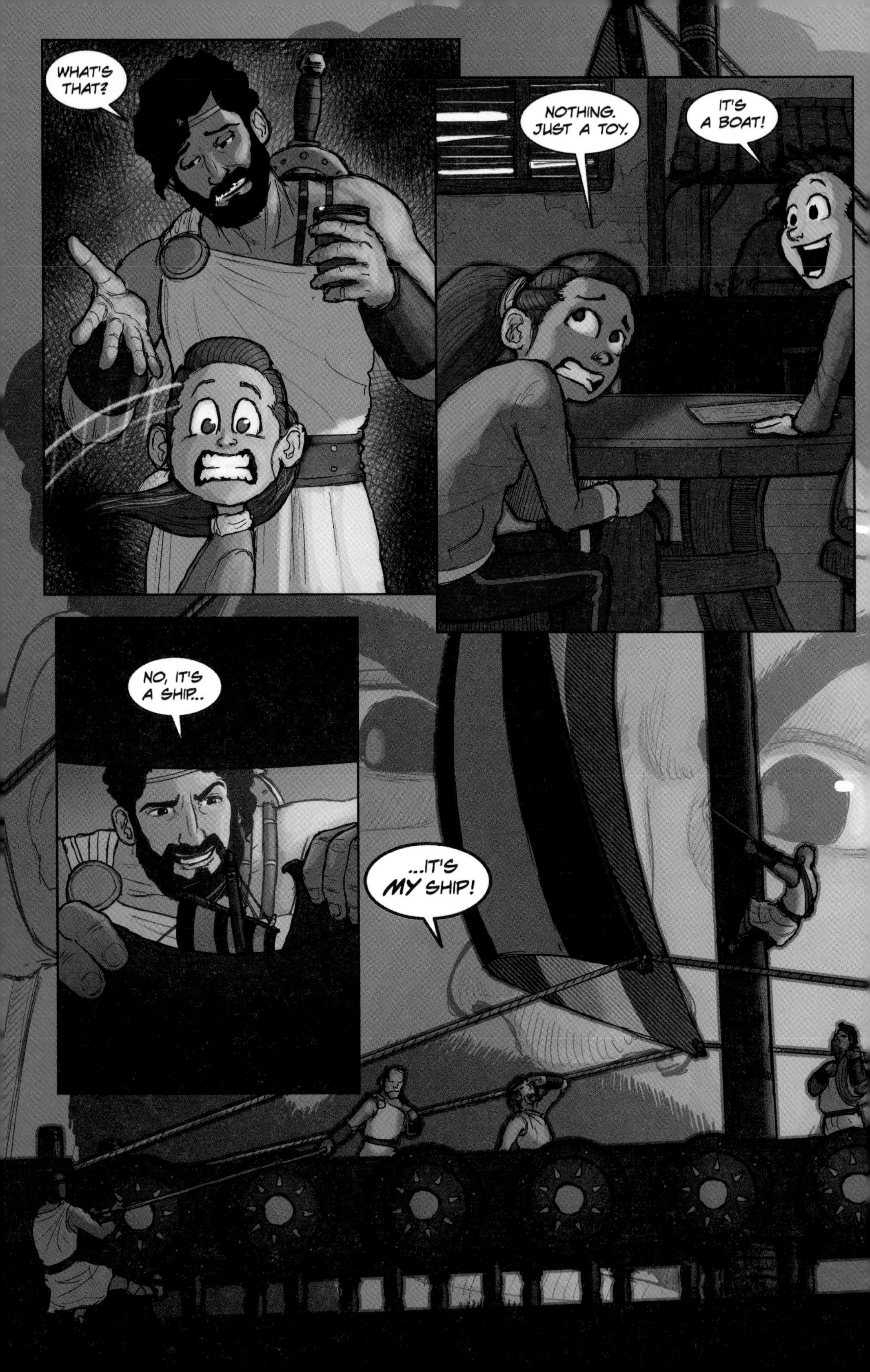
WHAT'S THAT?
NOTHING. JUST A TOY.
IT'S A BOAT!
NO, IT'S A SHIP...
...IT'S MY SHIP!

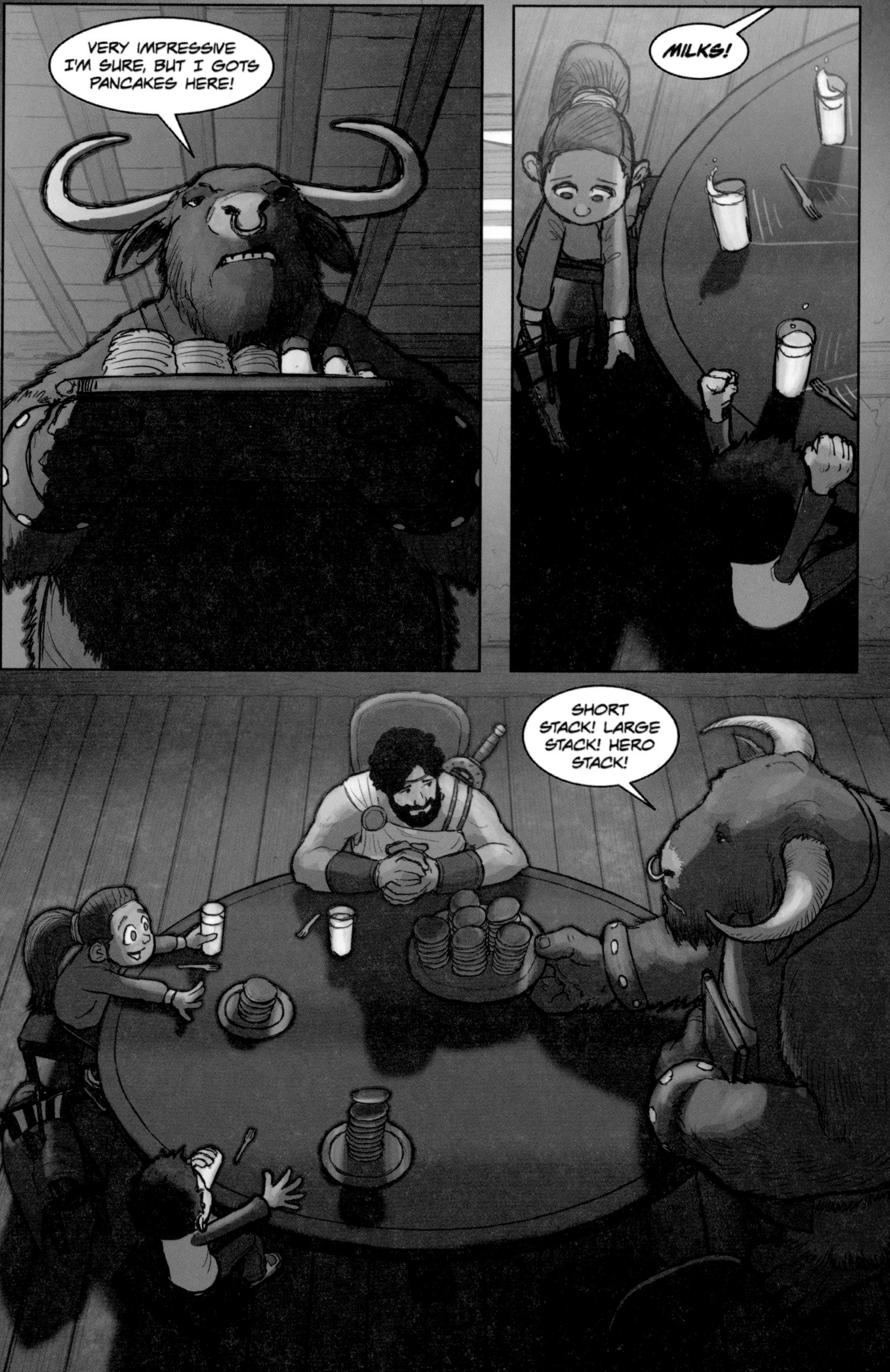
VERY IMPRESSIVE I'M SURE, BUT I GOTS PANCAKES HERE!
MILKS!
SHORT STACK! LARGE STACK! HERO STACK!

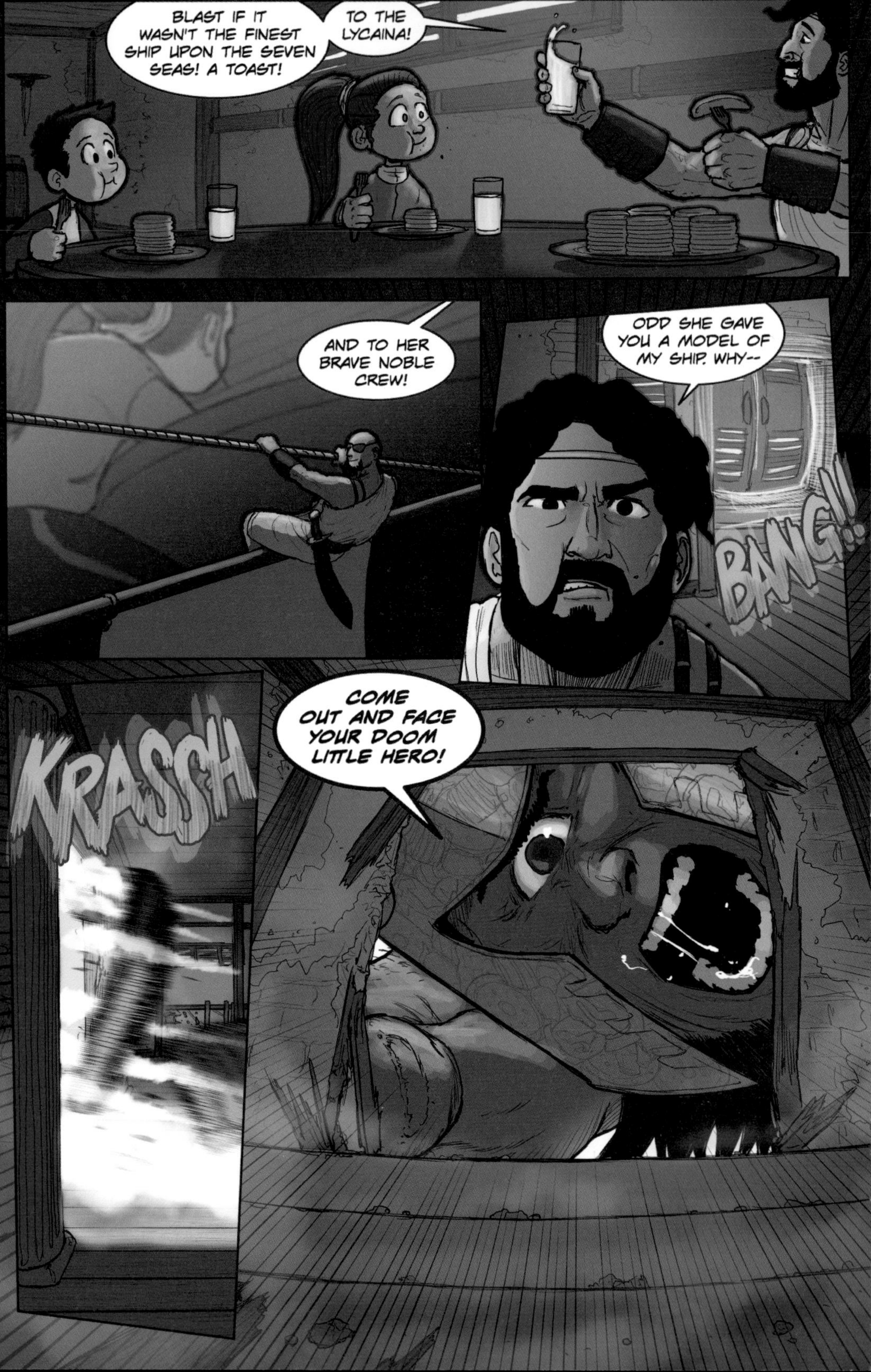
BLAST IF IT WASN'T THE FINEST SHIP UPON THE SEVEN SEAS! A TOAST!
TO THE LYCAINA!
AND TO HER BRAVE NOBLE CREW!
ODD SHE GAVE YOU A MODEL OF MY SHIP. WHY--
BANG!!
KRASSH
COME OUT AND FACE YOUR DOOM LITTLE HERO!

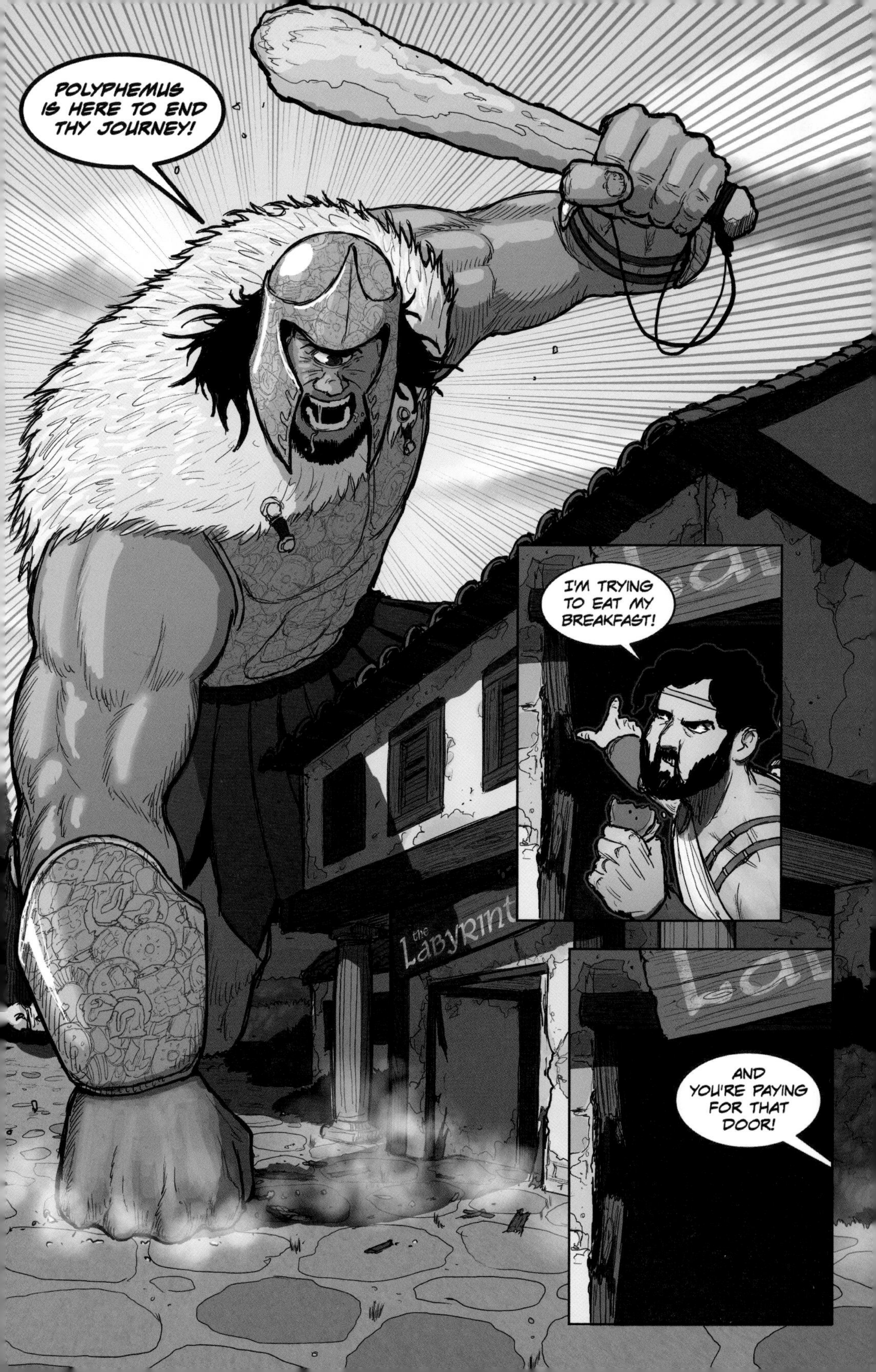
POLYPHEMUS IS HERE TO END THY JOURNEY!
I'M TRYING TO EAT MY BREAKFAST!
the LABYRINT
AND YOU'RE PAYING FOR THAT DOOR!

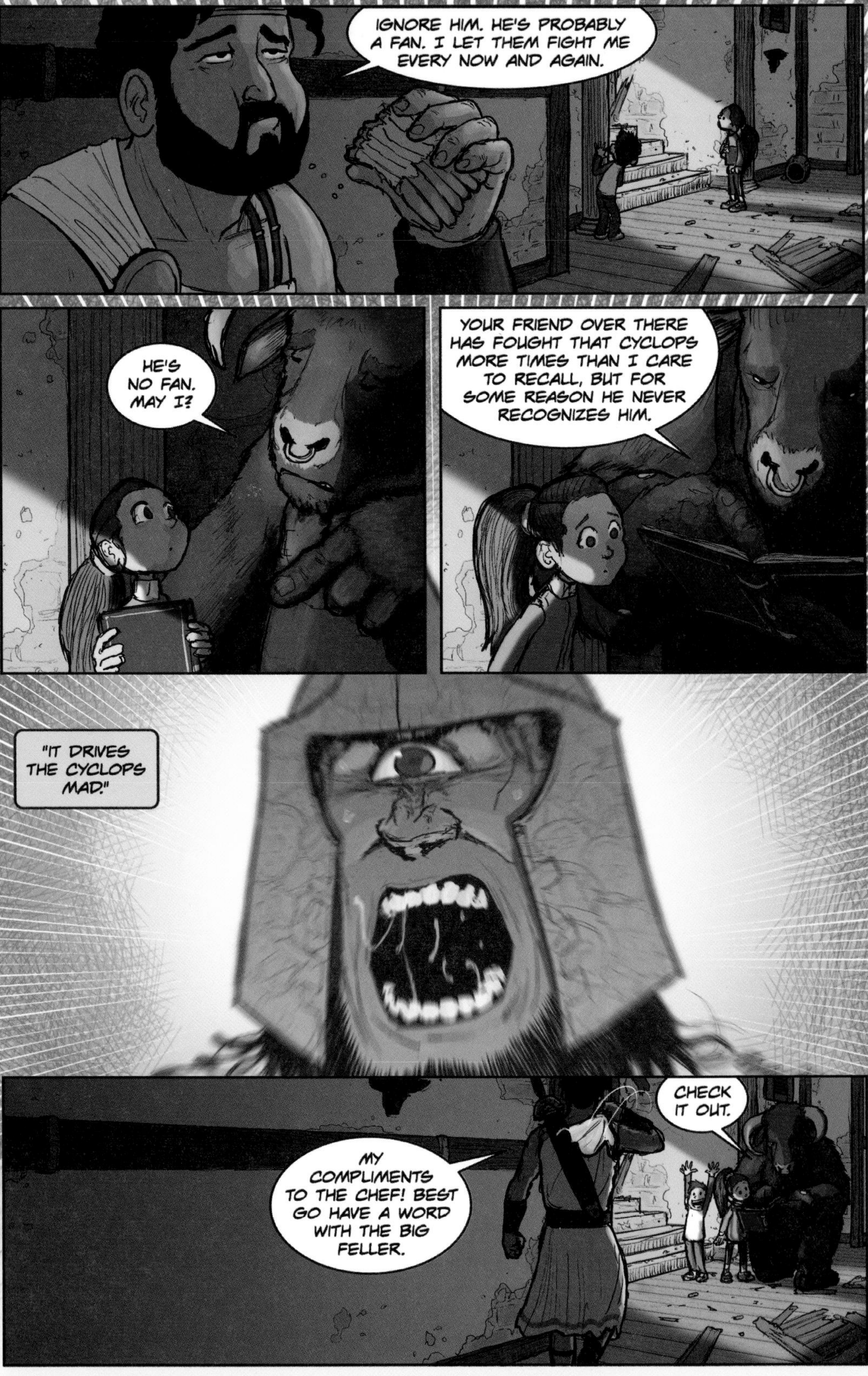
IGNORE HIM. HE'S PROBABLY A FAN. I LET THEM FIGHT ME EVERY NOW AND AGAIN.
HE'S NO FAN. MAY I?
YOUR FRIEND OVER THERE HAS FOUGHT THAT CYCLOPS MORE TIMES THAN I CARE TO RECALL, BUT FOR SOME REASON HE NEVER RECOGNIZES HIM.
"IT DRIVES THE CYCLOPS MAD."
CHECK IT OUT.
MY COMPLIMENTS TO THE CHEF! BEST GO HAVE A WORD WITH THE BIG FELLER.

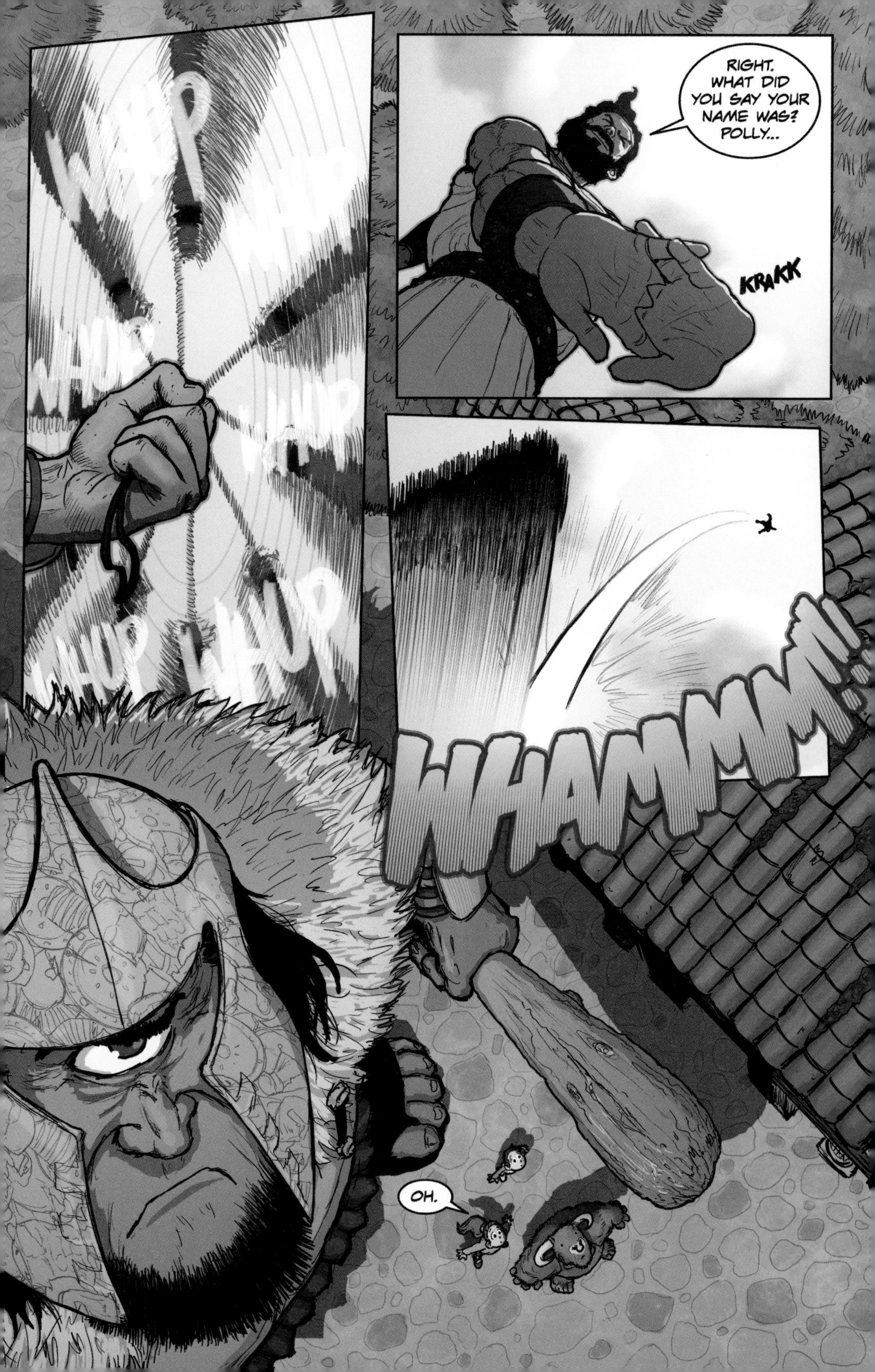
WHUP
WHUP
WHUP
WHUP
WHUP WHUP
RIGHT. WHAT DID YOU SAY YOUR NAME WAS? POLLY...
KRAKK
WHAMMM!!
OH.

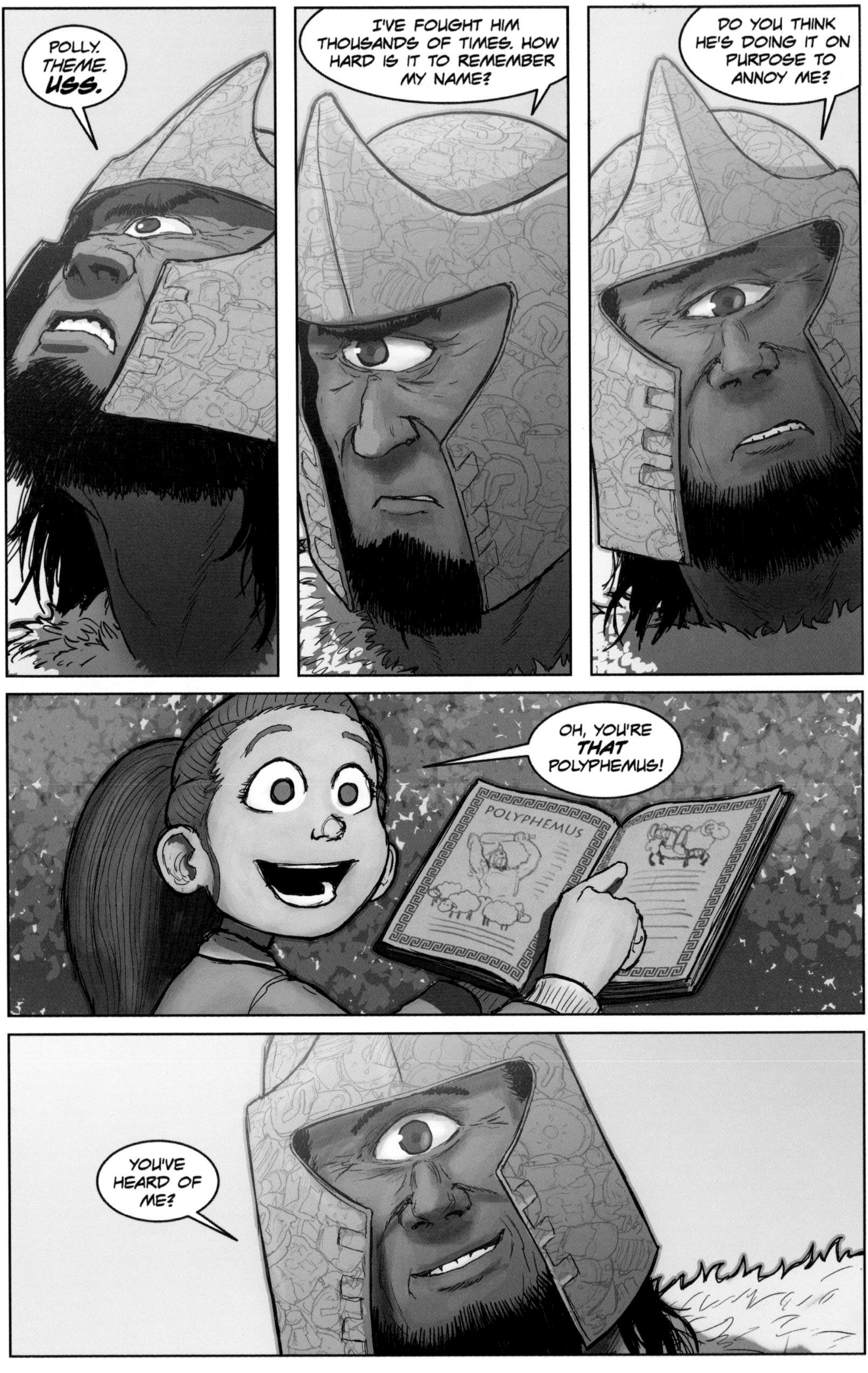
POLLY. THEME. USS.
I'VE FOUGHT HIM THOUSANDS OF TIMES. HOW HARD IS IT TO REMEMBER MY NAME?
DO YOU THINK HE'S DOING IT ON PURPOSE TO ANNOY ME?
OH, YOU'RE THAT POLYPHEMUS!
POLYPHEMUS
YOU'VE HEARD OF ME?

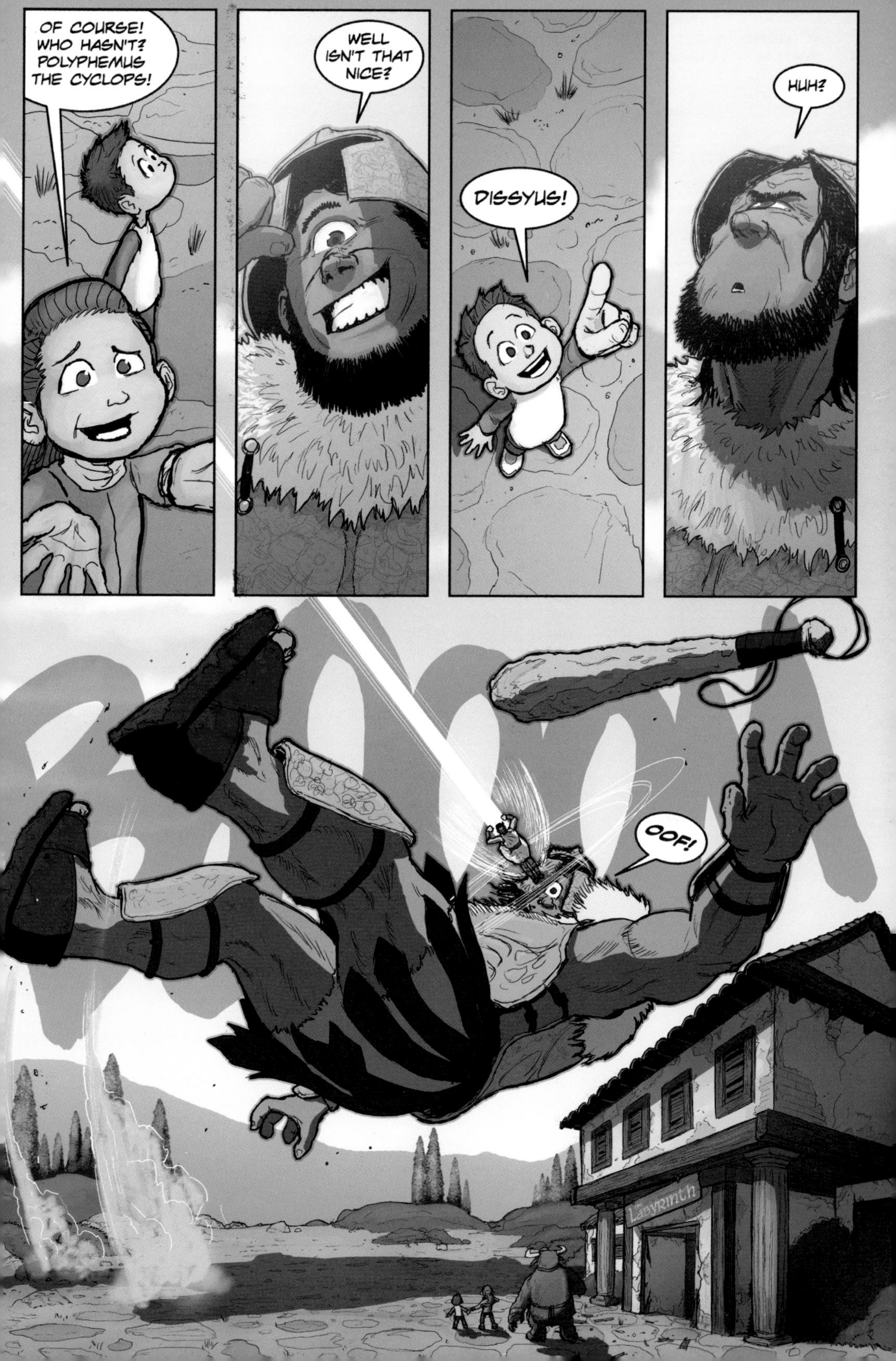
OF COURSE! WHO HASN'T? POLYPHEMUS THE CYCLOPS!
WELL ISN'T THAT NICE?
DISSYUS!
HUH?
OOF!
Labyrinth

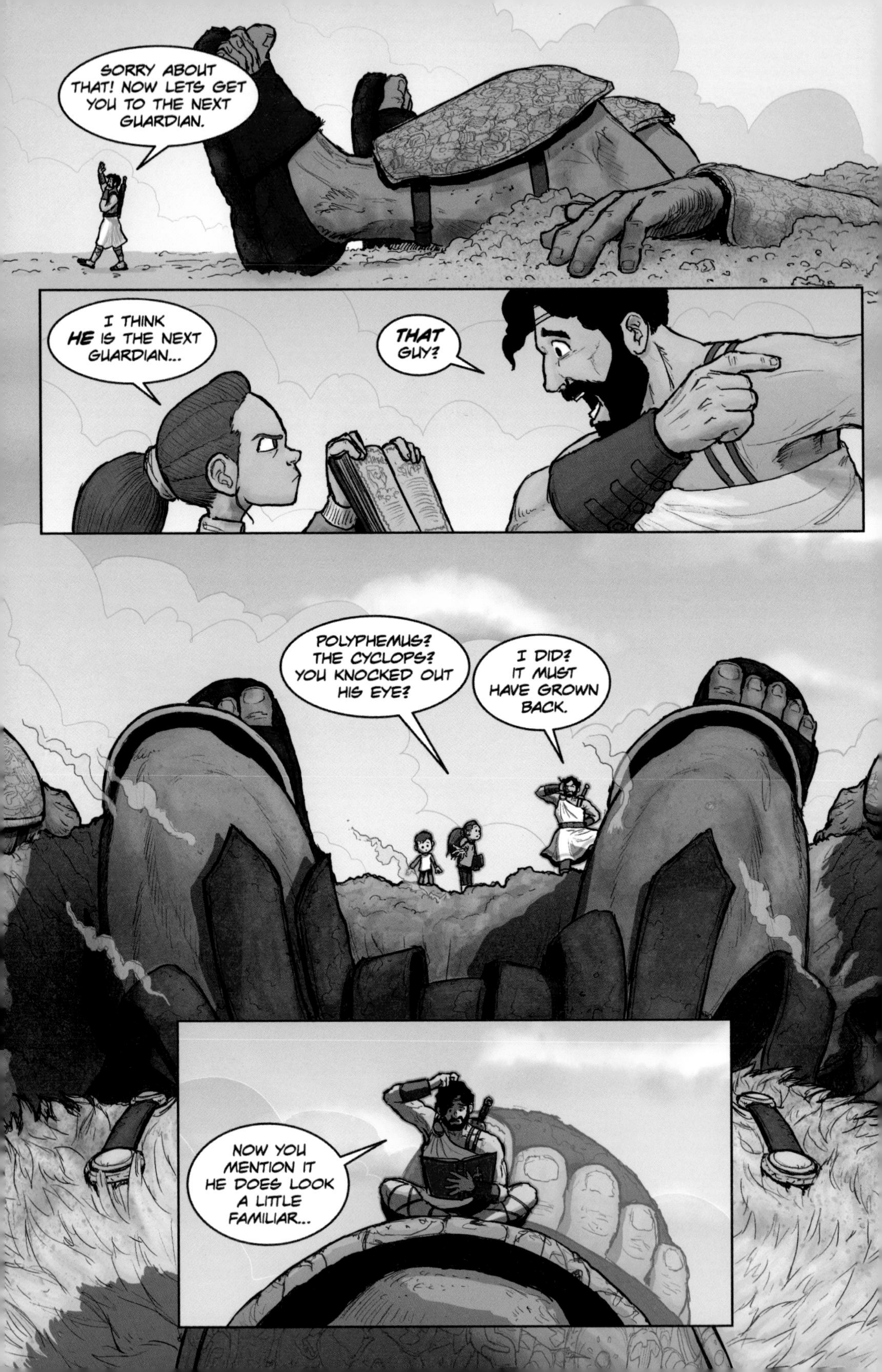
SORRY ABOUT THAT! NOW LETS GET YOU TO THE NEXT GUARDIAN.
I THINK **HE** IS THE NEXT GUARDIAN...
THAT GUY?
POLYPHEMUS? THE CYCLOPS? YOU KNOCKED OUT HIS EYE?
I DID? IT MUST HAVE GROWN BACK.
NOW YOU MENTION IT HE DOES LOOK A LITTLE FAMILIAR...

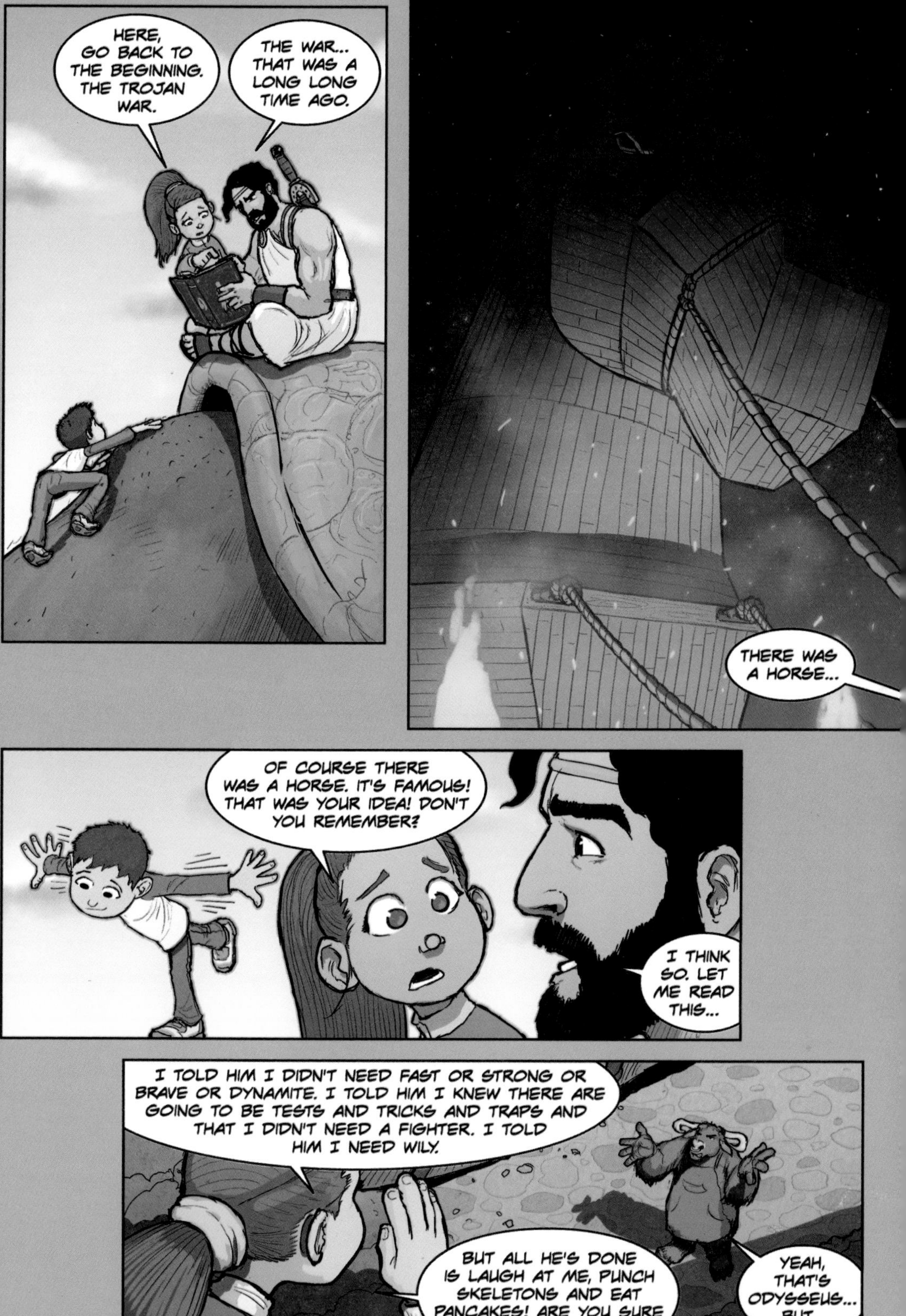
HERE, GO BACK TO THE BEGINNING. THE TROJAN WAR.
THE WAR... THAT WAS A LONG LONG TIME AGO.
THERE WAS A HORSE...
OF COURSE THERE WAS A HORSE. IT'S FAMOUS! THAT WAS YOUR IDEA! DON'T YOU REMEMBER?
I THINK SO. LET ME READ THIS...
I TOLD HIM I DIDN'T NEED FAST OR STRONG OR BRAVE OR DYNAMITE. I TOLD HIM I KNEW THERE ARE GOING TO BE TESTS AND TRICKS AND TRAPS AND THAT I DIDN'T NEED A FIGHTER. I TOLD HIM I NEED WILY.
BUT ALL HE'S DONE IS LAUGH AT ME, PUNCH SKELETONS AND EAT PANCAKES! ARE YOU SURE THIS IS ODYSSEUS?
YEAH, THAT'S ODYSSEUS... BUT...

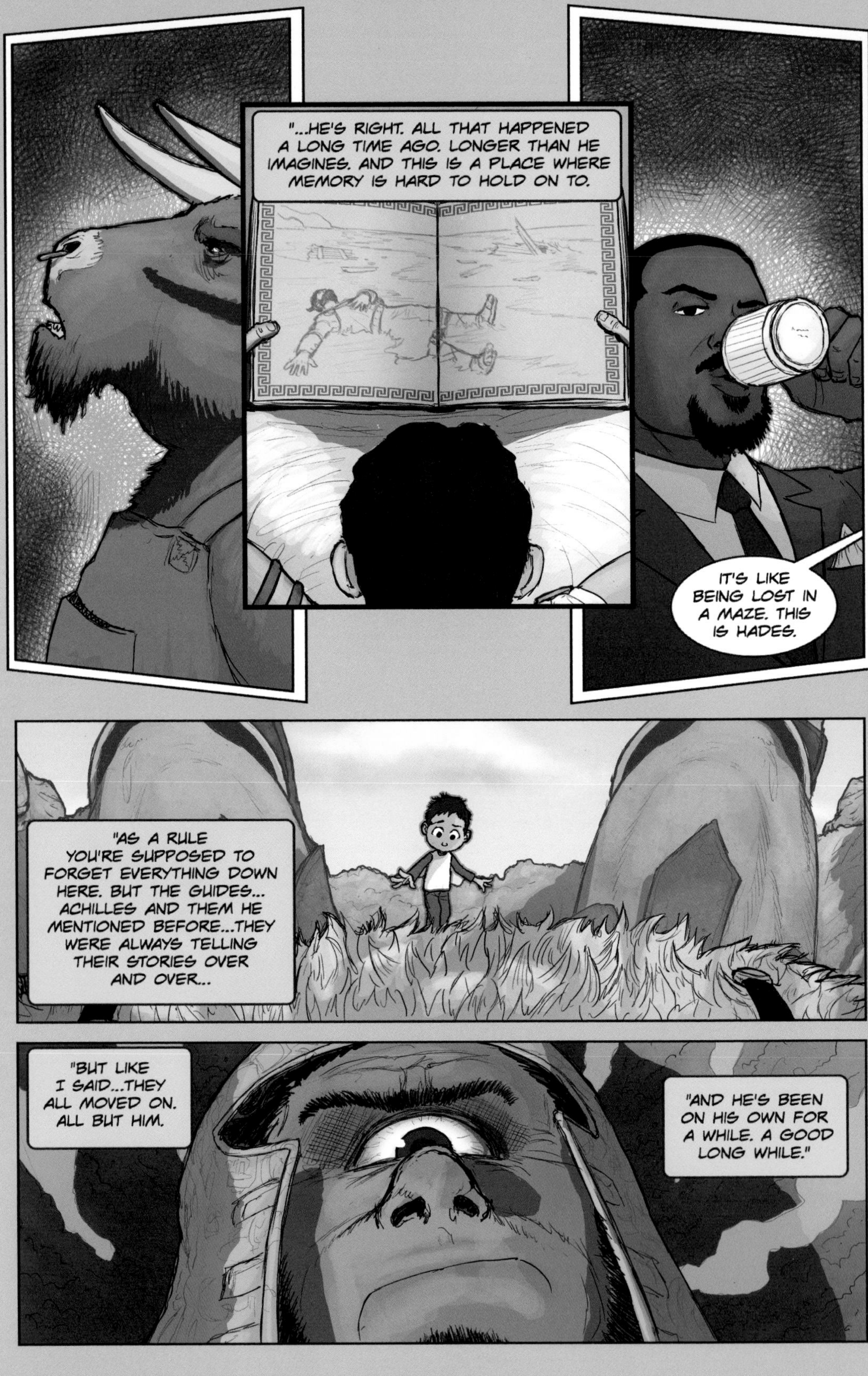
"...HE'S RIGHT. ALL THAT HAPPENED A LONG TIME AGO. LONGER THAN HE IMAGINES. AND THIS IS A PLACE WHERE MEMORY IS HARD TO HOLD ON TO.
IT'S LIKE BEING LOST IN A MAZE. THIS IS HADES.
"AS A RULE YOU'RE SUPPOSED TO FORGET EVERYTHING DOWN HERE. BUT THE GUIDES... ACHILLES AND THEM HE MENTIONED BEFORE...THEY WERE ALWAYS TELLING THEIR STORIES OVER AND OVER...
"BUT LIKE I SAID...THEY ALL MOVED ON. ALL BUT HIM.
"AND HE'S BEEN ON HIS OWN FOR A WHILE. A GOOD LONG WHILE."

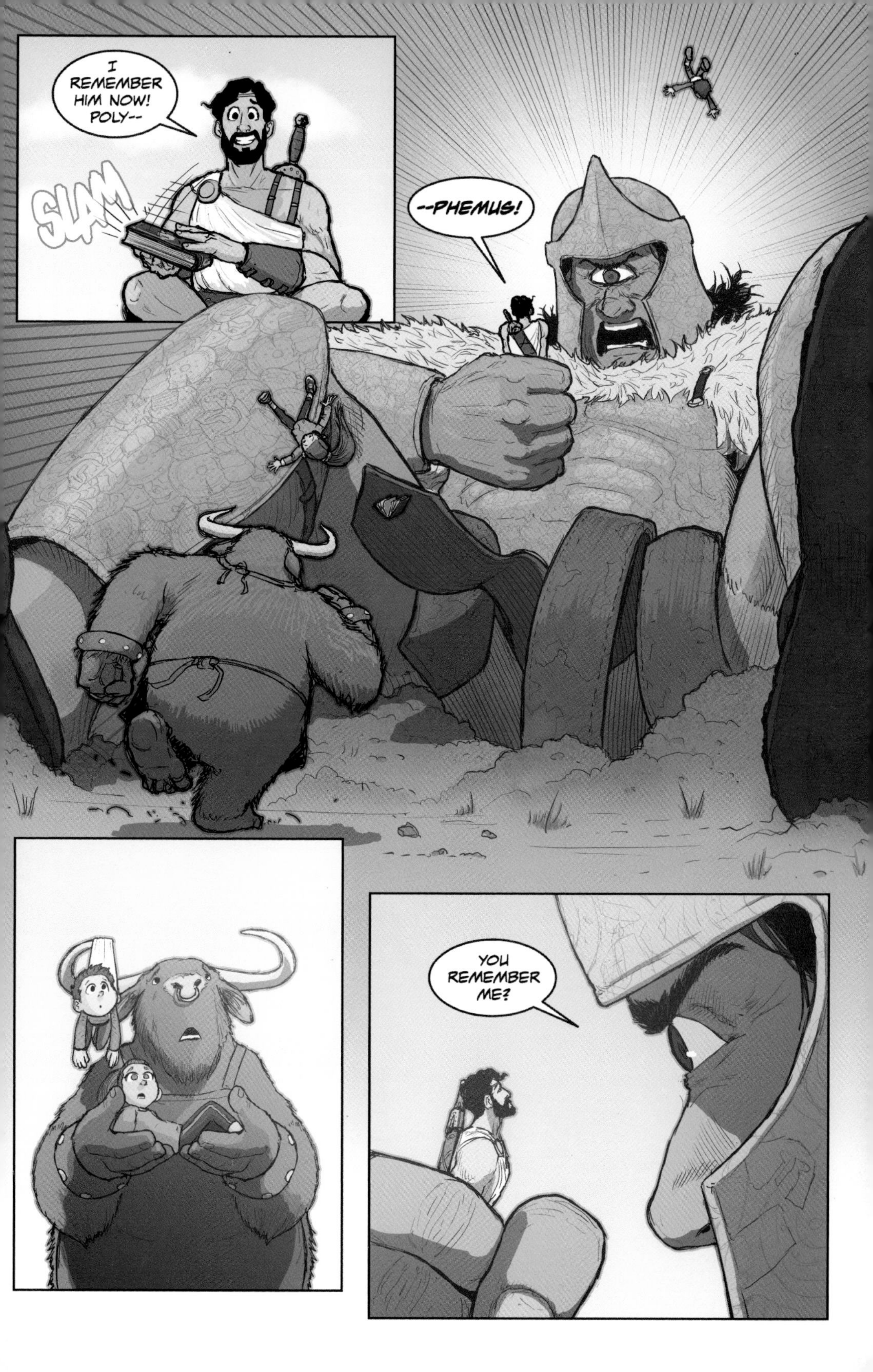
I REMEMBER HIM NOW! POLY--
SLAM
--PHEMUS!
YOU REMEMBER ME?

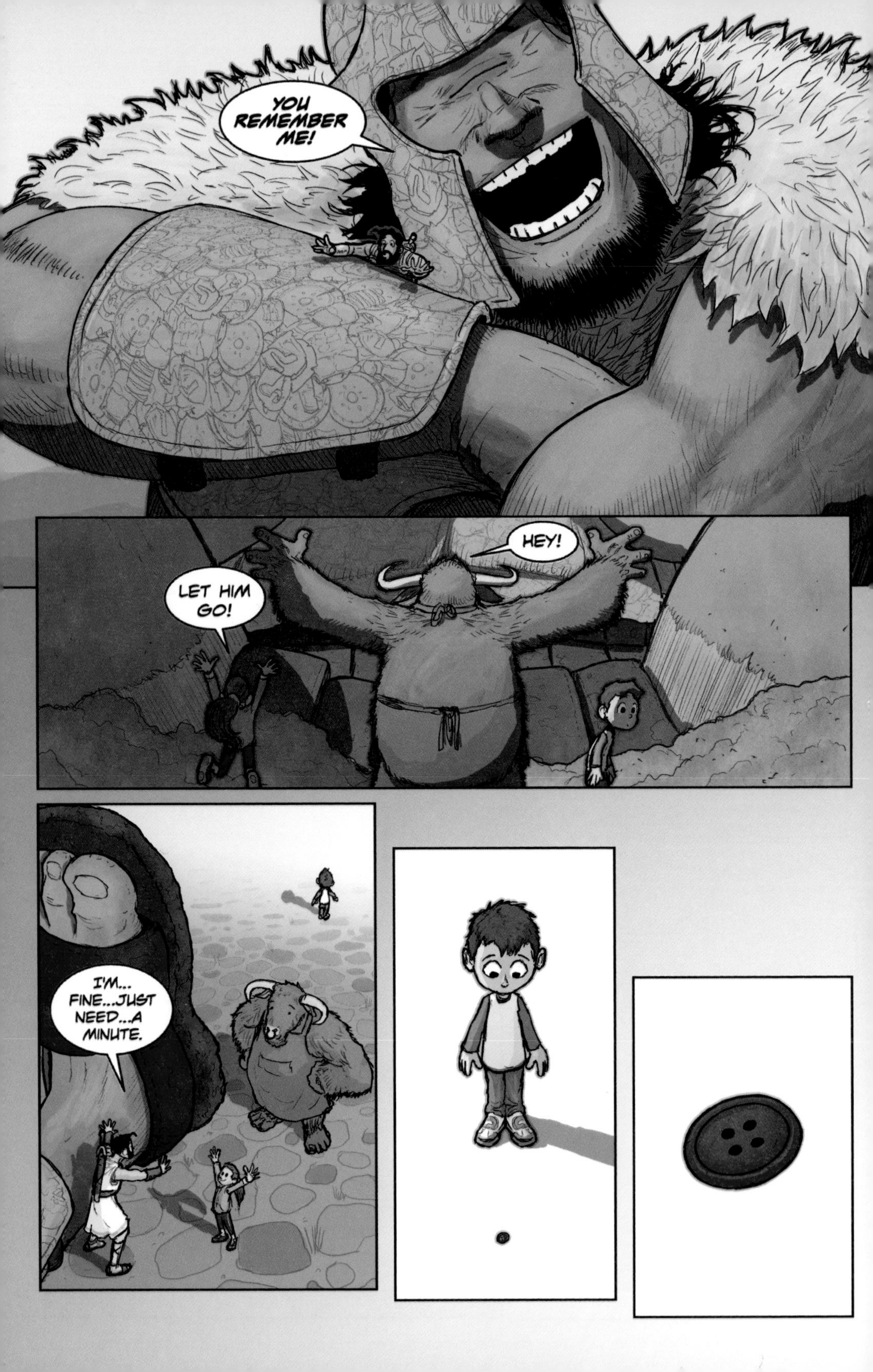
YOU REMEMBER ME!
HEY!
LET HIM GO!
I'M... FINE...JUST NEED...A MINUTE.

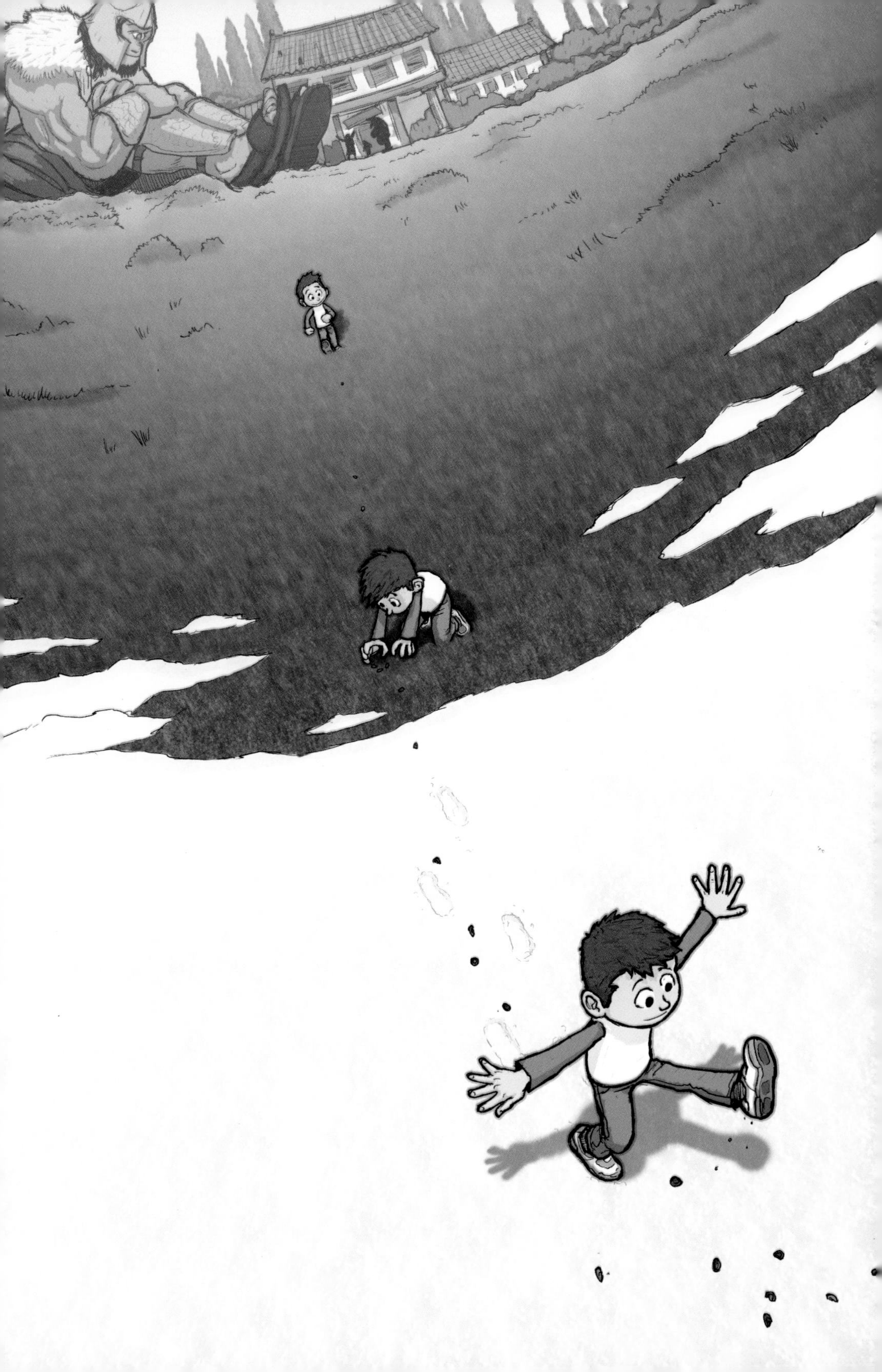

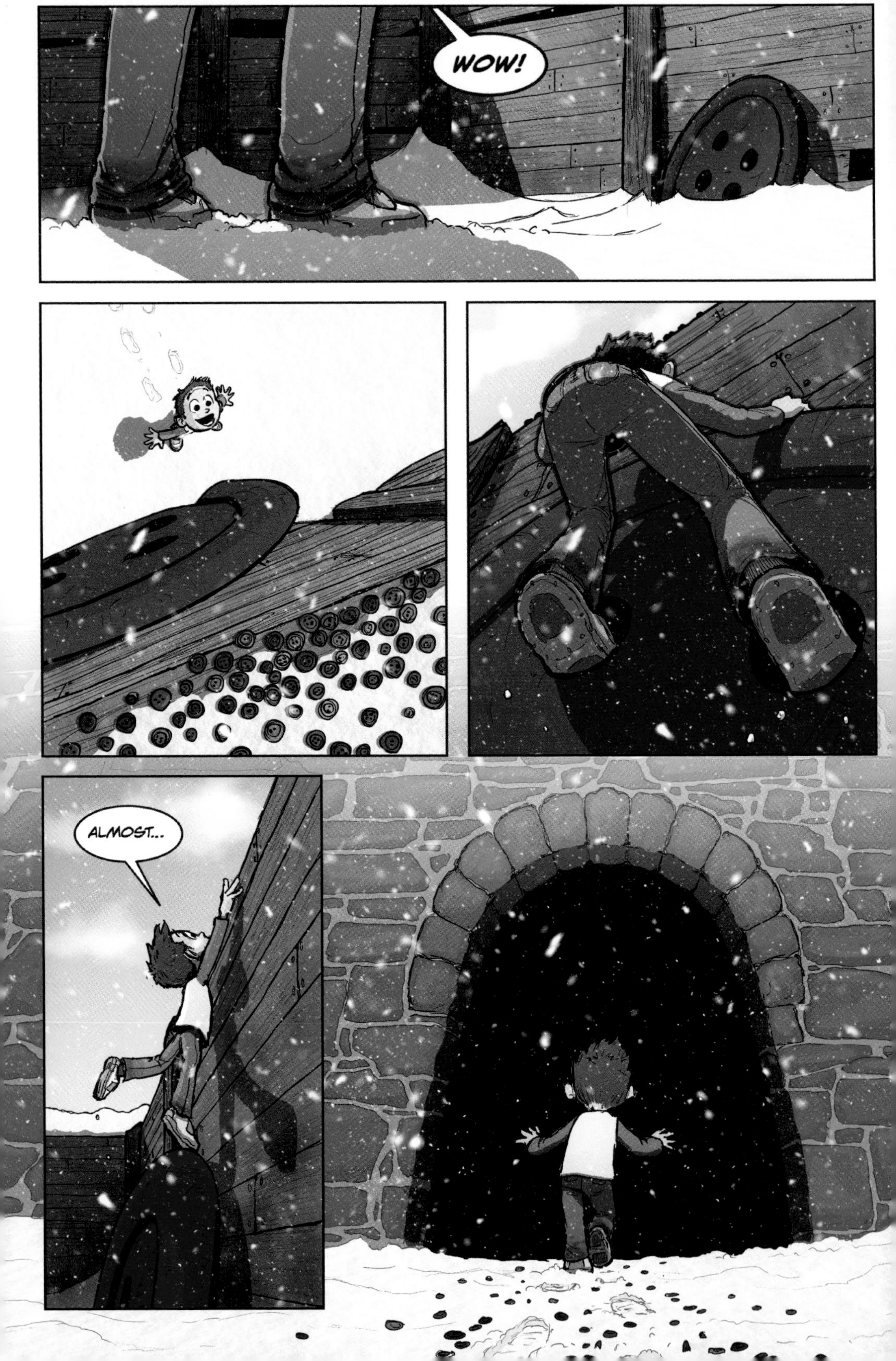
WOW!
ALMOST...

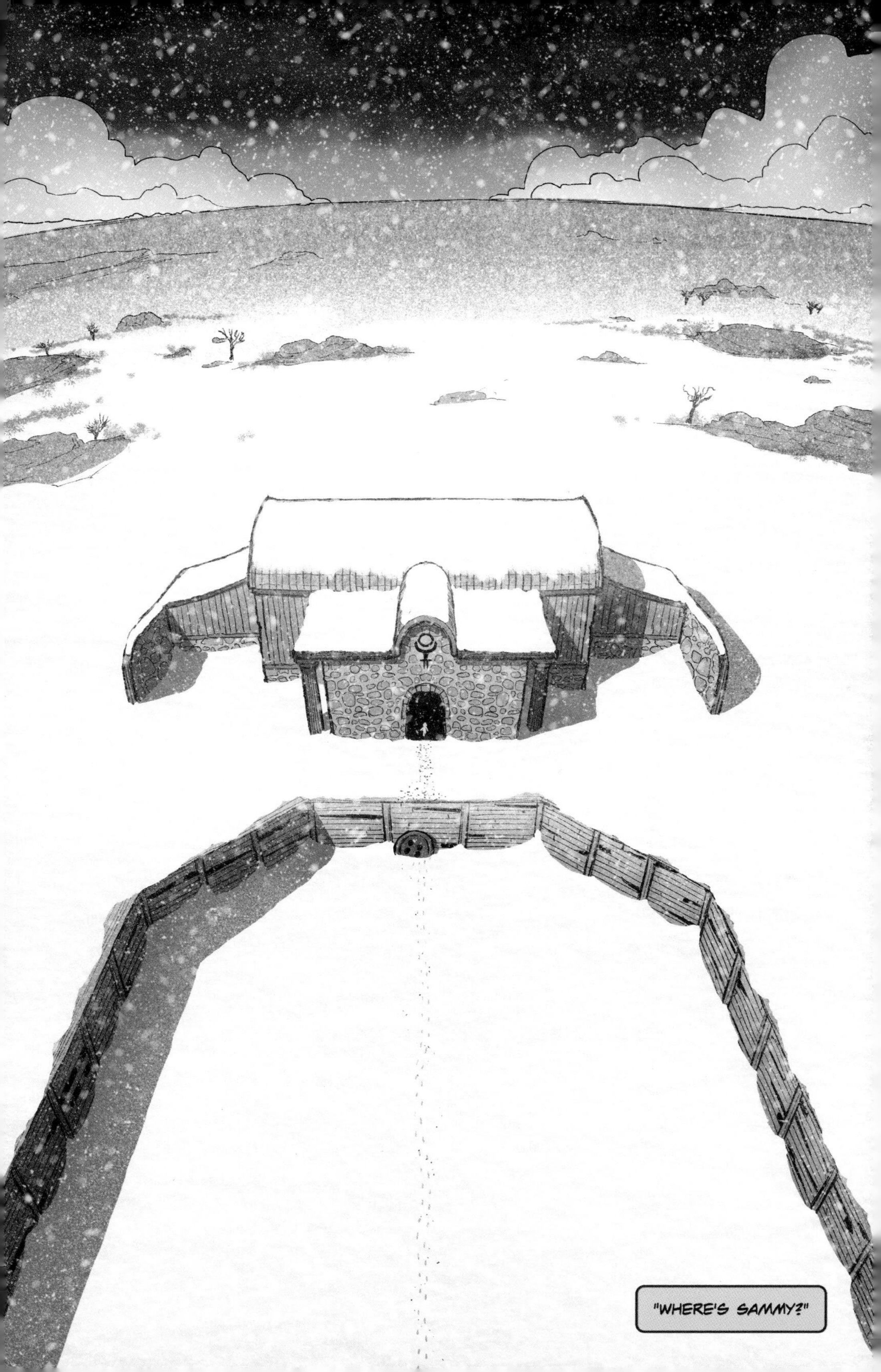
"WHERE'S SAMMY?"

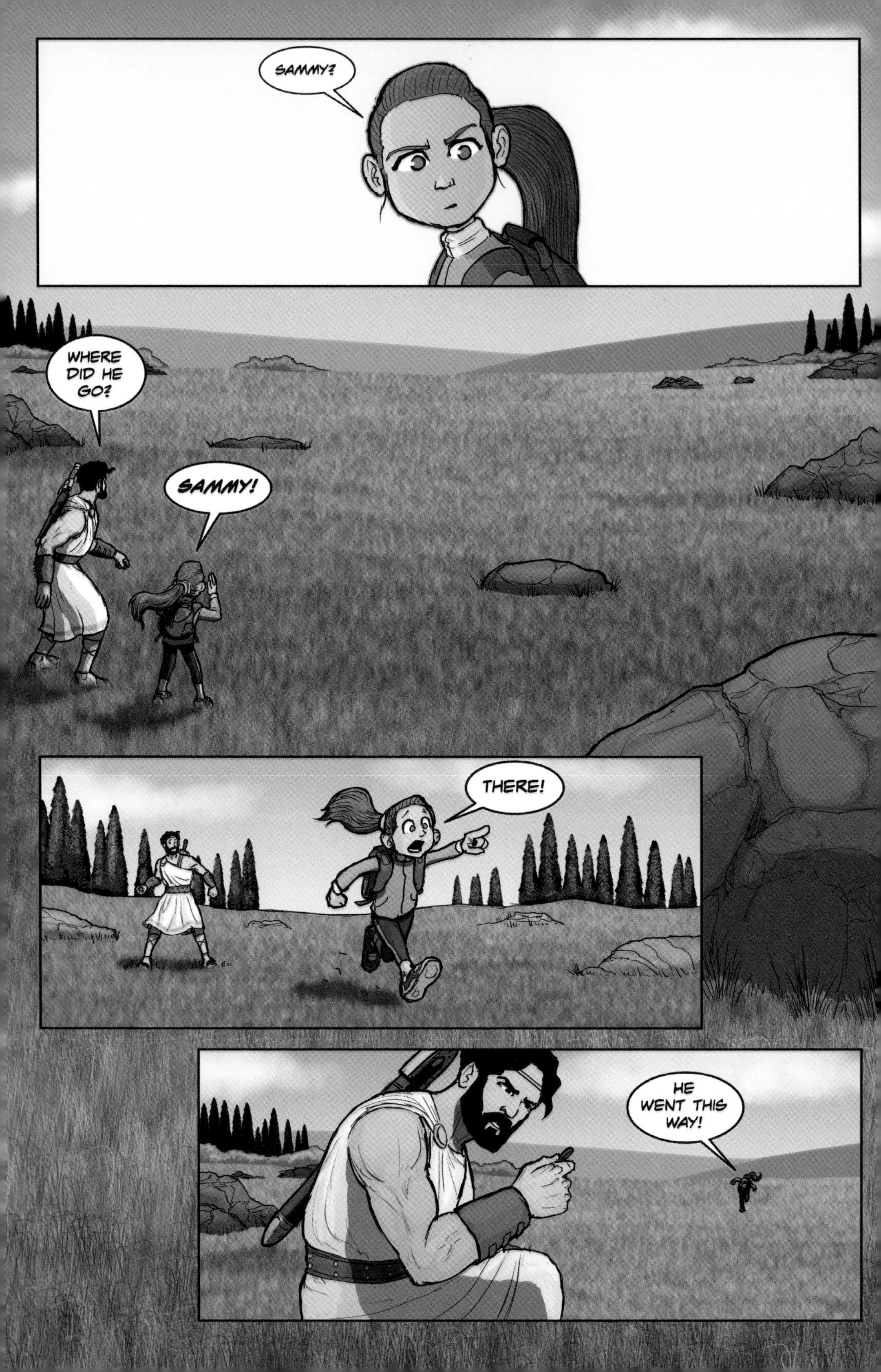
SAMMY?
WHERE DID HE GO?
SAMMY!
THERE!
HE WENT THIS WAY!

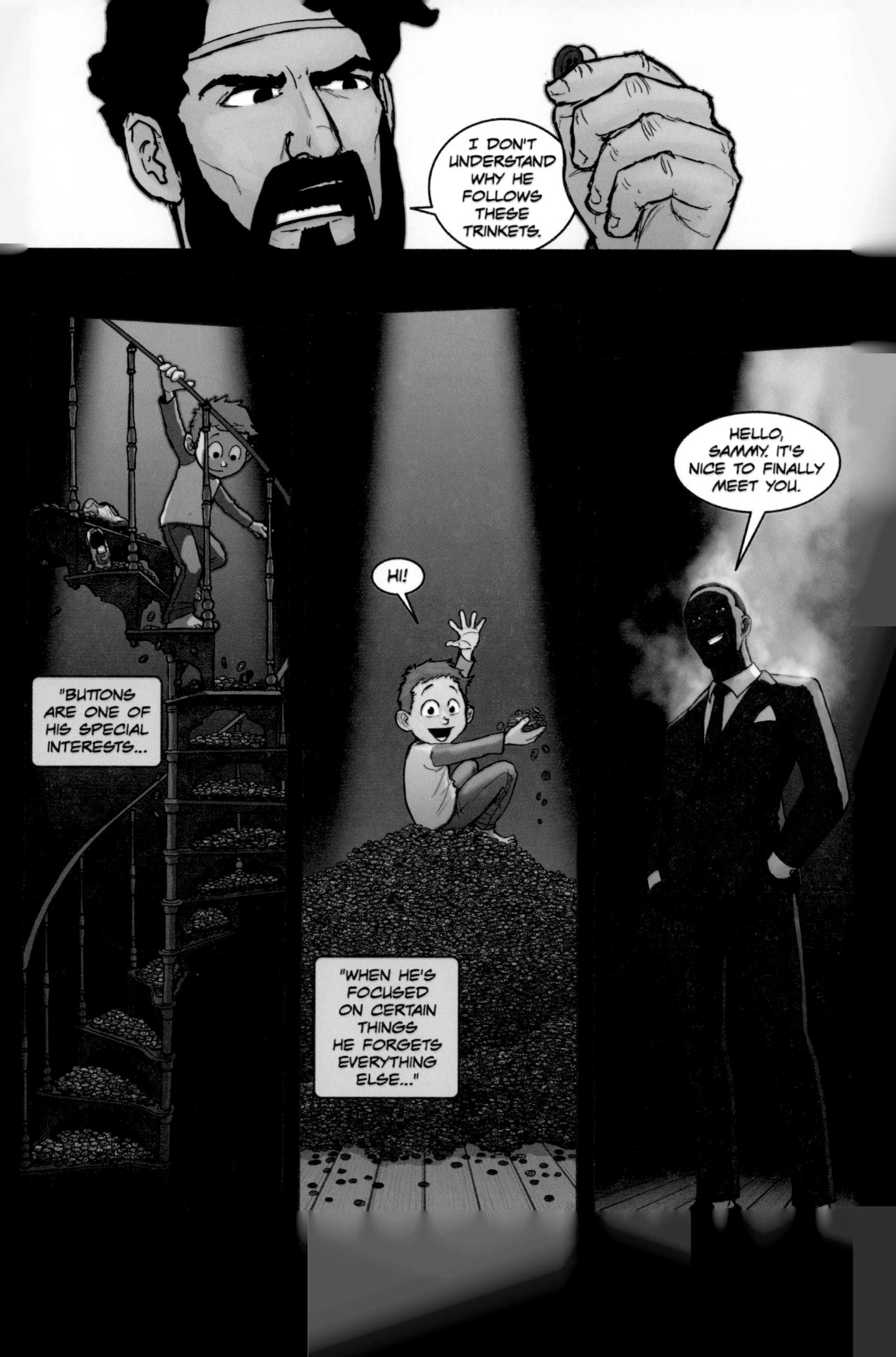
I DON'T UNDERSTAND WHY HE FOLLOWS THESE TRINKETS.
"BUTTONS ARE ONE OF HIS SPECIAL INTERESTS...
HI!
"WHEN HE'S FOCUSED ON CERTAIN THINGS HE FORGETS EVERYTHING ELSE..."
HELLO, SAMMY. IT'S NICE TO FINALLY MEET YOU.

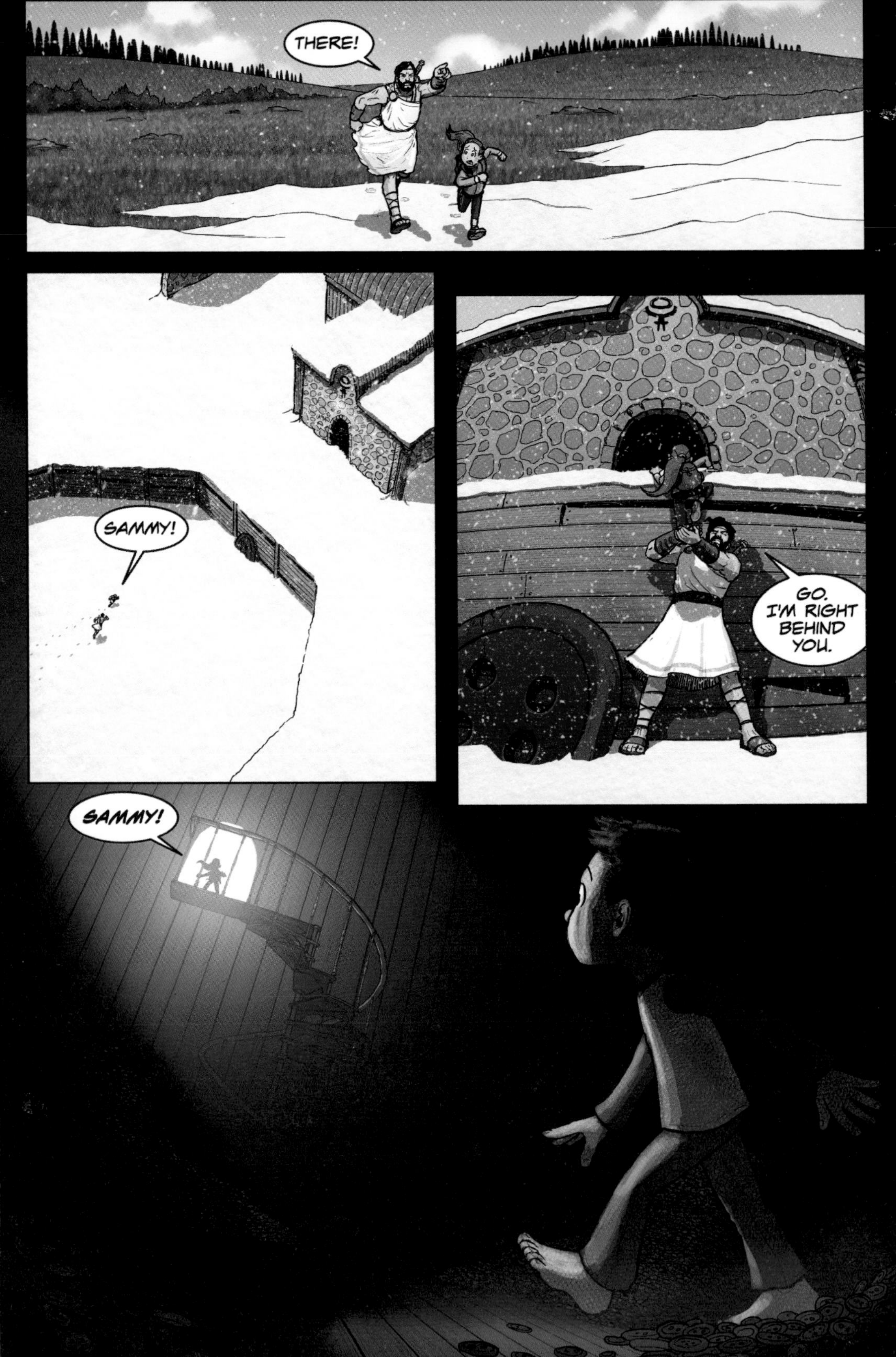
THERE!
SAMMY!
GO. I'M RIGHT BEHIND YOU.
SAMMY!

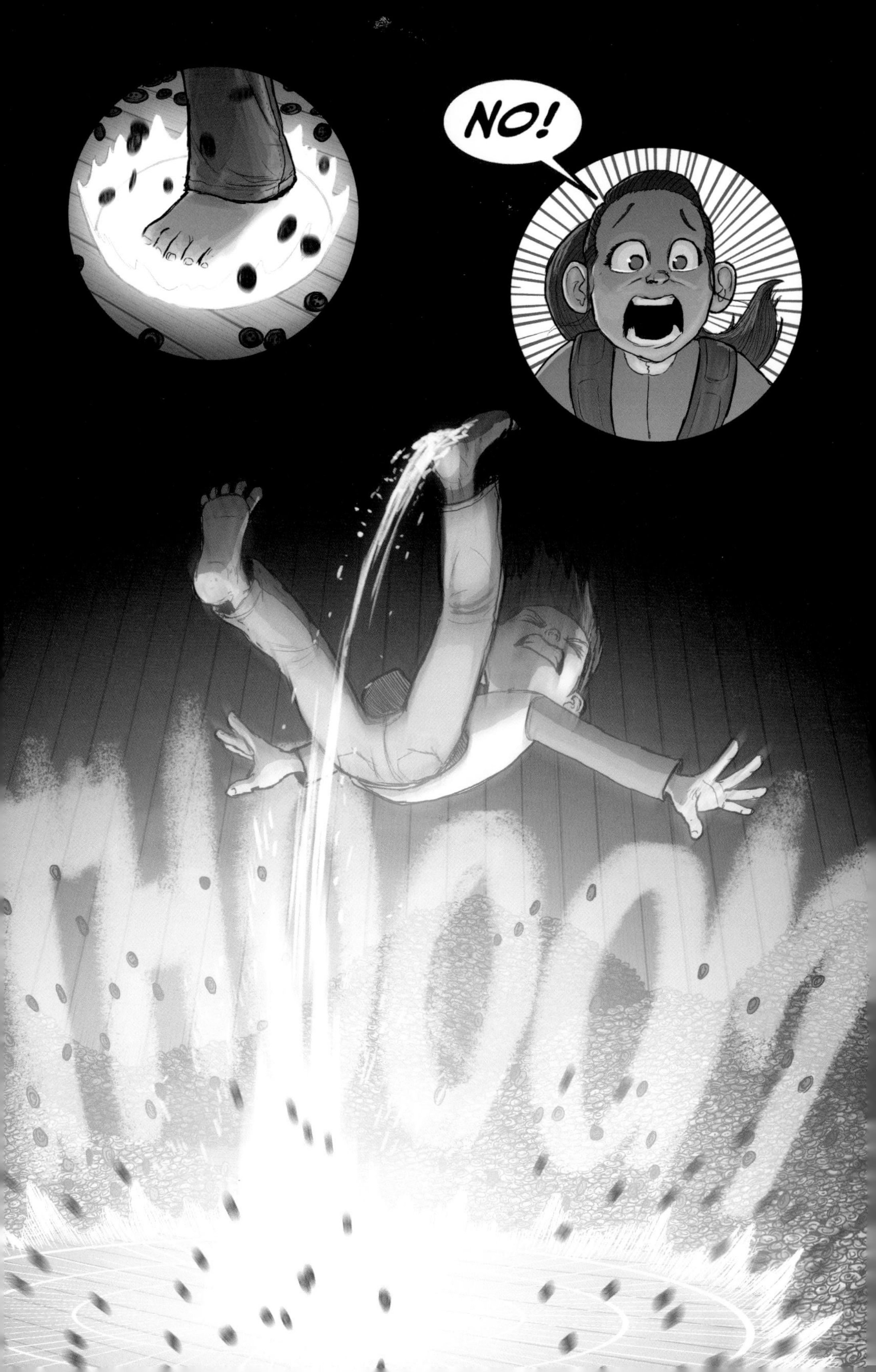
NO!

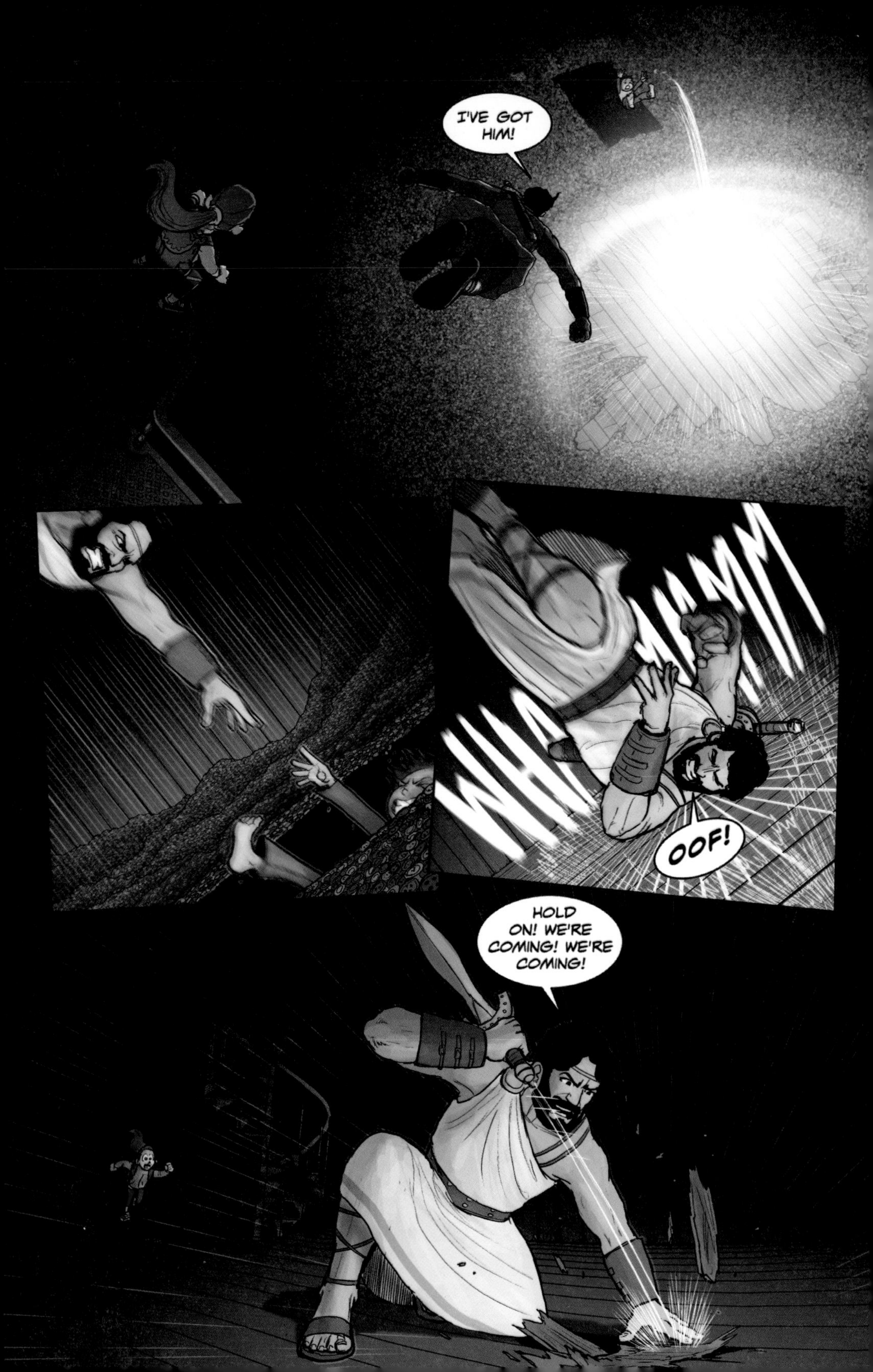

I'VE GOT HIM!
WHAMM
OOF!
HOLD ON! WE'RE COMING! WE'RE COMING!

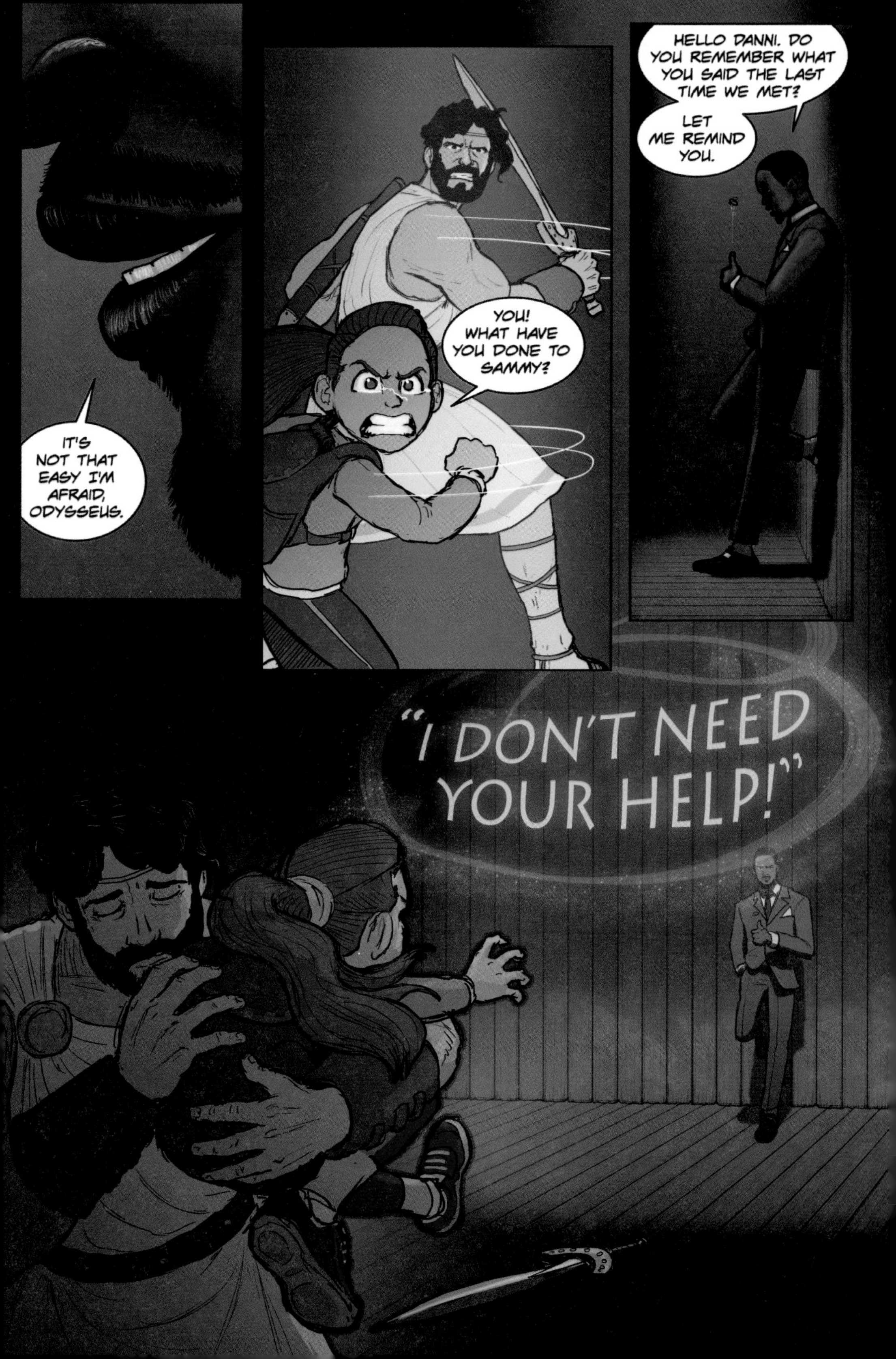
IT'S NOT THAT EASY I'M AFRAID, ODYSSEUS.
YOU! WHAT HAVE YOU DONE TO SAMMY?
HELLO DANNI. DO YOU REMEMBER WHAT YOU SAID THE LAST TIME WE MET?
LET ME REMIND YOU.
"I DON'T NEED YOUR HELP!"

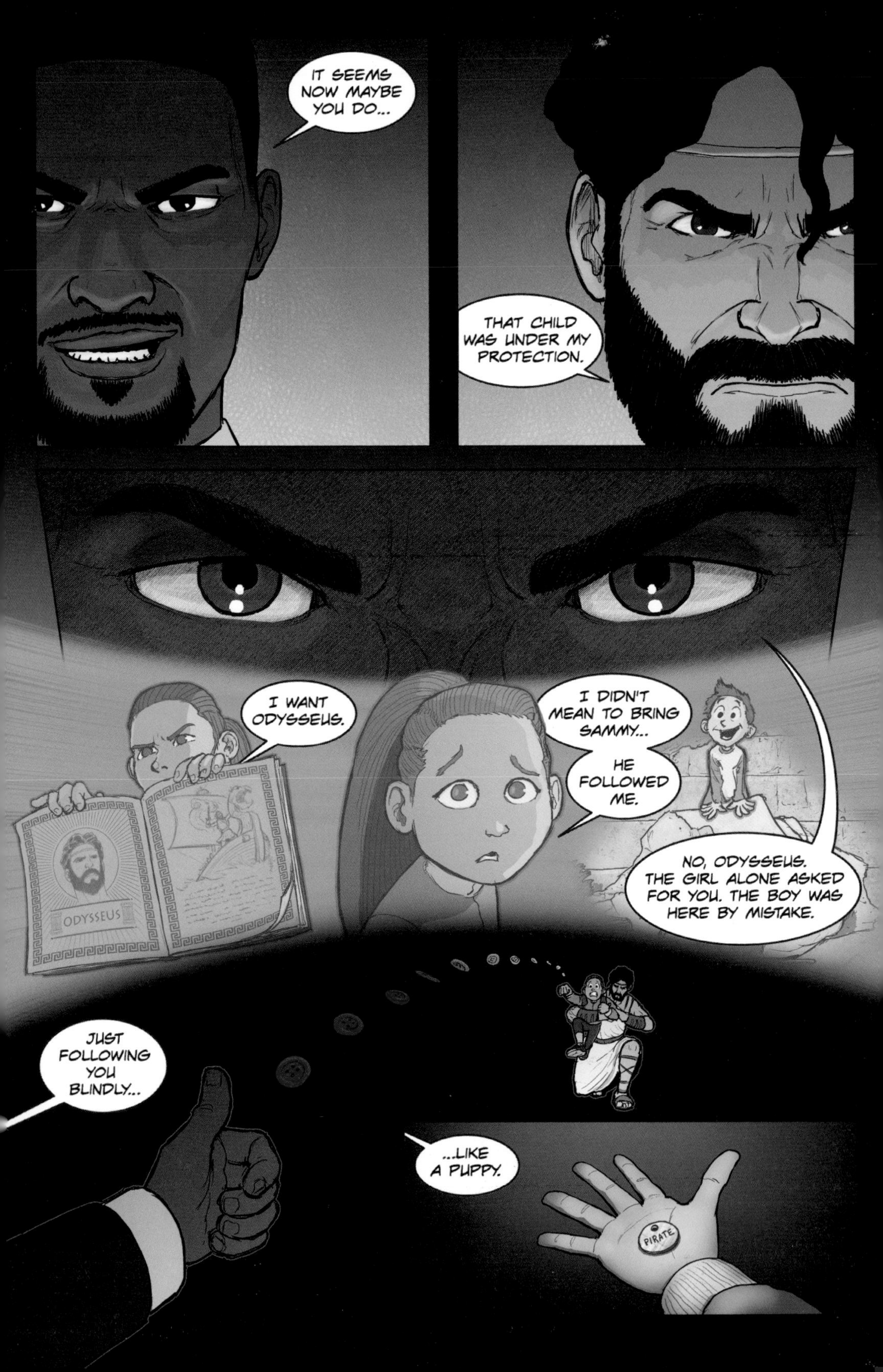
IT SEEMS NOW MAYBE YOU DO...
THAT CHILD WAS UNDER MY PROTECTION.
I WANT ODYSSEUS.
ODYSSEUS
I DIDN'T MEAN TO BRING SAMMY...
HE FOLLOWED ME.
NO, ODYSSEUS. THE GIRL ALONE ASKED FOR YOU. THE BOY WAS HERE BY MISTAKE.
JUST FOLLOWING YOU BLINDLY...
...LIKE A PUPPY.
PIRATE

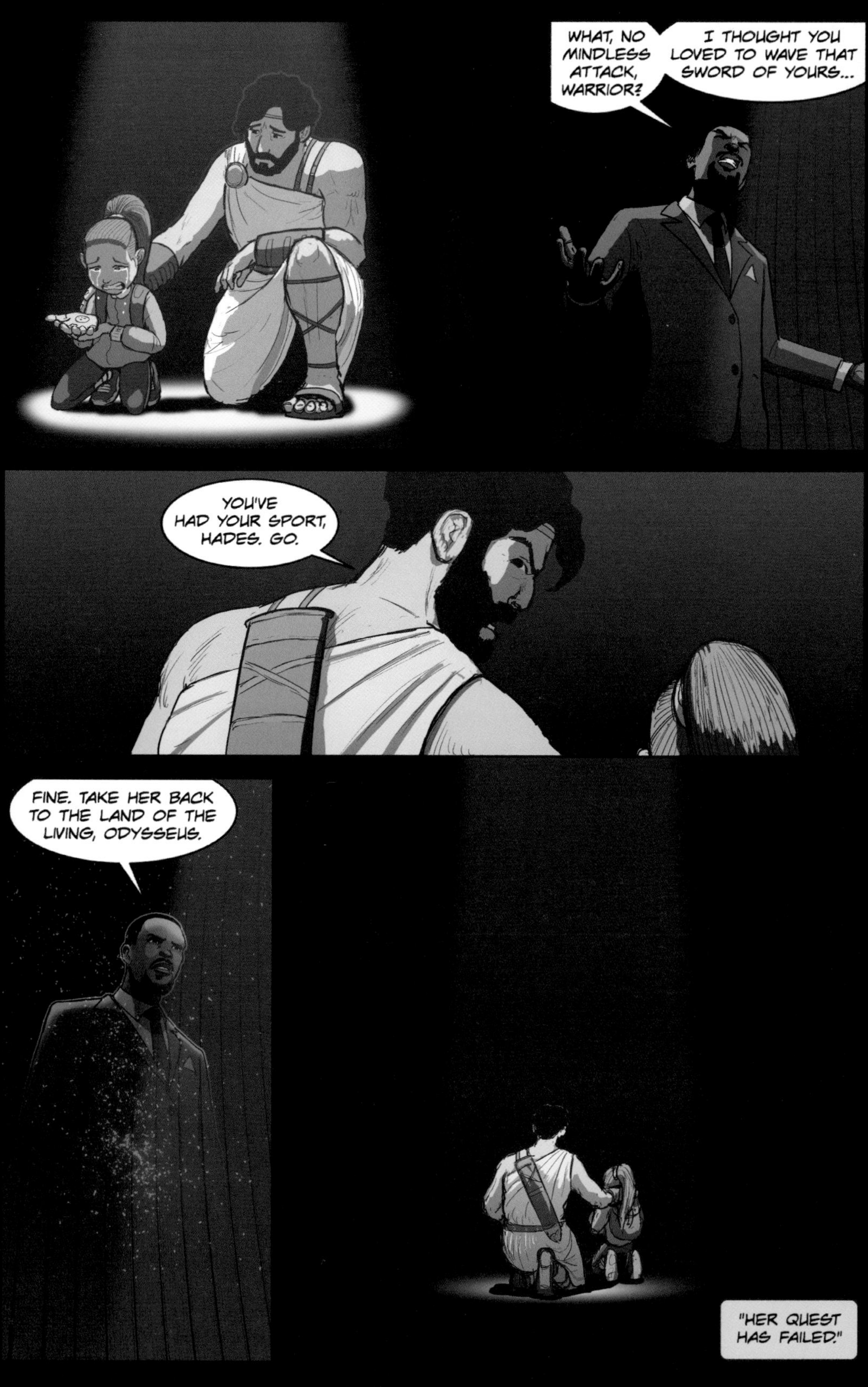
WHAT, NO MINDLESS ATTACK, WARRIOR?
I THOUGHT YOU LOVED TO WAVE THAT SWORD OF YOURS...
YOU'VE HAD YOUR SPORT, HADES. GO.
FINE. TAKE HER BACK TO THE LAND OF THE LIVING, ODYSSEUS.
"HER QUEST HAS FAILED."

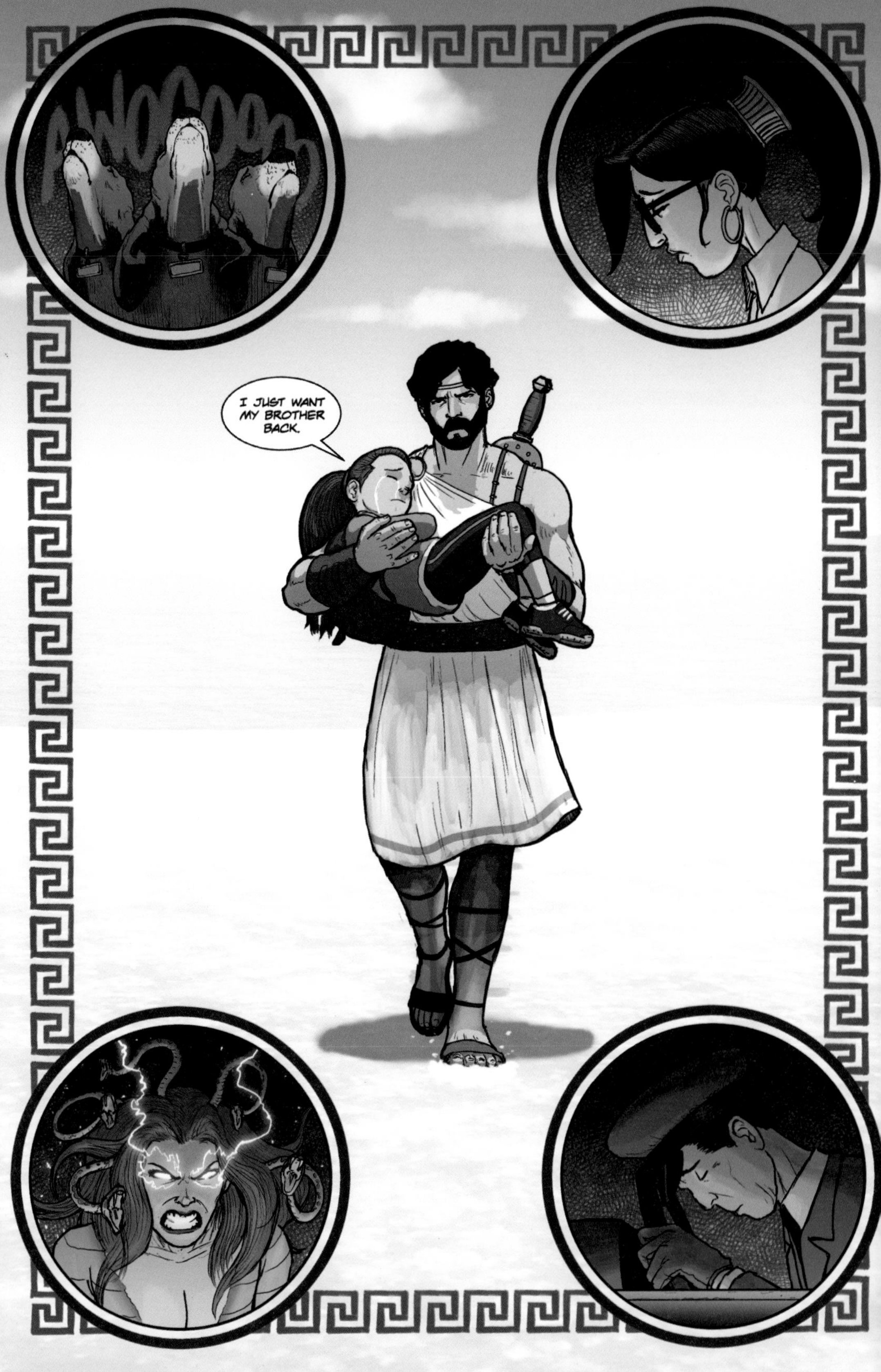
AWOOOOO
I JUST WANT MY BROTHER BACK.

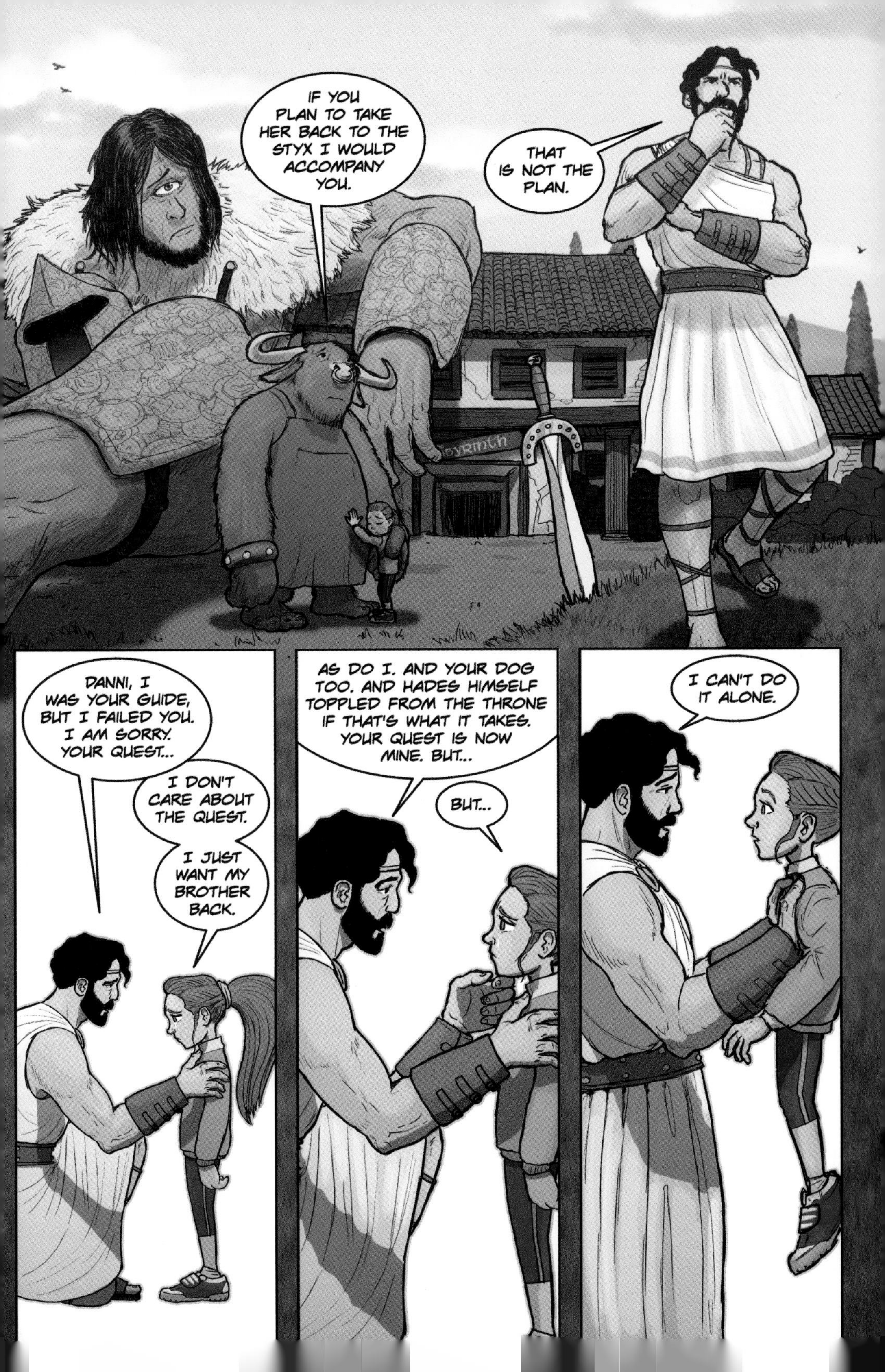
IF YOU PLAN TO TAKE HER BACK TO THE STYX I WOULD ACCOMPANY YOU.
THAT IS NOT THE PLAN.
DANNI, I WAS YOUR GUIDE, BUT I FAILED YOU. I AM SORRY. YOUR QUEST...
I DON'T CARE ABOUT THE QUEST.
I JUST WANT MY BROTHER BACK.
AS DO I. AND YOUR DOG TOO. AND HADES HIMSELF TOPPLED FROM THE THRONE IF THAT'S WHAT IT TAKES. YOUR QUEST IS NOW MINE. BUT...
BUT...
I CAN'T DO IT ALONE.

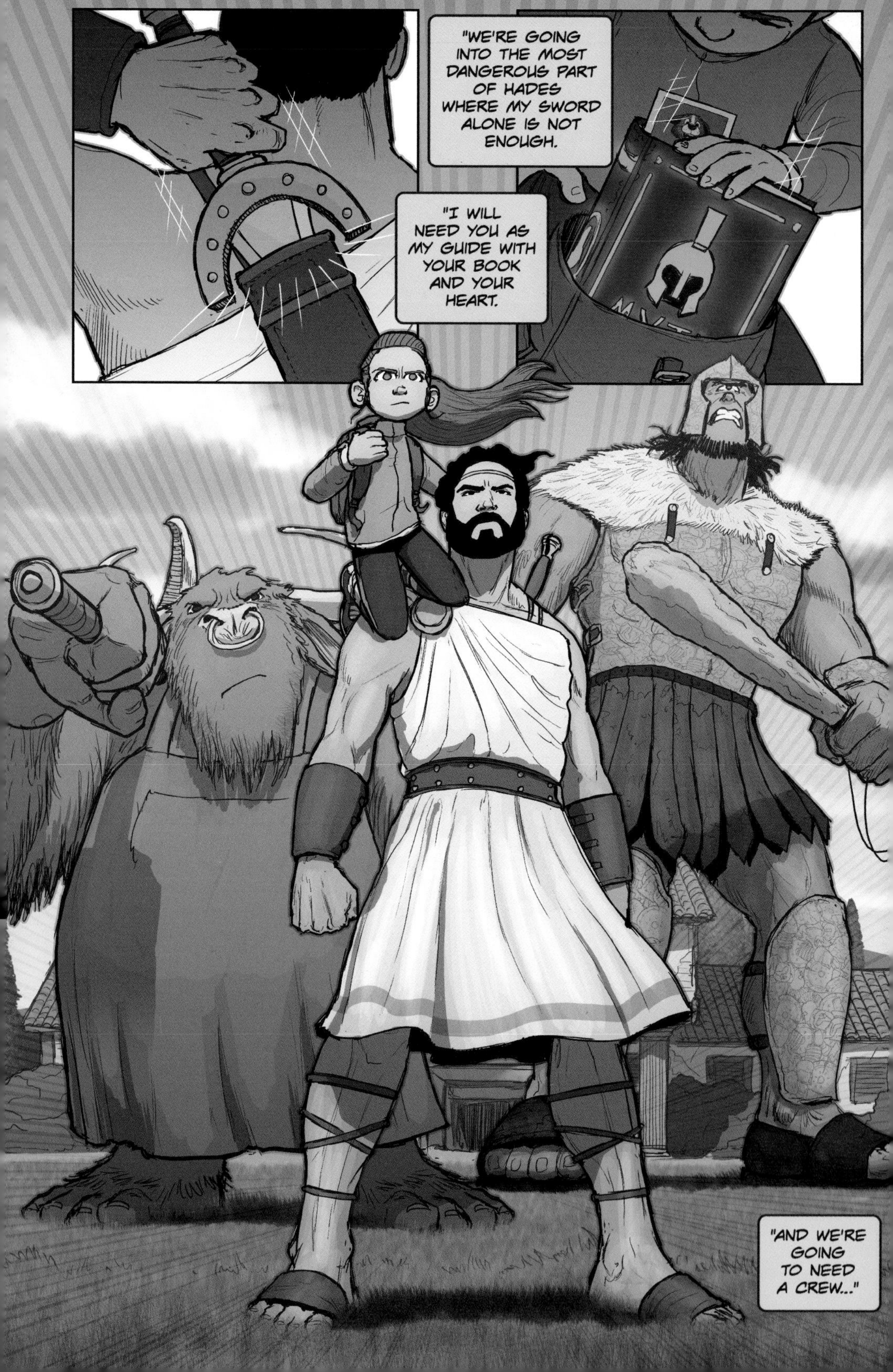
"WE'RE GOING INTO THE MOST DANGEROUS PART OF HADES WHERE MY SWORD ALONE IS NOT ENOUGH.
"I WILL NEED YOU AS MY GUIDE WITH YOUR BOOK AND YOUR HEART.
"AND WE'RE GOING TO NEED A CREW..."

TO BE CONTINUED IN

FETCH
BOOK TWO: THE RESCUE

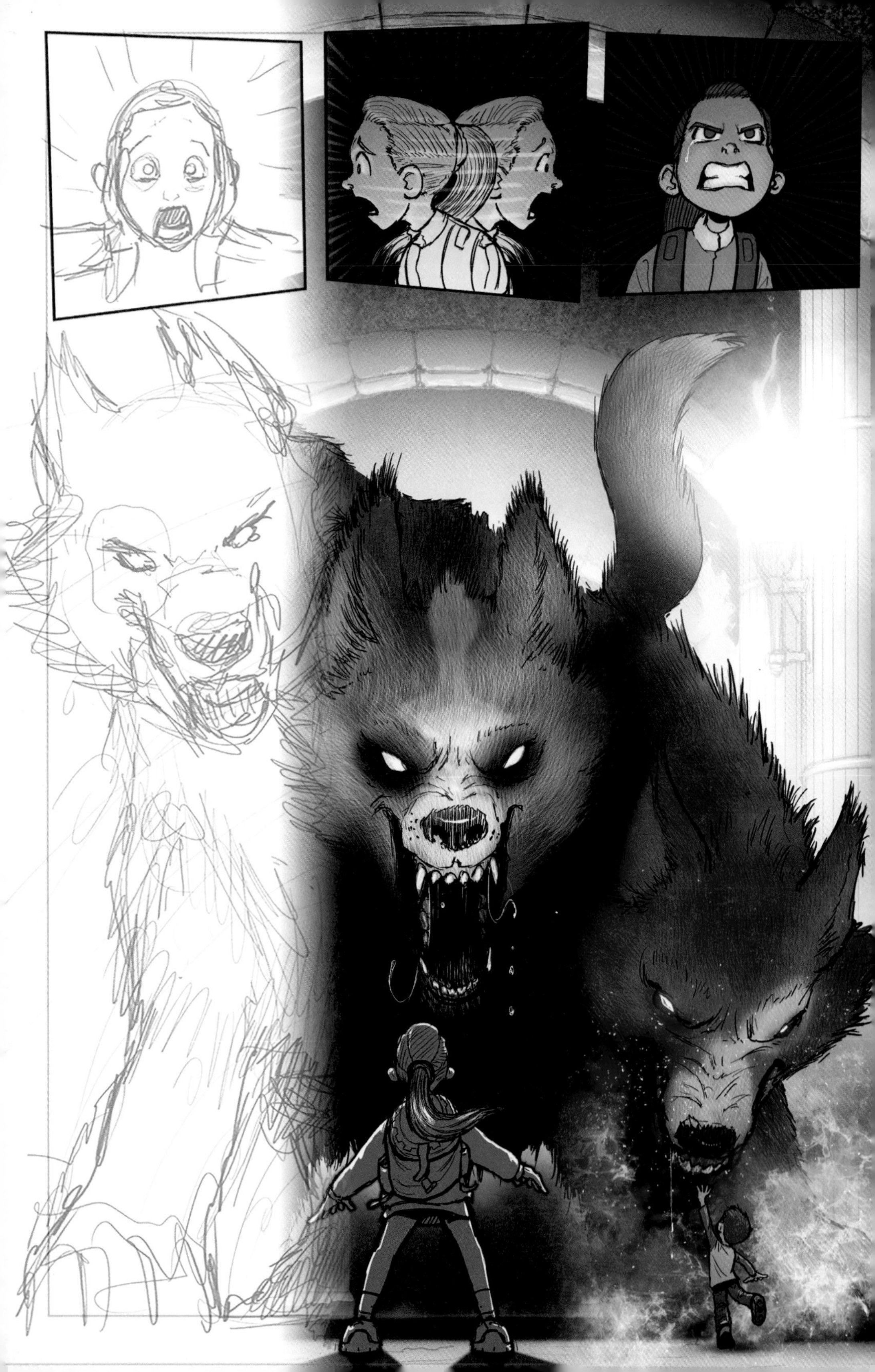

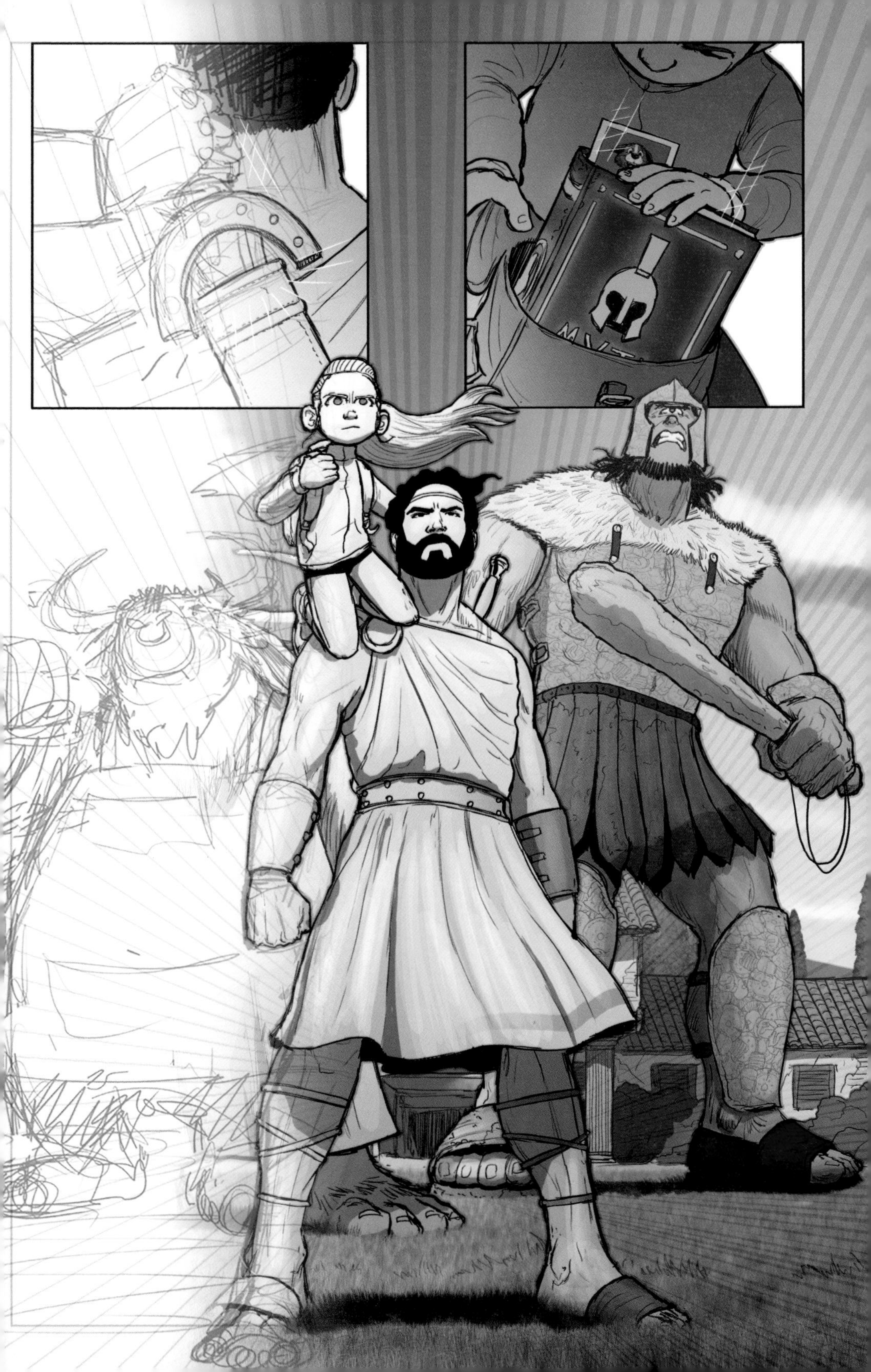

CREATOR BIOS

PHOTO BY KYLE CASSIDY

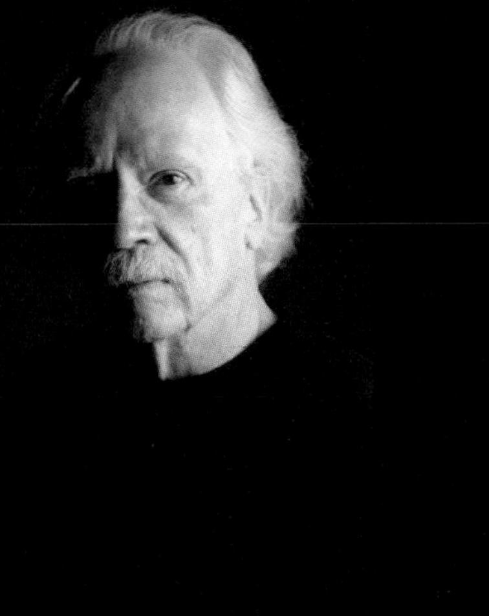

PHOTO BY DAN SANTONI

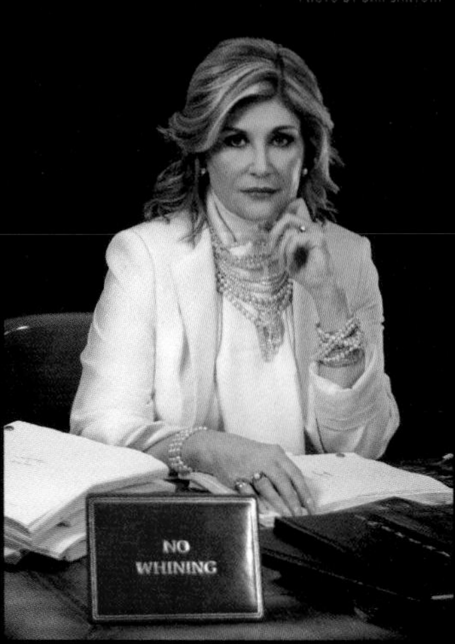
NO
WHINING

JOHN CARPENTER

John Carpenter's films are legendary: from the breakthrough ***Halloween*** (1978) to classics like ***Escape From New York, The Thing, Big Trouble In Little China*** and ***They Live***. His sci-fi love story, ***Starman***, earned Jeff Bridges a Best Actor Oscar nomination.

For the small screen, Carpenter directed the thriller ***Someone's Watching Me***, the acclaimed biographical mini-series, ***Elvis***, and the Showtime horror trilogy ***John Carpenter Presents Body Bags***. He also directed two episodes of Showtime's ***Masters Of Horror*** series.

He won the Cable Ace Award for writing the HBO movie, ***El Diablo***.

In the gaming world, he co-wrote the video game ***Fear 3*** for Warner Bros. Interactive.

In the world of comics, Carpenter co-wrote the BOOM! books ***Big Trouble in Little China*** with Eric Powell and the ***Old Man Jack*** series with Anthony Burch. He also co-wrote DC's ***Joker: Year Of The Villain*** with Burch. At Storm King Comics he is the co-creator of the award-winning series, ***John Carpenter's Asylum*** and the acclaimed annual anthology collection, ***John Carpenter's Tales for a HalloweeNight,*** as well as ***John Carpenter's Tales of Science Fiction, John Carpenter Presents Storm Kids,*** and ***John Carpenter's Night Terrors***.

SANDY KING

Writer, film and television producer and CEO of Storm King Productions.

With a background in art, photography and animation Sandy King's filmmaking career has included working with John Cassavetes, Francis Ford Coppola, Michael Mann, Walter Hill, John Hughes and John Carpenter.

She has produced films ranging from public service announcements on Hunger Awareness to a documentary on astronaut/teacher Christa McAuliffe for CNN, and major theatrical hits like ***They Live*** and ***John Carpenter's Vampires***. More recently, she directed and produced the John Carpenter Live Tour film and produced the horror/thriller, ***The Manor***, for BlumHouse/Amazon.

New challenges interest and excite her.

The world of comic books is no exception. King is the first woman founder of a comic publishing house.

Through Storm King Comics, she has created and written the award-winning ***Asylum*** series, the multiple award-winning ***Tales for a Halloween Night*** anthologies, the monthly, ***John Carpenter's Tales of Science Fiction***, and the graphic novel line ***Night Terrors***. In December 2019, King launched the new comics line, ***Storm Kids***, offering comics for ages 4 to 18 years old, and in 2021 received an Eisner nomination for the all-ages title, ***Stanley's Ghost***.

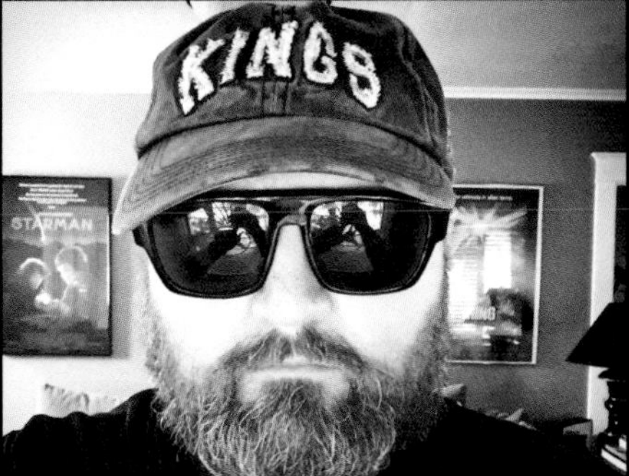
KINGS
STARMAN

MIKE SIZEMORE grew up reading everything he could as a way to escape his dreary surroundings in the rain drenched 70s of Northern England. A weekly injection of ***2000AD*** and an inherited love of Westerns set him on a path that lead to a Masters Degree in Literature and a life-long attachment to genre fiction and movies. His habit of throwing crazy ideas together eventually took him to Hollywood, and since then he has become an award-winning creator and WGA writer known for acclaimed web series, short stories, short films and comic books. Becoming friends with John Carpenter and Sandy King and being allowed to play in the Storm King Comics universe has been a dream come true. Working now with old school buddy, Dave Kennedy, and his equally talented brother, Pete Kennedy, and having his ideas brought to life by comic legends Janice Chiang and Tim Bradstreet is a pure delight. When he's not up all night thinking of new ways for robots, spaceships, monsters and planets to explode he's hanging with his long-suffering partner, Jess, and his very favourite creations, Connor (4) and Jaime (2).

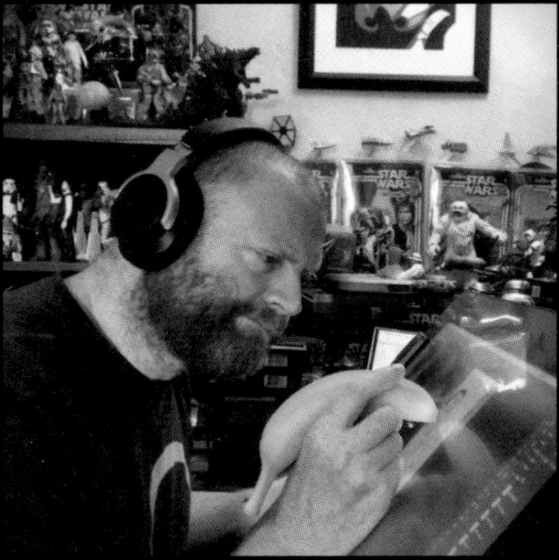
STAR WARS
STAR WARS

DAVE KENNEDY is a comic artist and illustrator based in the small town of Wigan in the north of England. His first memory was watching his grandfather draw a brontosaurus. This impressed him so much, he has spent his life trying to learn as much as he can about creating art. After many years working in the graphic design and games industries, Dave made the leap into comics and hasn't looked back - in no small part due to the pure joy of working with his insanely talented friend Mike Sizemore, but also due to having the opportunity to create with a lifelong hero of his - John Carpenter. With a passion for comics, cinema, books and games, Dave has stepped up to the plate to represent the Carpenter brand in the pages of the Storm King Comics titles ***Vortex, Vortex 2.0*** and ***Tales For a HalloweeNight***. He works alongside his supremely talented brother Pete, the crowned Queen of comic lettering, Janice Chiang and the incredibly supportive and motivated Sandy King Carpenter. Dave works in his home, amidst the love of his wife Tomomi and the chaos of his son Ren (4).

PETE KENNEDY must have fallen in love with stories before his earliest memories were formed, because there isn't a time he can remember where he wasn't hearing, reading, or watching them. In soaking up their every nuance of delicious prose, captivating illustrations, or entrancing visuals, he decided he'd like to help make some. Beginning at school with his favourite subjects of English and Art, he took a very serpentine path through life with a great deal of support from his family. Through the years this wonky path allowed him to explore his interests in Animation, Film, Writing, Comedy, Puppetry, Improvisation, and the incredible position of working alongside his amazing artist brother Dave in the world of comic books. Along with writer Mike Sizemore, the three worked on comics together, as well as the web series **Caper,** before eventually having the honour of working under the mutimedia-umbrella of master storyteller John Carpenter on several titles for Storm King Comics. Living in the town of Wigan in England's soggy but spirited Northwest, he is lucky enough to spend his non-work time with family and friends.

JANICE CHIANG is a comic pioneer as one of the first female letterers in the industry. From hand-lettering to digital, she has forged the way for countless female comic artists. Janice works with publishers old (Marvel) and new (DC's **Supergirls**, which won the Ringo Award 2018 for Best Kids Graphic Novel). She was also the letterer for the Eisner nominated Storm Kids comic **Stanley's Ghost** and two time Eisner winner DC Comics **Superman Smashes The Klan.** Comics Alliance honored Chiang as Outstanding Letterer of 2016 and ComicBook.com gave her the 2017 Golden Issue Award for Lettering. In May 2017, Chiang was featured as one of 13 women who have been making comics since before the internet on the blog Women Write About Comics. With her kind and forthright nature, Janice has built a loyal family within the comic community. Everyone has met her at one time or another, and everyone who runs into her says the same thing: "Oh my god, she's done so much, and she's so nice!"